**"I'm seen by tł** record."

Finn continued, "I refuse to let my past affect you or Lily."

"You had told me once that you'd been framed," Julia reminded him.

"And you believe me?"

"If you committed premeditated murder, I doubt the prosecutors would have made you a deal. Have you ever looked into the case again?"

Finn froze. He couldn't tell Julia anything about his case. He'd never want Julia to have a target on her back.

"Don't look to change me from a criminal to a martyr. Nothing matters but what's on my discharge papers."

"I know your heart, and you aren't a killer. I don't understand why you won't pursue it."

"Just drop it, Julia."

"If I'd been falsely accused, I'd fight like hell to prove them wrong." Julia had no idea that he was trying to fight it, but his last major attempt had ended in Miranda's murder.

"I don't need you diving into my private business." He was brusque, but if she asked the wrong people about what happened, Julia could end up like Miranda, and Finn couldn't let that happen.

Dear Reader,

When I wrote book one in the Fresh Pond Security series, I knew Jason Stirling's initial deception would create a lot of pain and chaos for the people he loved, but the loss of one particular team member, Finn Maguire, weighed on me. Finn had been a loyal member of the team, but Jason's lie tore that bond apart. Finn had been framed for a murder he didn't commit during his military service, losing his career and, tragically, his sister in the fallout. He valued honesty above all else, so when Jason betrayed his trust, he couldn't stay.

Finn had his own secrets to hide and his journey stayed with me. I wanted to give him the second chance he deserved.

In *The Heiress's Bodyguard*, Finn reconnects with his ex-girlfriend, Julia Gardiner, but their reunion is anything but simple. Together, they must protect Finn's four-year-old niece, Lily. As they fight to keep her safe, Finn and Julia must also confront their past and the love they once shared.

Of course, the Fresh Pond Security team (especially Jason, Fiona and Calvin) impacts the story. But at the heart of this book is Finn and Julia's journey toward healing, redemption and love. It's a story about second chances, not just in romance, but in life.

I'm so excited to share this chapter of the Fresh Pond Security series with you, and I hope Finn and Julia's story fills you with the same hope, suspense and heart that it has brought me.

Thank you for joining me on this journey. I can't wait to hear what you think.

With love,

*Veronica*

# THE HEIRESS'S BODYGUARD

## VERONICA FORAND

**Harlequin**

**ROMANTIC SUSPENSE**

**Harlequin®**
## ROMANTIC SUSPENSE™

Recycling programs for this product may not exist in your area.

ISBN-13: 978-1-335-47158-1

The Heiress's Bodyguard

Copyright © 2025 by Deborah Evans

Harlequin Enterprises ULC
22 Adelaide St. West, 41st Floor
Toronto, Ontario M5H 4E3, Canada
www.Harlequin.com

**Printed in Lithuania**

MIX
Paper | Supporting responsible forestry
FSC® C021394

**Veronica Forand** is the award-winning author of romantic thrillers, winning both the Booksellers' Best and the Golden Pen Award for the novels in her True Lies series.

When she's not writing, she's a search and rescue canine handler with her dog, Max.

A lover of education but a hater of tests, she attended Smith College and Boston College Law School. She studied in Paris and Geneva, worked in London and spent several glorious months in Ripon, England.

She currently divides her time living between Philadelphia, Vermont and Cape Cod.

### Books by Veronica Forand

### Harlequin Romantic Suspense

#### *Fresh Pond Security*

*Protector in Disguise*
*The Twin's Bodyguard*
*The Heiress's Bodyguard*

Visit the Author Profile page
at Harlequin.com for more titles.

For Edie and Kate, my BLE Mastermind Group.
For the past three-plus years, you've been there
for my highest highs and my lowest lows.
I'm so grateful for your support and love.

# *Prologue*

Finn Maguire stood under a stormy sky. Days of grieving his sister had left his eyes bloodshot and sore. As the gathering around her grave dispersed, he stared at the pine casket. Several people murmured condolences to him then hustled away, out of the rain. Finn barely heard any of it. His gaze remained on the casket, already lowered into the ground and blemished by a shovel of dirt and several wilted roses.

He'd learned a lot about life in these past few days. Just when he thought it couldn't get any worse, the sky would fall.

Only a few months before, he'd returned from Afghanistan, dishonorably discharged from the army, after being framed for the murder of Major Mark Donner. Donner had seemingly messed up paperwork on the shipment of several crates of weapons. Finn had wanted clarity on where the weapons had gone. Instead of helping Finn identify the discrepancy, Donner tried to shut him down. When a local faction had been located with the missing weapons, Finn confronted Donner, accusing him of arms dealing, only for Donner to turn up dead days later. Their shouting match at the officers' club and one lone drop of Donner's blood on Finn's boot had been the evidence used against him. With no way to prove his innocence and no understanding of who was controlling the illegal operation, Finn was forced out of the military in disgrace, his career and reputation shattered.

Finn arrived home ready to clear his name, to find out who had actually killed Donner. But whoever had really killed Donner and illegally sold those weapons wanted Finn silenced. Instead of killing him, they killed Miranda. They should have killed him, not her. Not his sister.

The police claimed it was a break-in gone wrong. It wasn't. She'd been murdered in front of her two-year-old daughter, Lily. To make matters worse, Lily may have witnessed the murderer carving what the police called an *X* on Miranda's chest. It wasn't an *X*. Someone had carved the Ordnance Corps insignia into her skin. A brutal reminder of whom he was up against. It was a message: "Shut up. Or the people you love will pay the price."

Finn's mind clouded with guilt and rage. Both Donner's and Miranda's murders had been a warning to stop him from digging for the truth. And it worked. The moment he saw Miranda's lifeless body, he knew what they were capable of.

He'd ignored their warnings. He'd kept digging. And now his sister was dead.

"Finn?" Julia's voice broke through the fog numbing his mind. She'd been Miranda's roommate when Finn had met her a few years before. It had been love at first smile for him. They'd been together ever since. Wearing a long black London Fog trench coat covering a black dress, she stood a few steps away, holding Lily, who was bundled in her arms under a warm blanket. The two-year-old was quiet, too young to fully understand what had happened, but something in her eyes had changed since that night. She hadn't spoken a word since Miranda's murder.

He looked at Julia, her face pale, wet with tears and rain. She'd been his anchor when he came back, the only thing keeping him grounded. She loved him even when he wasn't sure he deserved it.

But now, standing over his sister's grave, he couldn't bring himself to meet her gaze.

"You okay?" she asked, her voice filled with concern.

Finn nodded, though he felt anything but okay. He could feel Julia's eyes on him, searching for some explanation, some reassurance, but he couldn't give it to her. He couldn't tell her the truth—that Miranda had been murdered as a message to him, that Lily had barely escaped that night with her life and that the people responsible may not be finished until everything he valued was destroyed.

They were still watching. And if he remained attached to her, he'd place her and Lily at risk.

"I... I think I'll stay here for a little while," he said, gesturing toward the grave. "You should get Lily out of the rain."

Julia hesitated. "Finn, you don't have to be alone right now. We should—"

"I need to be alone," he interrupted, his voice tight. "I'll be fine." He tried not to be affected by the confusion and hurt in her eyes, but his heart broke as clarity came to him.

She nodded, pulling Lily closer to her. "Okay. I'll... I'll see you back at my place."

She lingered a moment longer, before turning away. Lily glanced over Julia's shoulder as they went, her wide, innocent eyes meeting his for a fleeting moment. He loved those two more than anything in the entire world.

Later that night, Finn sat on his couch, nursing some Scotch in the darkness of his apartment. He couldn't bring himself to drive over to Julia's place. He'd barely slept since Miranda's murder, and the funeral had clarified what he had to do to keep those he loved safe.

His sister was dead because of him. The people responsible were still out there, and they would come for Julia and

Lily next. Unless he stayed away from them. Made them unimportant.

He stared at his phone screen for what felt like forever before dialing Julia's number. It rang three times before she picked up.

"Finn?" Julia sounded exhausted. He wanted to pull her into his arms and hold her through all the pain, but that path had been buried with Miranda.

"I'm sorry, Julia," he said, his voice low, his sorrow threatening to break him. "I can't do this anymore. I have enough going on in my life. I can't be your crutch and your strength."

"My crutch? What are you talking about?"

"You're too high maintenance for me. My new position at Fresh Pond Security is going to take up all my time. Just focus on Lily. I'm not the family type," he said, his throat tightening.

"You're in pain, I get it. If you need space…" Her voice cracked.

"Don't. You're strong and sexy and amazing. Don't turn into a clingy, shrill hag." He hung up before he could hear her response. As deep as he'd thrust the knife into Julia, he'd wounded himself even more.

The silence that followed was suffocating. He drank down what was left of the Scotch and poured himself more. The people responsible for Miranda's death wouldn't stop until they'd erased every trace of the truth. And that meant anyone connected to Finn was a target. The only way to keep Julia and Lily safe was to walk away. To let them believe he was too broken to stay.

Finn buried his face in his hands. He'd thought losing his military career had been the worst thing to ever happen to him. But nothing prepared him for the fear and rawness of walking away from Julia and Lily.

Those bastards had taken everything.

And he was not going to stop until he destroyed them.

# Chapter 1

Big band music, a succulent French meal and fragrant wild-flowers adorning a converted barn created a perfect autumn evening, but Julia Gardiner wanted to go home. The hours of preparation to organize the event had drained every drop of her usual energy, enthusiasm and hospitality. She craved a snuggle with Lily, the four-year-old darling left in her care after the death of her best friend, Miranda. It had been almost two years since Julia had rushed to the hospital to find a crying Lily drenched in her mother's blood. There were still no suspects in the murder—only one very traumatized little girl.

Julia had been named Lily's guardian because Miranda's brother, Finn, couldn't step up. It had made sense in Miranda's will that Julia was named one of Lily's guardians. Julia and Finn had been together then, on the verge of something serious. But Miranda's death had done something to Finn. He'd become a different person. The man who had once been her future, and the uncle Lily adored, was now a ghost.

Adding to the strain of the evening, Julia had planned this fiftieth anniversary for Finn's aunt and uncle, Maureen and Walter Maguire. The whole room was filled with Miranda and Lily's family. Julia breathed in the fading scent of chateaubriand, candles snuffed out by their own melted wax and a pungent mix of perfume and sweat. The few guests who had abused the open bar seemed destined to remain all night, causing the corners of Julia's usual smile to lower. The sooner they departed, the sooner she'd be home with Lily.

Making matters worse, as if dreading being ignored by her ex wasn't already a headache, Richard, the anniversary couple's inebriated son, had spent the evening tormenting her with tactless jokes and inappropriate physical contact. Tapping into her years of evading drunks at parties, first as a carefree socialite and then as an event planner, she'd put several tables and a dozen people between her and the idiot, but he kept coming back. Avoid, evade, escape if necessary, but as an event planner, she couldn't afford to make a scene. Especially not at a family event.

She felt the floorboards shift a second before a large hand squeezed her ass. *Are you kidding me?* Her heartbeat quickened to a low thrumming. She turned around to find Richard leering at her, his handsome face marred by his smug expression, his breath thick with alcohol.

"Please remove your hand," Julia said, forcing the most professional smile she could muster, biting back three different swears and a scowl.

He slid his pudgy hand from her shoulder to her breast. "It's time for our dance." Spit splattered across her neck.

"I'm working and can't dance with the guests," she said, trying to pull away. This was a made-up, on-the-spot rule, but Richard didn't care about rules. He wouldn't let her go. Without drawing undue attention from the other guests, she grabbed his hand and twisted it back toward his body, stretching herself to her unintimidating height of five feet two inches. "The next time you touch me, I'll relocate your hand to a far more uncomfortable place."

He wasn't intimidated. At all. She didn't want a scene at the Maguires' party, not after all the support they'd given her.

"Where's your better half?" she called out, trying to re-mind him of his wedding ring.

"Over there." He pointed to the bar, where his wife's fore-head rested in a pool of spilled beer.

Her dress was cut scandalously low, exposing her spine, and her flaming red hair fanned out across the bar.

Julia kept her eyes on Richard's wife as the sharp scraping of wood against wood caught her attention. Richard shoved a chair, stumbling closer. Too close. She backed up, pushing his hands away from her waist. With nothing left to do, she slammed her heel into his foot and lifted her snarl into a smile. To the other guests and staff, they could have been discuss-ing the weather.

"Bitch." Richard stumbled back toward the bar. She sig-naled the bartender to cut him off behind his retreating back. She'd have to get security involved as well.

One more hour, two at most. Pride over a job well done fought with exhaustion. Exhaustion was winning. Her second-in-command, Helena, a beatnik wannabe in black leggings, a turtleneck and hair pulled tight into a long brown ponytail, appeared from around the corner with a tray of drinks. She rotated the tray toward Julia, indicating the Coke. "That glass is for you."

"Thanks." The caffeine would keep her alert and awake until the final guest left. The music played on, and the guests continued to linger in their groups, still drinking, still chat-ting. Julia took an energizing sip from her glass and stead-ied herself.

Helena glanced toward Richard. "I thought you'd drawn blood with that stomp."

"You saw that?"

"I'm sure I was the only one. Need any help? I can get Car-los from the kitchen."

"Get the security guard to watch him until he leaves and

make sure he isn't driving," Julia said, brushing her hair out of her face.

"Got it." Helena gave a knowing nod, then asked, "When's the band done?"

"In about a half hour."

"Can't wait." Helena shimmied away to the beat.

Julia took a few more sips, relaxing in the warmth her friend left behind. In less than an hour, she'd be driving home. She headed across the room toward the band, but a large hand moved low across her back. Her stress level spiked again, and without thinking, she whipped around and almost tossed the contents of her drink straight into the face of the man behind her.

On the plus side, she held the glass and all of its contents, but on the negative, the stranger wasn't a stranger at all.

She knew every part of this man, every muscle, every line on his face, every promise he'd ever made. Finn Maguire, the man who had crushed Julia's soul.

"What the heck are you doing here? You scared me," she whispered, trying to salvage the situation without the whole room noticing that the event planner had lost her cool.

"I've never seen you scared of anyone or anything." His deep voice, deeper than she remembered, sent a familiar warmth over her. She tried to ice it away, but that man always heated her blood.

"I have my moments," she replied, getting hypnotized by his beautiful face. The scar across his cheek, a souvenir from whatever hell he'd been through overseas, was less prominent, but still there, hinting at a past he wouldn't speak about.

"Aunt Maureen demanded I attend. So I came. What's going on?" he asked, always able to read her emotions.

She took a deep breath, trying to calm the tension. "Your cousin, the moron with a low tolerance for alcohol, has been literally on my ass all night."

He glanced over at the bar, where Richard was now half-heartedly trying to wake his wife. "I can't believe Richard would ruin his own parents' party. I'll take care of him." He paused, his eyes looking her over, taking her in. There it was. The caring, loving man he'd been and then wasn't. She couldn't deal with his hot-and-cold emotions. "Are you okay, Midnight?" he asked.

Midnight. Julia hated his nickname for her—it was a reminder of when they were happy, of nights spent tangled together, of everything they'd lost. His presence overwhelmed her senses, like stepping back into a past she'd fought hard to move on from.

They locked eyes, and her body reacted as though it was two years ago and his touch was still her world. Her heart ached with longing, with all the unanswered what-ifs. What if he hadn't left? What if he'd come home from Afghanistan unscathed? What if Miranda had never died?

"Don't bother with Richard," she said, her voice softer now. "I don't want to upset your aunt and uncle. This night is about them."

"Richard needs a restraining order from society at large," Finn replied.

She nodded, frozen in his presence. She should have returned to the guests, back to the safety of her work. But instead, she made her heart a bit more vulnerable again. She needed to understand why this man, who had once been her everything, was content to let everything fall apart. "How's the used car business?" she said, changing the subject.

"Lucrative, but not very exciting," he replied flatly.

Her heart clenched at his detached response. When he'd returned from Afghanistan, he'd been employed by Fresh Pond Security in a lucrative position, despite having been dishonorably discharged from the military. And from what she'd heard, he'd been happy and successful there, then one day he quit and became a partner with his cousin Richard and his friend Davis at their luxury car dealership. He'd never been a man happy with a desk job, but he'd done it anyway. It was as though he could never remain in a place where he was happy.

She wanted to reach out to him, to touch those strong arms that had once held her close and promised her the world. He was so close, and yet it felt like he was completely detached from her. "Is your new position too demanding to see your niece for an hour or two?"

His eyes darkened, and the air between them grew heavy, thick with unspoken pain. Without a word, Finn stepped back, putting distance between them. "I... I'm trying, Julia. I'm really trying. Give me time," he muttered before turning away and walking quickly through the crowd toward the bathroom.

Julia stood there, her last shred of energy draining out of her, as Finn disappeared into the crowd.

He was always disappearing.

# Chapter 2

Finn leaned over the bathroom sink, splashing cold water on his face, trying to wash away the weight of his confrontation with Julia. The sting of her blunt honesty, her elegance in that black dress and the way her smile lit up the room. She was a balm for his tortured soul and he'd pushed her away. Again. He hadn't just "chickened out" of reconnecting with them. It went deeper. Miranda was dead because of him. Someone still had a target aimed at his head and at those he loved.

And yet now, seeing Julia hurt, knowing how much they'd all lost, something shifted inside him.

He wanted another chance. This wasn't merely a casual longing; it was a constant ache that lived in his bones, a reminder of the life he'd once dreamed of. The fear, the guilt—they were still there, but they no longer outweighed his need to make things right. For the first time, he wasn't just running away.

The threat that followed him around seemed to have dissipated as his search for the truth involved very few trusted government insiders and nothing via the internet. Perhaps he could make room for Julia and Lily without placing them in danger. That's why he'd asked his aunt to have Julia organize the anniversary party. It was a small step toward rebuilding what he'd shattered, a chance to make amends, not just with her, but with Lily too.

Aunt Maureen called out from the dance floor, "There you

are, Finn. You owe me one before the band calls it quits." Her whippet-thin body swayed to the beat.

"How could I deny a dance to the woman burdened with raising me from adolescence?"

She tossed her hair back like a woman half her age. "Never a burden. More of a minor irritation."

"In that case, one dance and then I need to head out. I don't have your stamina." Aunt Maureen had been his and Miranda's lifesaver. When their parents had died in a car accident, their father's brother and his wife stepped in without any hesitation to raise two very opinionated high schoolers. Finn should have done the same with Lily, except he didn't think Lily should be raised by the person responsible for Miranda's death. He'd thought he'd been right to avoid her, but perhaps it had only been beneficial to him. She lost both Miranda and her uncle that day. It was time to step up.

He and Aunt Maureen headed onto the dance floor for a lively foxtrot, but interruptions prevented them from traveling more than five feet in any direction. His aunt, as the anniversary girl, stopped to hug a neighbor before he left. Then she pulled Finn over to an old friend from her high school to discuss the coming week's book club selection. Her enthusiasm changed every moment spent with her into a warm memory for everyone around her. When she appeared satisfied with her efforts off the dance floor, she moved back into the dance, her attention now on Finn.

"No date?" she asked.

"Tonight, I wanted to focus on you." He glanced over toward Julia. Just being in the same room as her would have made for a perfect evening, if he hadn't been such a jackass. Especially after his own cousin had already ruined her night.

"You're sweet, but the best gift you could give me is to find someone who makes you as happy as Walter has made me." Aunt Maureen meant well, but he wasn't ready to settle down. He never would be.

"Regrettably, in thirty-eight years, I haven't found such perfection." Except Julia. She'd fit perfectly into his life, his heart and within his arms. Before he'd gone away. Before he'd blown up his whole damn world.

Aunt Maureen smiled and slapped him on the arm. "You will."

At the end of the song, Finn escorted her back to Uncle Walter for the final dance.

Aunt Maureen remained with her arm in Finn's, refusing to let him go. "I have just the woman for you."

"That's not necessary." Finn looked over toward his uncle for help, but the seventy-year-old groom merely shrugged.

"Yes, it is necessary. Ah. There she is. Julia dear, please come over here." His aunt waved over Julia, as though she was Finn's fairy godmother manifesting his deepest desire.

Julia didn't seem too thrilled to see Finn again. He'd been discourteous and she'd done nothing to deserve it.

"We're having our last dance of the evening and both Walter and I want you both to be part of it. My only request of the evening." As she spoke, she placed Julia's arm in Finn's. "This woman is a gift from God by taking care of our Lily. You treat her well."

Julia was not wearing the expression of a woman who wanted to dance. "I appreciate your kind words, but I really need to work."

"Nonsense. It's my party. I get to make outrageous requests." Before anyone could reply, she pulled Uncle Walter onto the dance floor.

Julia looked over at her employees and around the room. Everywhere but at him. Her beautiful smile from earlier that evening had been replaced by a frown. He couldn't blame her.

"We don't have to dance," she said in a whisper.

"Of course we do. My aunt requested it on her anniversary. What kind of nephew would deny his favorite aunt her one request of the evening?"

She lifted a brow. "The kind who would kiss his aunt's ass and ignore his only niece."

"Please?" He tightened his elbow against her arm and escorted her to the dance floor, relieved she didn't pull away.

The band started playing "It Had to Be You," the slowest version Finn had ever heard. His aunt and uncle pressed into each other and turned across the floor in perfect symmetry. He placed his arm around Julia as though they'd danced together a hundred times.

She fit perfectly in his arms. After a minute, she rested her head against his chest. He'd forgotten what it had been like to hold her. Her head barely reached his shoulder and she lifted her eyes to look at him. Warm brown eyes filled with questions he needed to answer. It was time. He longed to kiss the top of her head, breathe in her presence, but he hesitated. One baby step at a time.

"Since you insist on my presence for the sake of your aunt, I'd like to insist on your presence in Lily's life," she murmured in his ear.

"I… I agree."

She stalled in the middle of the dance floor. "You do?"

"I was wrong to avoid you both. I want to see her again, if you'll let me. And I want to see you again too."

"I'll never limit your time with Lily, if you promise you won't intentionally hurt her again. She doesn't trust many people. But at one point in time, she'd trusted and loved you. She needs you."

"And you?" So much for baby steps.

"You had me. One hundred and ten percent of me. But you left and it nearly destroyed me. I can't go through that again."

"I didn't want to hurt either of you, I swear."

"But you did." Tears formed in her eyes and she pulled away from him, fleeing toward the kitchen.

Finn remained in place, staring after her. So much for their beautiful reunion. At least she agreed to his visits with Lily.

Only a few guests remained in the room nursing their last drinks, including Richard and Richard's wife, Kim. She yawned and lifted her head up from her alcohol-induced nap. Richard and his wife deserved each other. Both drank to excess and couldn't keep their libidos under control.

Julia loitered by the entrance to the kitchen, speaking to several of the servers. She directed them toward the final dishes on the tables. All business. She held another glass of Coke, probably to keep herself awake. Although she smiled and laughed with the waitstaff, she looked down at her watch a few times, her expression tight.

Finn should leave. He'd made a date with the cutest little girl in the world. He'd take that as a win.

Although he wanted to say goodbye to Julia and perhaps set up a time to go over to her house, she disappeared into the bathroom. As he turned to say goodbye to Aunt Maureen, he noticed Richard started weaving through chairs to follow Julia. The bastard headed straight into the women's bathroom. Pushing a few chairs to the side, Finn rushed after him. He opened the door just as Julia slapped Richard across the face. The asshole stumbled back and Finn caught his arms before he could retaliate.

"Richard, I don't know what you did to deserve that slap, but don't make the situation worse. Apologize and then I suggest you collect your wife and grab a cab home." He turned Richard's struggling body toward the door as a security guard came inside.

"Screw you." Richard pulled free, twisted around and swung toward Finn's face.

Finn blocked the punch and pushed him against the wall.

"Richard, go home. You're going to have many regrets tomorrow. Don't make any more."

"Sir, please leave the ladies' room," the security guard said to Richard, although he made no attempt to step toward him.

Julia tried to slip behind the security guard to leave. Finn held on to Richard, restraining his arms behind him. Richard slammed his foot onto Finn's toe. Then the son of a bitch headbutted him. The pain radiated from Finn's wingtip shoes to his temple. He fell back against the sink.

Richard grabbed Julia's arm before she got away. "I'm getting my dance right now."

She tried to pull free, but Richard tripped, yanking her off balance. Gravity favored Richard's size over hers. Finn could only watch as Julia slammed into the wall. Her head hit the wall first, then her shoulder. A smattering of blood sprayed across the white tiles as she fell to the floor.

Richard's eyes widened and he turned to escape. Coward.

The security guard stood like a deer in the headlights. Finn grabbed Richard to keep him there. There was no way he was leaving this room.

"Go to hell." Richard punched him in the stomach.

The pain almost knocked him to the floor, but he remained standing and responded with a right hook to Richard's jaw. Blood spurted out of his mouth and he collapsed on the floor as Julia struggled to stand.

The place looked like an IED had detonated. Blood everywhere. Not exactly the reunion of his dreams.

# Chapter 3

Everything had happened so fast, but Julia had the basics. She'd been assaulted by Richard Maguire and rescued by Finn Maguire. Security at the restaurant had been nothing more than an extra body in the way.

By the time the police arrived and interviewed everyone and Richard left in an ambulance, Julia and Finn were in the dining room again, sitting at a large round table that had been stripped down to the wood. Someone from the local paper had been notified of a fight and arrived to ask questions. The press were the exact people she didn't want to see. Not when her family were in the headlines in Philadelphia, one reason she moved to a different city. Julia had a fair degree of freedom living just outside of Boston because here she could be anonymous. Only Finn knew of her family fortune, and even he had only a limited knowledge of her family's assets.

He was far too close to her, his fingers brushing the hair from the spot where her head hit the wall. "You need an ambulance too," he said. "Or I can drive you to the hospital."

A night in the hospital was not on her to-do list. "The paramedic told me I could decide. And I choose to go home."

"It looks bad."

"It's a head wound. They bleed profusely. I'll be okay. I just want to go home." She wanted Lily.

"And if you have a neck injury?"

"I don't." She had a cut on her hairline. It was a tiny cut. She never even blacked out.

He shook his head. "If you had a medical degree, I'd believe you."

"Right back at you." She sat up and looked at him. "Are you okay? You have a bruise on your forehead." He would never admit to being hurt. He'd stood stoic and calm at his own sister's funeral.

"I'm good enough to be able to drive you home."

"Maybe you have a head injury. Or you hurt your neck with the headbutt."

"I'm fine."

"So am I. I'm perfectly able to drive home." Admittedly, she did have a headache, but she hated leaving her car at the party and not have it in the morning.

"I'm driving you home," he said as though his word was law.

She didn't argue. To be honest, her head ached enough to make her not want to drive. Besides, she liked Finn at her side. She wouldn't trust him with her heart, but he could act as her personal Uber.

They arrived at her house at 1:30 a.m. As she exited his car, he followed her to the door.

"Finn, I'll be fine from here. Thanks for the ride." She unlocked the front door and turned to say goodbye. Her heart and entire body longed to step closer to him, the traitors.

"Not a problem. Take care of that cut." He brushed her hair back again and checked on it under the front door light.

"At least my injury is tucked in my hairline. You'll have a shiner by morning, no doubt."

"It was a hell of an evening, but I'm glad to have seen you again. I'll call you about setting up some time with Lily," he said again, having stated the same thing at both the restaurant and during the ride home. His earnest expression almost melted her heart. Perhaps he had turned a corner and Lily would get her uncle back. Lily deserved more time with her biological family. Her great-aunt Maureen and great-uncle Walter took her for ice cream and to the zoo several times a year, but Finn was her closest connection to Miranda, and Julia wanted to strengthen that bond. That would be wonderful for Lily, but Julia had her own reservations. If he could break contact with them so easily in the past, what would prevent him from bolting when things became more complicated, uncomfortable or just boring? The thought scared her. She wanted to trust him, but he had some hills to climb to do so.

"That's fine. You have my phone number. Good night," she whispered, trying to remove Finn from Lily's line of vision. Her little girl had suddenly poked her head around Julia's legs, dressed in red-and-blue Cookie Monster pajamas. The four-year-old looked like Miranda, lanky body and dark curly hair.

"What are you doing awake?" Julia asked, seeing Dianne, Lily's nanny, raising her hands in a gesture of apology in the background. She couldn't be angry. Lily sometimes woke up and couldn't go back to sleep. And Julia would never force her. Perhaps this was an opportunity, one she should embrace. So she opened the door wider.

Finn crouched down and leaned back to not crowd Lily's space. "Hi, Lily. Do you remember me?"

She nodded. "Uncle Finn."

Finn chuckled as Julia stood there with her jaw hanging open. Lily never spoke to anyone. And one visit with her uncle pulled her out of her shell? The idea both thrilled Julia and annoyed her. In two years Lily hadn't spoken and he might have been the cure all along?

She looked between Finn and Lily. Lily stared up at him as though he was a rock star and she was a teenage fangirl.

"It's a pleasure to see you again." He reached out and shook her hand. Lily regarded him with as serious a face as a four-year-old could muster, and then she grinned.

Julia remained cautious. Perhaps Lily would have a delayed reaction. Finn could walk away and she'd be left to clean up Lily's broken heart.

"Lily, go back into the house and I'll get you a cookie," Julia said, hoping the bribe would work. "Uncle Finn is just leaving." She gestured for Lily to move back into the house, while trying to force Finn back to his car.

Lily grabbed his hand and pulled him inside the house.

Julia glanced at Finn and saw him winking at Lily. The suck-up.

"I don't think he likes cookies, Little Bear." Her glance turned into a glare.

He ignored her, keeping his attention on Lily. "I love cookies. Thank you, Lily. Do you have any milk? We can't eat cookies without milk."

She nodded and pulled him toward the kitchen.

"The perfect end to a strange evening." Finn laughed as he was escorted across the house.

Julia followed them into the kitchen. His large size was framed by the huge floor-to-ceiling windows overlooking a forest of trees hanging on to the last leaves of the season, mostly yellow, some orange. She looked toward the creek that cut through the backyard lit up by several strategically placed lights both for aesthetics and security. It really was peaceful there. She'd placed several benches along a pathway on the edge of the creek. It was her version of paradise.

Dianne stood by the kitchen island. She'd spent the night to watch over Lily.

"I'm glad you're okay. You had me worried when you called about the accident." Dianne dressed in what Julia termed casual grunge. Her outfits included ripped jeans, white T-shirts often worn with a black suit vest and black Converse.

"Why don't you go to sleep and I'll put Lily to bed," Julia said.

"Sure. I'll check on her when I wake up."

As Dianne headed to her bedroom, Lily pushed a chair over to the counter, climbed up and grabbed two chocolate chip cookies from the glass cookie jar. She hopped down, ran over to Finn and handed him one.

Finn leaned down to accept it. He towered over her. "These look fantastic. Thanks."

Lily bit into her cookie, but her eyes never left her uncle. Julia fought back tears. It was as though the last piece in their puzzle had arrived.

Julia poured two glasses of milk and turned the kettle on for tea for herself. This was going to take a while, as he appeared ready to settle in. But what could she do, kick him out when Lily seemed more than ready to build a relationship with him again?

By the time the water boiled, Finn and Lily were absorbed in a deep conversation about chocolate chip versus oatmeal-raisin cookies on the living room couch. Julia stood apart watching them as she prepared the tea. When she finished, she took her mug to the table to observe her precious little girl hanging out with the most confusing person she'd ever met.

Lily appeared sleepy. Julia shifted the little girl onto her lap and rocked her back and forth. Lily curled into her chest. Slowly, her eyes closed and Julia could feel the steady breathing of her daughter as she fell asleep.

"She looks like Miranda," he stated in a hushed tone. He'd turned his head to speak as close as possible to Julia without actually touching his face to hers. His breath, however, grazed her skin like the finest piece of silk. She wanted to lean in further, but not with Lily on her lap.

"And her uncle," Julia admitted, struggling to not place her head on his shoulder. They both had dark hair and blue eyes.

They both loved peanut butter and butter on their toast, and they both made her chest tighten when Julia thought of them.

"I wish Miranda could see how beautiful she is." His voice caught on something, perhaps heartbreak.

She gave into her yearning and leaned on his arm, pulling Lily in closer as well. It would be wonderful to remain sitting with Lily tucked between her and Finn. Her dysfunctional vision of a family.

"I think she'd love the fact that you're willing to do playdates with Lily."

The shortest, sweetest laugh came from him. "Playdates? Will you provide juice boxes and Goldfish crackers?" Finn's arm rolled off the couch onto Julia's shoulder. His thumb started to press into her muscle, relaxing her.

Cravings that Julia had tried to ignore flared up, like using a blowtorch on a pile of kindling.

"I...um...think I should put Lily to bed," she said, leaning closer to Lily and brushing her hand through her little girl's soft curls.

He seemed to get the point. Lifting his arm off her, he said, "I should get going anyway. I may stop by in the morning to check on you." Finn stood with her and walked to the kitchen to grab his jacket.

"No need, my nanny is sleeping over." His visit seemed to work out. Lily had fun. "Thanks for being so nice to her."

He looked back and waved as he went out the front door. Julia stared after him wishing she'd pushed their friendship a little more, but, in the end, was thankful she didn't. As the door closed behind him, tears flowed down her cheeks. The what-could-have-beens ripped through her mind. She'd been so prepared to go all in with him. But distance, murder and a whole new level of responsibilities got in the way.

At seven o'clock the next morning, Julia woke up to see her mother, Gabrielle, sitting on the edge of her bed. Her mother's black pants and white blouse were wrinkled. Gabrielle never wrinkled, not even her face. She must have really hurried to arrive at her daughter's side.

"Mom. How did you get here?"

"I took the jet. No one else in the family was using it." The Gardiner fortune provided her family access to a whole world of luxuries. One of which was a private flight from Philadelphia to Boston. Her mother's long, elegant fingers, decorated with a few subtle jewels, brushed across Julia's cheek. "When you called me last night about the press, you mentioned a head injury. Did you think I'd let you deal with all of this alone?"

"Thanks." She didn't want to tell her that Finn had taken her home and shared a snack with Lily. Her mother was still furious at him for breaking Julia's heart. "Let me check on Lily and I'll make us some tea."

"I'll meet you in the kitchen. I have to be home tonight for the gala for the art museum."

Julia nodded and got out of bed. Her head hurt at the place it had hit the wall, but the deep, throbbing headache was gone. She walked to Lily's bedroom, taking in the calm of the house.

Her home, a white three-bedroom colonial, sat on a small hill above Concord, forty minutes from Boston. Julia had chosen the isolated location for its peace and tranquility, tucked away from nosy neighbors and anyone else interested in the Gardiner family. A refuge for Lily to block out her violent past. Julia had added a six-foot fence around the back two acres to give Lily a play area. Lots of room to grow up feeling safe.

A squealing "Ma" and pattering footsteps came from Lily's bedroom. Lily, still dressed in her pajamas, leaped into her arms. Dianne followed and began to gather her things. She probably wanted to get home to study or to visit Kevin, her longtime boyfriend.

"Good morning, Dianne. Good morning, Little Bear." Julia kissed Lily on the tip of her nose. She could snuggle Lily all day, pain or no pain. She breathed in baby shampoo and straw-berry toothpaste. The smells of home.

Julia carried her across the room to the living room couch and sat. Lily bounced on her lap, smacking her hand on the cut on her head. Sucking in her breath, Julia shifted her away from the pain.

"You should be checked at the hospital," her mother in-sisted.

"I'm fine. I'll be back at work by this afternoon and home with my little bear by dinner," Julia said, kissing Lily's head.

"Seriously?" Gabrielle glared at Julia. If she could, she'd probably keep Julia home all week to rest, but Julia preferred to stay active.

"You should talk. I remember Dad yelling at you for going to work at the foundation with a temperature of 103."

"That was different. My children had already left the house by that point."

Dianne hurried her departure as the conversation heated up. "Nice seeing you again, Mrs. Gardiner. I'll be back by two." Dianne grabbed her bag and trotted to the door, leav-ing everyone a fading view of her short black-and-pink hair.

A few seconds later, the doorbell rang and Lily ran to the window to see who was there. Her eyes widened and her face fell. She ran down the hall as though the devil himself had arrived at the door. She was very shy with strangers, but cer-tain people sent her into crisis. Her therapist told Julia to be patient and she would be get over it. Lily had a long way to go to get over the trauma and Julia would be there by her side the whole way. Her sneaking to Julia's side and saying hi to Finn had been unusual. But Finn was family.

Julia looked down the hall toward Lily's room and then went to the front door.

A deliveryman with the physique of a college football

player and holding a large bouquet of flowers stared at Lily's retreating form. "Julia Gardiner?" he asked.

"That's me." Julia faked a smile and reached for the flowers.

"Here you go." He handed over the flowers. "Have a great day."

"Thanks," Julia said, glancing back toward Lily's room.

Leaning up against the closed door and holding the crystal cut vase filled with a rainbow of cheerful flowers, Julia inhaled the floral bouquet. A citrus scent brought back precious memories of summer picnics on Martha's Vineyard. The most peaceful place on Earth. She sighed. Looking up, she saw Gabrielle standing in the hall.

Her mother approached and hugged her, a brief gesture of support one mother to another. "Go check on Lily. I'll start the water for tea."

"Thanks, Mom." Julia inhaled deeply then headed to check on her little girl.

Soft sobs and little sniffles mixed with mild hyperventilating breaths echoed out Lily's door. Julia paused in the doorway. Her heart broke at all the pain this poor child had been through. "Lily? It was just a person delivering flowers. Do you want to see them?"

Lily, lying on her bed, the covers pulled up to her chest with her head on her pillow and her arms wrapped around a giant Smurf, shook her head.

Julia sat on the pale green rug next to Lily's bed and opened the small square envelope. "The card says the flowers are from your uncle Finn." That was fast. He'd only been home for a few hours. She glanced down at Lily wanting so much to heal all her broken pieces and her uncle's too. "They're very pretty. I like the red flowers best. What about you?"

Silence, except for an occasional sniffle.

Julia continued, "We should get rid of the blue flowers. I think they're kind of sad."

Lily turned her face and looked over the flowers in Julia's hands. "No. I like blue." The sound of her sweet voice crashed over Julia. It was as though they'd lived in a storm for a very long time and the sun finally shone through.

"You do?"

Lily bit her bottom lip and pulled the Smurf in tighter. "His eyes are blue like mine."

Julia sucked in her breath, trying to prevent her watery eyes from releasing the pent-up tears. She didn't want to upset Lily with her own despair. "I guess we should keep them all then."

"Okay," replied the tiny voice on the bed.

"Do you want to come to the kitchen for some breakfast with Grandma?" She reached over to rub Lily's back, calming herself in the process.

Lily shook her head.

Julia moved toward the door. "If you change your mind, there's a blueberry pancake sitting on the counter that is just for you."

She wanted to hug her, pick her up and carry her to the kitchen, but Lily needed space. Too much excitement might scare her, but too much concern could harm her as well, so Julia walked a tightrope between comfort and distance.

When Julia returned to the kitchen, her mother was pouring hot water into two earthenware mugs. Miranda had loved those mugs. They'd purchased them during a weekend in Vermont. Lily had been so tiny back then, but she'd presented her toothless grin to the old potter and every random customer in the studio. Completely innocent. Completely trusting.

"I didn't realize Lily still had so much anxiety." Gabrielle handed Julia a steaming mug of tea.

Julia sat down at the table, cradling the warmth between her hands. "Her psychologist told me Lily needs more time in a stress-free environment without feeling pressured. I was skeptical. But some people make her very upset. Mostly men, but she refused to go into the bank when a woman walked in before us. I can't find a common denominator, although I'm sure it's related to Miranda's murder."

Her mother sat next to her. "I think you're going about this all wrong. By keeping her so isolated from the world, you make everything more foreign and scarier. One man created a problem for her, but this isolation could turn every other person into a monster."

"I'm following the advice of her psychologist."

"Perhaps this person needs to be replaced. Has she given you a time limit on her being cloistered?"

"No. She said the time will come when Lily will speak and be more comfortable among strangers, but I shouldn't push it." Julia didn't want to mention that Lily had started speaking when Finn arrived.

"So you're not dating until she's cured."

"I'm not interested in dating anyone." Except Finn.

Gabrielle shook her head. "Terrific, she'll be in college and you'll be fifty by the time you start dating again."

"A boyfriend isn't on the top of my priority list." She'd already spoken to her mother about this a hundred times, but her mother didn't seem to listen, or perhaps she couldn't see any other person's opinion. She always was the most stubborn person Julia had ever known.

"I am impressed in the way you're adopting her, loving her and making her a huge part of your life and our entire family. Yet, you need to put the oxygen mask on in order to take care of yourself so you can successfully take care of her."

"I'm breathing fine, thank you."

Gabrielle shook her head. "By making yourself miserable, you'll end up making Lily miserable as well."

"I won't let Miranda down. Lily needs me more than I need a boyfriend." Julia stared out the window toward the creek winding through the backyard and thought about Finn.

Her heart was already breaking and he hadn't done anything wrong...yet. Having him back in her life just might kill her, but what was the alternative?

# Chapter 4

John sat at the edge of his bed, staring at the shitty wall in the shitty apartment in his shitty life. His days since leaving the military had become a monotonous cycle—wake up to a nightmare of the past, try to forget and repeat. The buzzing of his phone pulled him out of his thoughts. He glanced at the screen and tensed. Colonel Alec Rayburn. The man had once praised him for his work and then discarded him. Without Rayburn's extra financial support, John's world shrank into nothing. If Rayburn had a job for John, he'd accept. No matter what it was.

John hesitated before answering. "Colonel Rayburn."

"Private O'Donnell, good to hear your voice." Rayburn always called him Private, despite him rising to the rank of sergeant, but John would be called anything for some cash. "Got a little problem I need your help with."

"What kind of problem?"

"I'm having an issue with a Finn Maguire. He's been poking around—talking to someone in Internal Review about Major Donner."

The name struck John like a hammer. Donner. That's where he'd heard Maguire's name. With thousands of military personnel and private consultants at the base, they'd never run into each other. But John had planted the evidence that had destroyed Maguire's life. He hadn't known the guy would have the guts to keep digging, not after everything that had been taken from him.

Rayburn's voice interrupted his thoughts. "He obviously has too much time on his hands. I need you to fix that."

John's grip tightened around the phone. "How do you want me to handle it?"

"I want you to throw his life into chaos. His sister's dead, but he's still got a niece. I need you to…go after her."

John frowned, leaning forward. "Go after?"

"There's no father on the girl's birth certificate. Her mother lived near Boston, and you lived near Boston in the same period. Convenient, isn't it? You're about to become a dad, John."

The words settled into him like a cold weight. "You want me to pretend to be her father."

"Exactly. Get into his head. Play the role. He's already teetering. We just need to push him over the edge."

"What if they want DNA?"

"It'll be taken care of. You're no longer John O'Donnell. Consider yourself John Holland for the near future."

"Wouldn't it be easier to just get rid of him?" John had already killed Donner and Miranda after all.

Rayburn's reply was immediate. "No. If he's hurt, certain information will head to people who could put two and two together far better than he can. He needs to stay alive, but always on edge."

A long silence stretched between them before John replied, "How much?"

"Enough for you to retire from your job at the 7/Eleven."

John closed his eyes for a moment; the risk was enormous, but what option did he have? He had no savings, nothing to lose. Slipping into darkness again was like muscle memory.

"All right," he said. The more he thought on it, the better he felt.

"Good," Rayburn said, his voice cool and satisfied. "I knew

I could count on you. Let's make sure Maguire regrets ever asking questions."

The line went dead.

# Chapter 5

Finn sat in his office, his elbows resting on his desk. His head still hurt; the throbbing seemed more to do with his worry for Julia than the actual headbutt. He'd involved Julia in the party in an attempt to see her again. Instead, his cousin nearly sent her to the hospital. The thought of Richard pawing at her made him spitting mad.

Seeing Lily last night had made him realize just how stupid he'd been keeping himself away from the both of them. Lily deserved an uncle and he wanted to believe he deserved Lily in his life. Julia? Well, time would tell if they could fix the rift between them. The connection seemed as strong as ever, but he'd abandoned her when she'd needed him. He couldn't waltz back in and expect forgiveness in one night. But he had patience. She was worth it.

A knock on his door hurt both his head and his ability to concentrate. He had a killer headache, caused by the heaps of paperwork on his desk and the ink-colored hematoma on his forehead courtesy of Richard.

The door opened to reveal Davis, Finn's business partner and closest friend from high school. He walked in, looking every bit the international playboy that he wasn't. If image had value, Davis would have a house in the Riviera and a spot on a polo team. "Nice move, Rocky."

"What?"

Davis raised his eyebrows. "The minute I leave the party,

you slug Richard in the face, send him to the hospital and then calmly ask, 'What?'"

"I'd do it again in a heartbeat. He attacked Julia." Thinking about Julia's head injury, Finn clenched his fists as his heart hammered into his ribs.

"Typical asshole Richard move," Davis agreed. "I couldn't bear to watch him further humiliate his parents with his drinking. Had I known what was to come, I would have lingered until the end if only to give you an eyewitness to his actions. The DA wants to press charges against him, but she's waiting for Julia to corroborate your story. The police, however, are giving major pushback. Must have something to do with Richard's recent donation to their memorial fund." Davis often obtained detailed information of closed-door meetings throughout Boston. Whatever the source, the insider knowledge could only help Finn in this situation.

Davis dropped down into a chair, and crossed his foot over his knee. He tended to hang out in Finn's office when something pressing had to be discussed. Finn resigned himself to having a guest in his office indefinitely.

"I spoke to Walter," Davis said. "He said his idiot son Richard needed to get his jaw wired shut. I guess Richard can't annoy us at board meetings for a while."

"Too bad they can't make it permanent," Finn said.

"The perfect kind of investor—silent." Davis hated Richard as much as Finn did. His father and Walter had started the car dealership nearly fifty years ago. Richard and Davis took over their fathers' roles. Davis ran the whole dealership and Richard pranced around, pretending to be important. Richard, however, had a way of spending the dealership's money without working to bring in income. When they hit a rough spot, Finn offered to take a home equity loan on his condo to buy an interest in the company and a new purpose in life. Finn and Davis owned 51 percent combined, which kept Richard's spending under control. "Richard's drunk ass should rot in prison, but he'll get off. Kim will support him no matter what, hiring the best attorneys possible. And they'll want to make your life miserable. Feel free to sell your shares. I'd understand."

Finn's stomach soured at the thought. "Richard would never agree. He'd never give me my investment back and that would bankrupt me. I don't have many other options."

"Except to return to Fresh Pond Security." Davis had told Finn to return to his old job because he seemed happier there.

Returning, however, wasn't an option. When his boss, Jason Stirling, admitted to lying about his real identity in an attempt to hide from the head of a drug cartel, Finn left the company . Jason had not only putting the team at risk, but Jason's wife and son as well. Finn couldn't work for someone he didn't trust, but working with Richard had its own issues. If it wasn't for his money being tied up in the dealership, he might have tried to find something…anything else.

"I prefer you annoying me every day," Finn replied. He did like working with Davis, but Davis was happy running a car dealership. Finn wanted his old life back in private security.

"How's Julia?"

"She went right back to work. She should have stayed home."

"You should check on her in person tonight."

"I sent flowers to her house. She texted a quick thanks, but I should keep my distance until she sends me an invite to see Lily again." He wanted to respect her space.

"You're not some stranger. You're her ex and Lily's uncle."

"I saw them last night. I'll catch up to them later."

"Suit yourself, but she may be too busy to see you after today."

"What are you talking about?"

"Your ex-girlfriend's face is all over the newspapers. Julia

Gardiner. It says her family's foundation is one of the largest in the country. Didn't you know that about her when you dated her?" Davis threw the newspaper article on Finn's desk.

In the photo, Julia appeared like an American aristocrat in a designer dress at some fundraiser. The only information he had about her family was that her father and mother lived an upscale life outside of Philadelphia. Apparently, they had billionaire-level wealth. "I knew she came from an affluent family, but not this level. She never spoke about her family situation. She likes her privacy."

"I wouldn't advertise that fact either. With that much money, she's got a target on her back."

Finn stared at the photo again. She would have more than one target on her if he became too involved with her.

After going over some sales numbers with Finn, Davis didn't leave. He remained in his chair, grinning with too much expression, even for him.

Finn finally acknowledged Davis's ridiculous countenance. "What's going on? You're far too happy, even knowing Richard can't speak for a while."

Davis beamed. "While you were beating up Richard, I left the party and went to the Kelleher Rose Garden with Calvin and asked him if he'd take the next step with me."

"Seriously? You proposed?" A stupid question. Of course, he'd proposed. He'd been living with Calvin for three years. They were inseparable. Calvin had been the one to recommend Finn for a position at Fresh Pond Security when he'd left the military. Finn owed him a lot.

"We went for a drink and walked over to the gardens. I proposed by the half-moon bridge."

Finn smiled at his friend's happiness. "It couldn't have happened to two better guys. I'm really happy for you." Davis and Calvin had been steady and faithful to each other since they first met. They deserved this moment.

"Thanks. The wedding won't be anything huge," Davis said. "Calvin prefers small, simple and subtle."

Finn thought about Julia and the destruction of the event she'd planned. "I know the best event planner around. Let her do your engagement party on my dime. If you like her, she can help with your wedding."

"I assume you're speaking about Julia? I don't know. Wouldn't this bring you into contact with the woman whom you've resolved to avoid?"

Finn shrugged. "I feel bad about what happened to her last night. Richard is my cousin after all. And I'm trying to be more involved with Lily."

"And Julia?"

"One step at a time."

Davis threw up his hands. "By all means then, plan away, but don't break her heart again—and keep the color scheme monochromatic."

"I know what Calvin likes. I'm sure she can make it happen."

Davis finally stood. "Good luck then."

Finn followed Davis to the door and closed it behind him. He stared at his phone for a few minutes, then dialed.

"Hello?"

"Julia?"

"Speaking. Is this the man who sent flowers this morning?" She sounded quieter than normal.

"It is." The person who tried to help you but failed. "How are you feeling?" He needed a visual. Did she have bruises from hitting the wall?

"I'm fine. A butterfly Band-Aid and a few Tylenol work wonders." She tried to make light of it, but he could hear her fear. "I made it to the office this afternoon, so I'm functional."

She should be at home resting. He tried to speak without sounding too forceful. "Shouldn't you take some time to heal?"

"I have some pain medicine if I need it and I'll go home early."

"When do you see a doctor?"

"I don't need a doctor, but I happen to have an appointment with my internist in two weeks. If it doesn't feel better, I'll move the appointment up."

"Look, if you need anything, I can help."

"Thanks, but I'm pretty self-sufficient," she said, her voice growing more distant.

"I'm sure you are."

"How about you? Are you okay?" she asked.

"I'm fine except for a nice bump on my head and a sore toe. I was also calling because it seems I'm in need of your services." Not only would providing her extra business bring some consolation for the pain she suffered, but he could also check on her.

"What service do you need?" she asked, turning professional.

"I'm planning an engagement party and would love your help."

She paused. Finn waited her out, curious as to her reaction. Which kind of made him a jerk, but he wanted to gauge her interest in him.

"Oh. Congratulations?" Was that melancholy he heard under the words?

The asshole in him felt good about that. "Not for me. For my friend Davis Malone and his partner. Davis is the financial brains of the car dealership."

Julia took a deep breath and let it out, creating a light whistle in the phone. "I remember Davis. He's quite the charmer."

"Still is."

"And his future spouse?"

"His name is Calvin Ross. He worked through the party last night so you wouldn't have seen him."

"And you want to throw the engagement party?" she asked.

"He's one of my best friends. Neither he nor Calvin have much family around here." He could take care of both Davis and Julia. A double good deed.

"Okay. When are you planning the party for?"

"Three weeks from now?" That would be enough time to make sure she's okay.

Julia paused. Her voice, attempting to be cheery, darkened again. "No problem. I'll have my manager Helena call you to set everything up."

Finn's throat tightened. Was she passing him off? "I thought you handled these events," he blurted out like a nerdy kid with his first awkward crush.

"I'm really busy right now, but Helena's terrific. If you give me the cell number of one of the grooms, I'll have her call them. Look, I have to go, but I appreciate your call."

As he hung up, he felt dismissed. She couldn't get rid of him that easy.

His phone rang before he even placed it back on his desk.

"Hello?" His voice scratched with fatigue and wariness.

"Finn." A voice from the past he hadn't expected to hear from again. Jason Stirling.

Finn gripped the receiver tighter. "What's going on?"

"I'm calling to check on you," Jason replied.

"I'm good."

"Give me a break. Calvin was at the party before all hell broke out. Davis filled him in on the details. You can't still want to work with your cousin, and I have a job opening..."

"No."

"At least hear my proposition."

"I'd rather get suckerpunched by my cousin than work for someone I don't trust."

There was a pause, a silent space where Finn wanted Jason

to say the right combination of words to convince him to come back and make everything right between them. But he didn't.

"And you trust your cousin? The one who attacked Julia?"

"I don't trust anyone anymore."

"I get it. But I think you know, deep down in your soul, we'll always have your back. If you ever want to return, or you want anything at all, I'll always leave the door open to you."

After the call, a rush of emotion came over Finn. He didn't want to care about his prior work at Fresh Pond Security and the people he'd worked with, but damn he missed them all.

# Chapter 6

Finn listened to the purr of the engine turn into a roar as the red Ferrari V-12 F12 backed into the showroom. A small crowd had gathered outside to watch the car described as everyman's dream car be placed on display until someone rich enough to afford the crazy price tag decided to buy.

"Can I get that in a navy blue?" Davis asked, wearing an outfit every bit as pretentious as the car.

Finn laughed. "For the right price, we'll make it green with yellow polka dots."

"How did you obtain this? There's a two-year wait at the main dealership for this model."

Finn grinned. "This baby became the center of a custody dispute in a really nasty divorce. I received a call after the judge declared that the parties needed to sell it." Major acquisitions, like this one, made his job challenging and fun.

"Divorce. So ugly, yet such an opportunity as well. *C'est la guerre.*"

"Agreed." Finn turned back into his office with Davis following along. "Did you get the information on the party?" He'd handed off the planning to Davis, who was more than happy to set the menu and arrange the evening. Finn would handle the bill. He didn't want to spend time with Julia's second-in-command. He wanted to spend time with Julia and find out how she was doing.

Davis nodded and sat in his usual chair. "Yes, I had lunch

with Julia at the Driftwood Cafe. It's the perfect location. Reasonably priced for the crazy friend who wants to pay for it, but very elegant."

Finn frowned. So Julia didn't want to step back from Finn's event, just Finn himself. It was for the best, but the cut made him even more protective of her. "And how is Julia?" Finn needed a physical description. A picture would be even better.

"She looks great, almost no sign of the injury. You'd know that if you called her."

"I am visiting Lily in a few days. Julia's and my relationship is strictly business." Finn glanced at his computer screen one second too late.

"Seriously? Your eyes reveal far more than your mouth does. I'd say you're smitten."

"Smitten? What kind of word is that?" Julia could never be right for him. The heiress and the criminal, a match made in hell.

Davis leaned back and tented his fingers together. "The perfect word actually. I remember seeing you guys together at Miranda's birthday party a few years ago. Neither of you could keep your eyes off each other. And you haven't dated another woman since then."

"First, I'm too busy to date anyone. Second, I care about Julia as a friend, the same way I care about you."

"No, it's more than that."

The phone rang, interrupting their conversation. After Davis left to return to his office, Finn answered the phone.

"Kim's here," Aspen, their office manager, warned.

*Great.* "Thanks. Don't let her back here. I'll come out."

"I'll try." Aspen hung up.

Bracing himself for Hurricane Kim, Finn wandered out to greet the disturbance in the showroom.

Kim stood next to the F12 wearing a beige rag wool sweater

and worn tan riding pants tucked into tall brown boots. Her red hair was tucked into a leather headband.

Putting his hands in his pockets, he strolled over to her. "Hello, Kim. Nice to see you."

"Screw you, Finn. Richard still has his mouth wired shut and you're to blame. I don't care what the police report says. You beat up my husband."

"He tried to molest a woman. I'm surprised the police didn't charge him with attempted rape. It's a joke he only received misdemeanor assault charges." He backed up. Her explosions could involve violent confrontations and he didn't need any more bad blood between him and the rest of his family.

She stepped toward him. Arrogant and aggressive. "You wouldn't have this office if it wasn't for Richard feeling bad for you. He let you buy into the dealership. You owe him everything and this is how you repay him?"

"He needed my capital. Still does. He also needs the profit Davis and I generate to make up for his slacking."

Kim poked him in the chest. "Maguire Exotics would fold if Richard ever pulled his investment."

Before Finn could remove her hand, Davis showed up in full stride to greet her. "Kim, how wonderful to see you. Spend the morning at the stables?" He approached swiftly and gave her a European kiss on each cheek. His teeth sparkled as he smiled at her.

"You are such a charmer. Thanks. Yes, I rode Mickleby for two hours this morning. He's doing great."

"Terrific. I wanted to tell you some fantastic news. Calvin and I are having an engagement party and we need you there to make it the social event of the season." Davis had a difficult job keeping Richard and Kim happy while ignoring their business advice. They craved the prestige of the company but neither of them had a competent bone in their body. The checks he sent them each month kept their interference limited.

"Of course I can make it. How fun." Kim loved being the center of attention and someone else's event was usually her preferred stage. Being in the spotlight was great, but stealing it from someone else felt divine.

She angled herself to cut Finn off from the conversation. He could now see only the back of her head. Eventually, she hugged Davis goodbye and strutted away without looking back toward Finn. No loss.

"Thanks. She was about to create a scene," Finn said.

"I figured I could take her mind off the *incident* and let her continue to think I adore her."

"You're a pal."

Davis turned and they both walked back to their offices. "No, it's self-preservation. If they sell their investment, we're screwed."

"That won't happen. They prefer the income."

"Perhaps, but better to be safe than insolvent."

# Chapter 7

John could see Julia's house clearly. For such a rich bitch, she certainly had a small house. If he had her millions, he'd live in a fortress overlooking the ocean.

Her huge windows acted like plasma television sets, screening her life to him from dusk to dawn. She really should pull her shades down after sunset, but if she wanted to remain oblivious to the dangers lurking outside at night, all the better for him. Single woman, no neighbors. She flirted with danger and John couldn't wait to flirt right back. He loved watching Julia arrive home in the early afternoon only to leave again after dusk, dressed in some dress designed to be pulled up over her hips as she was shoved against a wall. As he sat outside the house, he imagined receiving the money Rayburn promised to him and also a payment from her for the physical pain she was causing him as he sat and obsessed over all he could do to her.

During his nightly observations, he mostly focused his attention on Lily. She looked like Miranda now that she was older.

He walked back down the road to his car and slowly drove away. He had taken enough photographs of Lily from the back woods to ensure that he'd recognize her instantly. He'd also memorized Julia's quirky but steady schedule. Babysitter arrives at 7:00 a.m. Julia leaves fifteen minutes later most mornings. She must work a short day, because she usually returned to play with the kid at about two. Several hours and a slutty little dress later, she's back out the door to entertain whoever's paying her. Her nights generally didn't end until two or three in the morning. Repeat ad infinitum.

Rayburn called.

"The plan is in motion," John exclaimed before Rayburn could say hello. "The child is as good as mine."

"It's not enough. I want you to screw with his business too."

"His business? The car dealership?" John had no idea how to disrupt a business, but he'd look into it.

"Keep him occupied on all fronts."

"Okay."

The phone went dead before John could respond.

He looked down at the place where his watch, a steel TAG Heuer, had adorned his wrist until recently. A gift from Rayburn, he'd had to sell it when his funds dried up. Rayburn was the only way he'd get back to where he'd been.

# *Chapter 8*

The simple white envelope arrived certified, return receipt requested. Julia signed for it and walked into the kitchen. Standing by the table, she picked up a knife and slid it through the crease to open the letter.

After reading the first few lines, Julia felt her neck muscles tighten. By the end of the letter, her entire body clenched so tight, she almost collapsed. Already tired from handling an event the night before and spending the morning at the office, she leaned against the wall to give her weakened bones additional support.

Dianne, dressed in shredded jeans and a Death Rocks T-shirt, hustled over to her side. "What's wrong? Are you all right?"

"Can you stay for a few more hours? I need to handle some things." Julia forced herself to straighten up. She couldn't let Lily see her fall apart. Not now.

"Sure. I'll call Kevin and tell him that I'll be late. He'll be cool about it."

"Thanks. I appreciate it." Julia glanced back at Lily, who was in the kitchen eating some apple slices. She went over to her and kissed her on the cheek. "I need to go out for a little while. You get to spend some extra time with Dianne."

"Can I come?" Lily asked, looking up at Julia with the most innocent blue eyes. She had been speaking more and more after her meeting with Finn. He had promised to visit the next day and Lily was thrilled.

"No. I'm going to a busy office and you'll have more fun with Dianne." Lily's darn eyes would be Julia's undoing. She squeezed Lily's shoulders and kissed her cheeks again, refusing to think about how important the little imp was in her life.

"Please," Lily pleaded.

"Not today, Little Bear." Julia smiled at her and then rushed to grab her pocketbook and leave the house before she fell apart.

A few miles away, she pulled into the parking lot at the state park. The huge oak trees growing majestically in a patch of small pines soothed her. She took several deep breaths, and strengthened her backbone for the fight ahead. She read the letter again, and then picked up the phone. After canceling a dinner meeting with a client, Julia called her mother.

"Mom. I need you." She tried to sound stable, but the cellular connection to her mother turned everything around and shot the significance of the letter right back through her heart.

"What's wrong?" Gabrielle asked.

"It's Lily." Julia's voice broke. The tears that had held off suddenly flowed from her eyes. Her nose also filled up and leaked down her face. A mess. She became almost inconsolable for a few minutes.

"What is it, Julia? What's going on with Lily?"

Taking a huge breath, she tried to speak, but the tears and the sobbing overtook her again.

Gabrielle stayed silent during Julia's breakdown. When the crying slowed, Gabrielle spoke again. "Julia?"

"I'm…here," she said wiping her eyes with her sleeve.

"Deep breathing, honey. Just breathe. Take your time. What's wrong?" Her mother's voice provided the balm that stopped her shoulders from shaking and slowed the torrents of tears.

After few smaller sobs and a sniffle, Julia released the news, "I received a letter today. A court document. Lily has a father and he wants custody."

"Lily has a father? I thought Miranda never listed who he was." Gabrielle's voice stayed solid, strong.

Julia tried to emulate her mother's steel nerves. She spoke slowly, holding off the sobs that threatened to rise again. "She never mentioned a father to me and there isn't one listed on the birth certificate. Mom, this legal document is real. I'm holding it in my hand."

"Isn't the adoption this month?"

"Two weeks until it's final, but this could completely derail it." More tears broke through. She'd never considered that someone would prevent her from getting permanent custody. Although the anguish in her own heart twisted everything she'd planned into the future, maybe she should be happy for Lily, but her gut told her there was something wrong about this potential reconciliation. "Can I really beat a person who claims he's the father? And should I? Maybe Lily should live with her father." No, Julia couldn't fathom that possibility when this man had been absent for so long.

Gabrielle was silent for a few moments and then said, "What proof does he have that he's the father? Is he willing to do a paternity test? Call the attorney who is handling the adoption. See if she can meet today, even if it's past five o'clock. I'll pay double her normal hourly rate for an incentive. Have her look at every possible angle on this. As of right now, you're the custodial guardian. That means something. Don't panic."

"Thanks, Mom. I should be okay. You always seem to give me some of your backbone when we talk."

"Call anytime, I have a lot of backbone to spare. Do you have a friend who could go with you to the attorney's office? Helena maybe?"

"Yeah, I can call a friend. Thanks."

After she hung up, she made an appointment with her attorney, who was exceptionally accommodating and supportive. Then she called Finn. She needed him now. She didn't care if this pushed the limits of their non-relationship. He was Lily's uncle and should be involved.

Finn answered on the first ring. "Hello? Julia?"

"I'm so sorry to bother you at work." She tried to hide her heartache and fear, but her voice cracked and the tears began again.

"Julia, what's wrong?"

Between hiccups, she explained to him about the letter and the attorney's meeting.

"Where are you?" he asked.

"I'm in a park near my house. I didn't want to worry Lily so I left her with Dianne." Outside her window, a youth soccer practice started in a large open field. Loads of children running around without a care in the world. She bit her lip until she tasted the metallic tang of her own blood on her tongue.

Finn, although sympathetic in tone, belted out questions and orders. "What time is the appointment with the attorney?... Where is she located?... Calm down. Lily needs you... Cry later... Okay?"

By the time he finished grilling her, Julia's breathing had returned to normal and she felt much better. "Should I meet you at her office?"

"No. I'll drive. Can you go home? I'll pick you up there."

"Are you sure?"

"Go home," he ordered.

"All right. Thanks."

"What are friends for? I'll see you in an hour."

When they had both hung up, Julia drove toward home. She dabbed her eyes with some bottled water and tried to make herself appear happy and confident for Lily. She didn't need to worry about her appearance, however, because Dianne and Lily were playing in the backyard on the slide. Julia slipped into her bedroom and changed out of her jeans and into the linen pants she'd worn to work earlier. A brush through her hair, another across her teeth, a little makeup and she looked decent on the outside, despite her heart breaking. She headed out to the backyard to play with Lily for a few minutes. Her makeover seemed to do the trick, because Lily remained a happy and confident little kid climbing up and down the slide on the play structure.

Finn arrived at her house too quickly. He must have broken speed records to get there. He called her and waited outside so Lily didn't get upset by him arriving and then leaving. His car, a Bentley Continental, was as ostentatious as it could get. Not exactly the downplayed existence she'd imagined him in over the years, but she couldn't complain. It was incredibly comfortable and allowed her to relax for the first time since receiving the envelope. Or perhaps it was Finn's close proximity that eased her fear.

# Chapter 9

Bridget Kovach could have been mistaken for a suburban PTA mother from Kansas. With her long blond hair flowing straight down her back and her trim athletic figure covered by a peacock-blue wrap dress, she appeared wholesome and nurturing. Looks could be deceiving. Older male attorneys often underestimated her ability. Meeting her for the first time, they'd send confident looks toward their clients and then speak to her with slow enunciated speech to make sure she understood all those large Latin words. Once she finished manipulating the Massachusetts family law code to create miraculous results for her clients, those same attorneys took her more seriously. Much more seriously.

Julia's mother had found Bridget after asking some of her friends for a referral for the best family law attorney in Boston. Although Julia's initial case for adopting Lily would have been as easy to Bridget as a trip to the local nail salon, the interruption in the adoption process by Lily's possible father proved that mothers always knew best.

Julia never appreciated hiring such a shark until the moment she sat down in Bridget's office with Finn. Having the top family lawyer in the city on her side eased some of the stress plaguing her since receiving the notice of the claim for paternity that morning.

Bridget looked up from the piece of paper that had jolted Julia's life. "He wants an emergency hearing tomorrow. He must have some clout somewhere, because I called the court and they confirmed that Judge Miller is permitting a temporary custody hearing in the morning. Not to worry. Since he's had no contact with her since birth, they won't change custody immediately. They'll focus on what is in the best interest of Lily. Right now, that's you."

"How can a guy come out of the woodwork like this?" Finn asked. His support made the bitterness and fear clawing at Julia more bearable.

"When there's an unknown birth father, notice by publication is generally all that's needed to sever parental rights in an adoption. If no one objects in writing or in person by the hearing date, then the case moves forward. This guy filed his objection within the window. The adoption hearing is not for two weeks and he's already filed his objection."

"What's his name?" Finn asked, his harsh voice directed at the bastard trying to take away Lily.

Julia responded, "John Holland." The name sounded like some boring bureaucrat. He'd probably want to force Lily into a life of organized dreariness.

"I never heard of him. Have you?" Finn asked Julia this time.

"No. When Miranda became pregnant, I was commuting back and forth between Philadelphia and here during my father's cancer treatments. I didn't pay attention to whom Miranda was with at the time."

Finn placed a hand on her back and rubbed. His touch absorbed some of the strain and she leaned toward him.

When Bridget finished typing on her keyboard, she glanced between Finn and Julia, perhaps making an assumption that they were more than friends. She didn't get ahead in her field by missing the connections between people. "I don't know what's going on between you two, but for the time being, you're only friends. Finn, you're Lily's uncle and a great advocate for her. Julia, you're her legal and physical guardian. Together, you can argue for Lily's best interests, but if the judge focuses on a possible relationship between you, Finn's criminal record could hurt Julia's claim for custody."

Finn took his hand off Julia's back as though he'd been burned.

"That's all we are," Julia replied. She'd never admit to wanting anything more with him. She didn't want to lose his friendship and she didn't want to lose Lily. A real relationship would be too risky, especially now.

A frown creased Bridget's face. "Sure. Make sure this friendship doesn't blossom into anything else until Lily's adoption is final."

Like two children being chided by their teacher, Julia and Finn remained silent.

Bridget typed a few things onto her keyboard. "I did some background research on Mr. Holland after you called. It seems he manages call centers located in foreign countries. His most recent job took him to India for three years. Perhaps he thought Miranda would take care of Lily until he returned, without a cost to him. When he found out she'd died, he probably decided to go for custody out of guilt."

"Who would abandon a child, not pay child support, or have any contact with her, and then push for custody? Guilt alone wouldn't make someone want to uproot his life, especially if Lily was already in a good situation. It doesn't make sense," Finn said.

"We'll figure out everything about this guy before the final hearing. I'm requesting a paternity test and I'll get an affidavit from Lily's psychologist about her fear around men. That should slow him down for at least a few weeks." Bridget's eyes returned to her computer. All business.

"Does he have a chance?" Julia didn't want the answer. She wanted to remain oblivious to all of the roadblocks to her adoption of Lily, but fighting with her eyes wide open would provide a better chance at keeping her.

Bridget looked up, her blond hair shining in the sun and her blue eyes beaming rays of wholesome goodness. Then she shot Julia in the heart. "If he passes the paternity test? Yes. He has a chance at some form of custody."

# Chapter 10

Finn escaped with Julia from the attorney's office and found a small diner. Her normal radiance had been replaced with tired eyes and a pinched expression. She walked with the gait of an eighty-year-old in need of a hip replacement. She needed food in her stomach and a little fire in her belly as well.

A young college-age waitress came over and asked Finn what they wanted. He ordered them each a cheeseburger, fries and a large chocolate milkshake. Julia needed some nourishment and something to comfort her after such a trying day. Finn would have given her a shot of Scotch, but the strongest liquid the diner served was coffee.

The waitress winked at him as she walked away. He ignored it, but Julia noticed. She glared at him. "Terrific, I'll have a heart attack before the hearing. Do I look like a person who can't order for herself?"

Finn shrugged his shoulders. "No, you look like a person who needs a friend to take over for a few minutes so you can concentrate on Lily. And a salad doesn't quite fill me up."

Julia scowled. "I'm glad your needs take precedence over mine."

He smiled. "You could have spoken up. I'm sure the waitress would have listened to you."

"She couldn't get her eyes off of you, so I doubt she would have heard a word coming from my direction." Jealousy looked really good on her.

"Do you want something different?" he asked.

"No."

He leaned back and crossed his arms. "Then why are you upset?"

"Because I want a choice. I need to make a decision."

"You make decisions every day. You run your business, calling all the shots. You're raising Lily as a single parent, so you decide everything regarding her well-being and, on top of all that, you're a grown woman who can pick and choose who to hang out with and what to eat. I thought I'd make a decision for you so you could relax for once and eat guilt-free. You've lost weight since the first time I've met you and, as your friend, I want to make sure you're okay."

"I'm fine." She spoke defensively as if she needed to prove that she had everything under control.

"I'm glad."

She could be fierce when she wanted to be. She needed to get into that role for the upcoming fight with John Holland. Finn didn't know too much about family law, but proof of paternity probably trumped the claims of a nonrelative. As Lily's biological uncle, he might have had a better chance of upending a custody fight. Perhaps he should have fought for his innocence instead of taking the deal, although his manslaughter conviction and the time served in the military prison would negate any blood relationship they shared, despite the crime being a misdemeanor and not a felony. The resentment over being labeled a criminal ate at him. He had to admit it, Julia was the best person for Lily. Not only because of her wealth, she was a beautiful soul, a hard worker, and a sweet but strict parent.

He paused while the waitress placed the milkshakes on the table. When she left, he spoke again. "You really are a great mother, by the way."

"Thanks." Her expression softened and she picked up the

glass to take a sip of the milkshake. When she put it down, she had a slim mustache over her lip. When they'd been first dating, she always left some milkshake over her top lip, and Finn had always kissed the sweetness off her. He needed to close his eyes to avoid letting his heart fall for her more. It wasn't the time or place to relive the best moments of his life. They'd laughed together, loved with every part of their being and should have been together for always. But not anymore. He wouldn't allow her to end up like Miranda.

Julia picked up a french fry with her fingers and smothered it in ketchup. After taking a bite, she peered up at him. The sight of a dot of ketchup directly below her nose caused him to grin.

He reached over and wiped the ketchup from her face with his finger, rubbing it onto his napkin. "Do you want me there tomorrow?"

"Yes. I think it might help. Could you take the time off?" she asked.

"Absolutely." He'd have to ask Davis to handle a meeting with a potential buyer.

"Thanks. You'll make a great husband someday. To the right woman." Her words stung. He wanted all of that with her, but he cared too much about her future to jeopardize it.

Picking up his milkshake, he took a long, slow sip of the richest milkshake he'd ever had. The icy liquid cooled his throat and gave him a few seconds to rethink the conversation. "I'm not cut out for marriage. It's not in the cards."

Julia swallowed the enormous bite of cheeseburger she'd taken and wiped the grease oozing over her fingers onto a paper napkin. The heiress was exhausted, and he was glad she could relax with him.

After drinking some more of her milkshake to swallow the rest of the burger, she said, "How do you know you won't meet someone? You deserve a partner in life and you're wonderful with children. Lily adored you when you were in her life."

Finn grew serious. He reached across the table and grabbed both of her hands. He needed all of her attention. "You heard the attorney. I'm seen by the bloodstains on my service record. I refuse to let my past affect you or Lily or anyone else around me."

"One moment in time can't destroy a life," she insisted. "You had told me once that you'd been framed."

"And you believe me?"

"If you committed premeditated murder, I don't think the prosecutors would have made a deal with you. Have you ever looked into the case again?"

Finn froze. He couldn't tell Julia anything about his case. He didn't want her or her family trying to "help" him. Her father had extensive connections in Congress, but Finn would never want Julia to have a target on her back.

"Don't go looking to change me from a criminal to a martyr. Nothing matters but what's listed on my discharge papers." He pulled back his hands.

Julia sat quietly, picking at some french fries. "I know your heart, and you aren't a killer. I don't understand why you won't pursue it."

"Just drop it, Julia."

"If I'd been falsely accused, I'd fight like hell to prove them wrong." Julia shook her head as though annoyed by Finn's stance. She had no idea that he had tried to fight it, but his last major attempt had ended in Miranda getting a knife to the chest.

"Why don't you focus on your work and Lily? I don't need you diving into my private business." He was brusque, but if she or her family asked the wrong people about what happened to Finn in Afghanistan, Julia could end up like Miranda and he couldn't let that happen.

They both ate in silence for a few minutes and then Julia insisted on being driven home.

"Should I come inside to see Lily?" Finn asked, remembering his playdate.

She shook her head. "Not today."

# Chapter 11

The next morning, Julia arrived with Finn at the Middlesex County Probate and Family Court, located in a modern glass building in Lowell. Finn had arrived, looking perfect as usual. But his words the day before, telling her to stay out of his life, had kept her up all night. She didn't want to focus on him when all of her attention should be on Lily, but his rejection of her assistance stung. Didn't he realize that she had certain resources that could be useful to him in clearing his name?

She filed away her heartbreak and focused on Lily. Small groups of people had congregated outside the doors to the courtroom. A few children stood in the hallway as well, accompanied by mothers or grandmothers or maybe social workers. The present and future of most of the people gathered there would be affected by the outcome of their court appearance.

If Julia could help it, Lily would never be present at such a legal proceeding. She'd left her little bear at home with Dianne, protected from this intrusion on their life. Lily didn't need to know about the man who wanted to remove her from her home until the last moment possible, if ever.

Across the room, Julia saw Bridget and breathed easier. Bridget's legal expertise rivaled Finn's physical presence as a balm to Julia's nerves. Bridget, dressed in a navy power suit with a pale gray blouse and pearls, stood outside talking with what looked like a few other attorneys, all in suits.

When Bridget saw Julia and Finn, she said her goodbyes to the suits and walked over.

"All set?" Bridget asked, reaching out to Julia.

Julia clasped Bridget's hand for a moment, absorbing some of her confidence and strength. "I guess so. I'm not sure what to do."

"Your job is to look like a great mother with a very supportive friend by her side." She turned to Finn and shook his hand. "Could you sit in the row behind us so that it doesn't look as though you're a party to the hearing as well? We want Julia to have support, but having what looks like a boyfriend can make the judge and even the opposing party question your role in Lily's life. We don't want to add additional issues to this case."

Finn nodded. "Sure."

They stood near the entrance to the courtroom for a few minutes until their names were called.

"Take a deep breath. Stay relaxed and as calm as possible." Bridget touched Julia's arm and then stood straighter and led them into the courtroom.

Julia stopped abruptly, causing Finn to bump into her. She swallowed hard, trying to open her throat, but terror had lodged in it.

"Sorry. Are you okay?" he asked, placing his hand on her back in a gesture that felt comforting, and yet possessive.

Julia pointed to the cause of her alarm. "Is that the guy?"

Bridget turned around and whispered, "Probably. The woman sitting next to him is the attorney who signed the petition."

The man wore a white button-down shirt and a thin black tie as well as a black wool vest. His stocky frame gave him a brutish look. His dark hair seemed to have been sheared off by a barber before he arrived. Not exactly the type of guy Miranda usually dated. She preferred pretty boys and this man seemed more bulldog than golden retriever. He carried a small black briefcase and was accompanied by what appeared to be a brand-new attorney straight from law school.

Bridget led them inside the courtroom and pointed to the seats on the right side of the court for Julia and Finn to sit in. Then she walked over to the opposing party.

Julia strained to overhear their conversation.

Bridget shook hands with the other attorney. "Gwen, nice to see you. I see you passed the bar."

"Easily," the other attorney said with a grin. "Meet my client John Holland."

They shook hands.

"I'm Bridget Kovach, attorney for Ms. Gardiner."

Gwen pointed in Finn's direction. "I see she brought her latest stud."

Julia could see Bridget smile toward Gwen, yet the smile was infused with a spark of pure hatred. "Careful, neophyte. Finn Maguire is Lily's uncle and her mother Miranda's brother. He's here to support Julia Gardiner. If you'll excuse me." She turned and walked back toward them.

"Do you know Mr. Holland's attorney?" Julia asked.

"She interned for me last year, before you became my client. I'm convinced she copied all of my standard forms and documents in order to set up shop with a minimum of effort. Can't prove anything, but I know she's guilty. She's also not above using every trick in the book to win her cases."

"Could she beat us?" Julia's heart weighed down with uncertainty. She couldn't lose Lily.

Bridget shook her head. "I doubt it, but I'll double-check every one of her pleadings to make sure she doesn't try to gain any advantages through unethical means."

Finn sat behind them and didn't say a word. Julia felt relieved to have him with her and understood that his role would be as a friend. If the opposing party thought of him as her boyfriend, an entirely new bunch of issues would arise in the custody case.

The arrival of the judge silenced the room and focused everyone on the case. Judge Miller, a middle-aged man with a beer belly and a wrinkled black robe, briefly spoke to the court reporter seated in front of him and then began the proceedings.

Gwen made her case first. She argued that Mr. Holland had already started the process of obtaining partial custody of Lily, but had been transferred to India soon after the birth of the child and decided to wait to file the claim until he returned. "In fact, he has a valid paternity test and only needs it approved by the court to take his rightful place in the child's life."

"What?" The word burst from Julia's mouth. Her stomach lurched and her composure fell apart.

Bridget squeezed her wrist and tried to calm her down. "Relax. I'll get to the bottom of this," she whispered to Julia and then stood up and spoke to the judge. "Your Honor, when was this test taken? There has been no DNA taken from Lily since she was placed under Ms. Gardiner's guardianship."

"The paternity test was taken three weeks after her birth at the hospital where Lily was born. It's in the hospital records. I'm surprised you didn't request the records when you first took the case," Gwen said to Bridget with a tilt of her head and mock expression of shock.

"Ms. Holt, please refrain from making extraneous commentary to the opposing attorney. I'm the one making a determination, not Ms. Kovach," Judge Miller said, frowning at Gwen.

"Sorry, Your Honor." Gwen bent her head in some sort of contrived contrition.

Bridget, still standing, said, "I'd like to request a copy of the test."

Gwen shuffled through her file and then looked back up to the judge. "I don't have a copy with me, except the one I provided to the court, Your Honor."

"Get her one by the end of the day," the judge said.

"Absolutely."

When Gwen had finished presenting her case, Bridget spoke. "Your Honor, after a three-year absence, pretty much this child's entire life, a man arrives to claim her as his daughter. Where was he during the trying few years that this little girl has lived through? There are no records of child support or any other communication between this man and his alleged daughter. Indeed, he may or may not have a valid paternity test, but that in no way makes him capable of being the parent of a special needs child."

Gwen jumped out of her seat and turned toward Bridget. "Special needs?"

The judge remained in his seat with a frown creasing his already creased forehead. "Ms. Holt, what did I tell you about yelling out to the opposing counsel?"

"Sorry, Your Honor." She sat again, but the fire in her eyes told Julia that Gwen wanted blood: Bridget's.

"Ms. Kovach, please explain Lily's special needs issues for the court," Judge Miller asked.

Bridget positioned herself to face the judge and then tilted her stance ten degrees toward the opposing party's table. "Lily's mother was brutally murdered approximately two years ago. The crime has never been solved. Lily, only two at the time, was found sitting by her mother's bloody body when a neighbor found them." She took a pausing breath, patting Julia on the arm, and then continued. "The trauma of such an extreme and disturbing event in Lily's life causes her to have flashbacks. She exhibits signs of traumatic stress disorder and has had difficulty speaking. She's under the care and treatment of Dr. Teena Gupta, a recognized psychologist in the field of child abuse traumatic stress disorders and their symptoms and treatment. I have an affidavit from her acknowledging that any disruption from her current treatment including introducing a stranger into the equation could set back her progress by months." She handed the affidavit to the judge.

"Thank you," said Judge Miller.

She then crossed the floor and handed it to Gwen. "As *required*, I also copied it for opposing counsel."

Both Gwen and John looked it over. Neither spoke to each other and their faces slowly tightened.

Bridget pivoted back to the judge. "Because of the unique and delicate condition of the child, I would like to request that a guardian ad litem be assigned to this case in order to look out for the best interests of the child."

"Granted." The judge looked up from the document and then to the court clerk. "Clerk, please assign Ms. Pearson as the GAL on this case. I think she'll do the most thorough investigation under the circumstances."

After Bridget sat down next to Julia and Finn, the judge spoke. "In light of the child's special needs, I am keeping temporary custody with Ms. Gardiner and will allow visitation of the child for Mr. Holland only after a complete report is given to me by the GAL regarding Ms. Gardiner's and Mr. Holland's respective abilities to care for the child. I'd like the GAL to also interview the psychologist for Lily to determine any and all medical and psychiatric issues that I'll need to understand before I make a final decision. Let's return in four weeks. I think that's more than enough time for the investigation."

The judge stood up, prompting everyone else to do so as well. When he left the room, Julia sat back down, drained of all of her energy.

Bridget stood, creating a barrier between John and Julia.

John pivoted around her. "Julia?"

"Yes."

"I'm sorry to put you through this. My job hasn't allowed me to come sooner. I want to do what's best for Lily."

The weasel wanted sympathy?

Her eyes burned. They would either burst into tears or explode in a fiery rage. "I'm what's best for Lily," Julia replied.

She felt Bridget pull her toward the center aisle. Bridget and Finn flanked both sides of her and led her out the door, away from John Holland.

# *Chapter 12*

Julia didn't linger after the court date. She went back to work and then to spend time with Lily. Finn asked about seeing her, and Julia made a tentative date for them to get together.

He spent the night in his apartment dreaming of a beautiful woman who had tilted the axis of his world. He wanted to be with her and focus on her pain to try to eliminate it, but as he stared up at the slowly turning ceiling fan, reality stared back. He'd been leading her on. He couldn't be a father to Lily and a permanent part of Julia's life. He needed to back off before someone hurt her. She had enough risks in her life with her wealthy family. He would support her in the court case and then fade away. They'd all be better off.

When he arrived at his office the next morning, his secretary and Davis ran up to him. Literally, ran to him. He stopped in the hallway and watched as Davis edged out Aspen to arrive first.

"Do you own a cell phone?" Davis said without his usual smile.

"I need to charge it. What's going on?" Finn shouldn't have remained so long at home, but he needed time to think and get a grip on his crumbling defenses.

Davis clutched a letter and handed it to Finn. He looked over the words; Richard wanted to sell his ownership in the dealership. Although they hated working with Richard, his investment kept them afloat. They didn't have the capital on their own to keep the business running without a large bank loan or outside investors. It wasn't impossible, but would take every spare minute to research and plan. As if Finn didn't have enough to think about.

"We're screwed," Davis said, nearly screaming.

Luckily, Finn had shut the door when he entered the office so their staff didn't hear Davis's rage. Davis marched back and forth in the small office. Finn, protected behind his desk, followed his friend with his eyes.

Davis never showed anger, swore or harbored animosity toward anyone but the most heinous villains. For him to lose his cool so forcefully, so unapologetically, warned Finn that they'd be fighting a battle neither of them could afford to lose.

Slamming one fist down, Davis exploded. "Bastard. This is revenge, plain and simple."

Finn backed away from his friend's anger and tried to quash his own simmering rage. He needed to keep his head while Davis vented. "Not Richard's revenge on me for the broken jaw. More like Kim's revenge on me for hitting her husband and not hitting on her. My guess is that she wants a new house in Palm Beach and she's pushing Richard to sell this investment. I'll suffer and their money becomes liquid."

"I didn't think she'd go after me as well. What the hell have I ever done to her?" Davis asked.

Finn almost smiled at Davis's comment. "Don't inflate your importance in her life. She likes the idea of you, but I don't think she ever particularly liked you. And since you're my friend, she has even more reason to dislike you. Richard, on the other hand, at least could tolerate us. He may not have liked working with us, but he loved the consistent dividends and bragging about the new cars on the showroom floor."

"I don't care whose idea it was. I've worked too hard to go back to preparing taxes for small business owners who give me their paperwork the day before the filing deadline and expect tax-free miracles. This letter says that Richard's hiring an appraiser this week to value the business. If it comes in too high and we can't pay out his interest, we'll be forced to sell."

"Relax. We have the right to obtain our own appraisal. I'll get on it immediately. We'll also find a new investor." Finn tried to sound confident, but with only sixty days in the buy-out clause, there really was a chance they'd have to sell the business. Finn had already put all the equity he had into his investment. Together, Finn and Davis had tied up all of their assets in the company.

Finn tried to reassure him further. "We'll call our attorney to see if there's any way of delaying the buyout. Then we'll start looking around. We have a client base of the richest men and women in the city. Most of them like us. Maybe someone has always dreamed of ownership in a luxury car company. It'll take work, but we'll do it."

"Maybe we should cancel the party this weekend. We have to focus on this," Davis said in a quiet voice. He looked down at the notice again.

"No." Finn stood up, needing movement to release some of his own stress. "You and Calvin need to celebrate. Besides, I've already committed the money for it, so you'd better enjoy it."

The frown on Davis's face softened. "I may not enjoy it, but I definitely appreciate it." He rubbed his temples and inhaled. "Calvin does too." He backed away from Finn's desk and sat back into his favorite chair.

"You both deserve it. I'm glad Julia could make it all work for both of you." Finn, still standing, picked up a pen on his desk and began to spin it through his fingers.

Calmer, Davis lifted his eyebrows and asked, "Why do I get the feeling that you're keeping your emotional distance from her on purpose?"

Finn didn't want to discuss his personal problems with

Davis or anyone. Davis, however, wouldn't relent until he had a good reason.

"She has too much baggage," Finn answered. Why the hell was Davis focused on his personal life right now? They had much bigger issues to deal with.

"Too much baggage? It amazes me how you can ignore your own happiness. In fact, I think you prefer making yourself suffer." Davis's voice had a hard edge. So much for the unified front.

Finn glared at him. He should get off this topic fast, because neither one currently had enough good humor left to laugh off each other's comments. "I'm fine." His clipped response demanded an end to the topic.

Davis, however, carried on. "You have almost no friends, no intimate relationships, and you punched out one of your only relatives. And while I appreciate being one of the few people you can tolerate, you really should get out more. Maybe you should get a dog. If it survives one year, you know you have the ability to sustain a more meaningful relationship."

"I don't want a dog. What the hell would I do with a dog?" Finn snapped back at him.

"Love it?" Was he trying to get Finn's blood to boil?

Finn shook his head. He would not bring a dog into his life for it to become a potential target. "Love is for idiots."

"Thanks." Davis's earlier anger reappeared.

"Present company excluded."

Davis stood with the notice clenched in his fist. "Too late, you've insulted Calvin and me. And for the record, love does suck sometimes. It's not easy making room for someone else in your life. Compromises, disagreements and loss are all part of it. Try loving someone knowing that holding hands in public with that person could get either one of you beat up or worse. You have no damn idea how hard it can be loving Calvin. But I'll never regret even one minute of my time with him. If we're separated sooner than forever, I'll accept the heartbreak and the pain as a risk worth taking. It's life. Something you know nothing about."

"I know nothing about life?" Finn yelled, tossing the pen onto the desk. "I loved my parents. Gone. I loved my sister. Gone because of some crazed person who may or may not have been going after me. I loved my life in the military, I was tried for a murder I didn't commit and was kicked out." He moved around the desk to stand directly in front of Davis. "So don't tell me that I know nothing of love. I don't want love. You risk it all with Calvin. That's your choice. I've had enough loss in my lifetime."

Finn slammed his fist into the wall. Pain radiated from his now-bleeding knuckles across his arm as the plaster cracked open. Finn opened the door and stormed out of his own office. He couldn't deal with any more emotions. They all sucked.

Davis followed him. "Wait up."

Finn kept walking until he was outside and in the parking lot. Davis blocked his access to his car.

"Get out of the way," Finn insisted, but his bluster faded. He was taking out his anger on the wrong person.

Davis didn't appear upset by Finn's earlier outburst. Instead, something in his eyes showed pity. Finn hated pity. "What do you mean Miranda's murder might have something to do with you? Does Calvin or anyone at Fresh Pond Security know?"

Finn froze. Had he said the words out loud? He'd never shared that with anyone. He'd only offered slivers of information with others in order to gain something in return. Like the woman from the Pentagon who had sent him off in a direction that offered nothing. Not that he'd investigated the case in the past few weeks. Too much was spiraling out of control to focus on something from the past. But the minute his time freed up, he'd dig further. Not as much to clear his name, but definitely to find and destroy the person who had murdered his sister.

"Just leave it alone, Davis. We need to focus on the dealership and I have to help Julia with Lily's custody."

From the look on his friend's face, Finn knew Davis wouldn't leave it alone. And that would put everyone in danger.

# *Chapter 13*

The Driftwood Cafe had transformed into a sea of dark blue tables with cream-colored candles standing among ivory blooms in pewter bowls. Minimalist like Calvin. Elegant like Davis.

Julia's heart almost skipped a beat seeing Finn across the dining room. He'd been so reassuring to her the week before. The time together reminded her of how wonderful it had been to have a supportive partner in her life. Granted, he only offered that smallest part of him, the part that didn't involve his heart, but with Lily's adoption in such a precarious state, she'd take any bit of him he cared to offer. Her heart almost stalled out when a tall blonde sauntered up to him and embraced him. An embrace that continued and continued.

Finn looked up from the arm candy and stared across the room toward her. He didn't smile. Was that regret in his expression? Or was Julia imagining emotions that weren't there.

He turned away, back to long legs and big breasts. They looked good together in a cover-of-a-romance-novel kind of way. He'd said he was single, not celibate.

Julia wasn't jealous. She had Lily and a business to run. So what if she imagined Finn preferring to come to the party alone, like he had at his aunt's anniversary party? Sure. It was a selfish thought, but she deserved some selfish thoughts to keep her loneliness at bay. Suddenly cold, she wrapped her arms around her waist.

She focused her attention on the rest of the room and hustled around making sure the buffet contained every delicacy ordered, the open bar remained open and the music filled the air. Busy work would help take her mind off of Finn and allow her to avoid him.

"Here's the woman of the hour." Davis strode up to her with Calvin a few steps behind, typing into his phone.

"Hi. Is everything the way you wanted it?" Julia asked.

"Better. We love it." Davis smacked Calvin in the arm. "Don't we?"

Calvin looked up, smiled and then grew somber again. "Love it. If you'll excuse me." He walked away toward the lobby.

"Don't mind him. He's trying to do something for work and has decided to deal with it in the middle of the party. I suppose I should be used to it."

"Perhaps. I know he works with computers, but what exactly does he do?"

"He works with a security and protection company. The one Finn used to work at to be accurate. He's the technical brain of the operation. Major corporations hire him to find flaws in their computer security. Sometimes he tracks people down who try to break into servers. Sometimes he tries to break in himself in order to show his clients certain flaws in their systems. I think it's the former right now."

"I bet he has your house wired up."

"He's a bit excessive, but aren't all brilliant people?" Davis's annoyance in Calvin's work habits disappeared and a deep respect shone through his words.

Julia thought of Finn. "Perhaps."

They both looked over at Finn trying to speak to some gray-haired gentleman while Blondie practically humped his leg. *Nice.* Guess Finn didn't embody all of the heroic qualities she'd assigned to him after the bathroom brawl. She needed to train her focus back on work.

"If you'll excuse me, I have to speak to someone in the kitchen," Julia said, smiling against the heartbreak like it was her birthday.

Davis smiled at her and placed a gentle hand on her forearm. "Absolutely. Thanks again for everything, Julia."

"It was my pleasure."

She walked to the kitchen as quickly as she could and closed the door with a thud, exhaling as though she'd escaped a serial killer. She turned around and saw the entire kitchen staff staring at her. Straightening, she smiled again, freezing that expression onto her face, and sauntered through the kitchen with as much dignity as she had on reserve until she exited the back of the restaurant.

Hurrying past a large blue dumpster that smelled of one thousand rotted things and skirting towers of wooden shipping pallets, she made her way to a small deck overlooking the river. Someone had arranged several folding chairs and a card table near the edge. Lots of cigarette butts littered the ground nearby. Perhaps it was for staff.

She stood next to the railing and took several deep breaths. The moon provided a perfect backdrop to the skyline lit up like a fairy wonderland. A beautiful scene, but it wasn't enough to cheer her up. No longer able to hold them back, tears cascaded from her eyes. How could she love a man who wouldn't love her back? She didn't have room in her life for this. She had to be strong for Lily. She didn't need to be tortured by thoughts of his muscled chest and arms, black hair that curled slightly as it touched his collar and blue eyes that completely seduced her even when he so clearly didn't want any part of her life.

Footsteps behind her made her swing around. When she turned, a wall of the pallets came tumbling toward her. The pallets smashed into the ground beside her. She dived out of the way, but slammed her elbow into the asphalt and landed in a puddle of something that wasn't water. What the hell had happened? The tapping of someone's very feminine shoes faded away and she stood up in a panic.

The black Badgley Mischka dress she'd worn was torn at the knee and smelled like a garbage truck. She couldn't even wipe the tears from her eyes as her fingers were covered with a nasty grime.

The wind picked up and blew an empty plastic bottle into her leg. Julia kicked it away, then rushed over and picked it up before it fell into the water. She tossed it into the dumpster and headed back into the kitchen, suppressing the need to run with every step.

# *Chapter 14*

John watched Julia scamper back into the restaurant. She looked vulnerable. Very much like Miranda had looked only a few years before.

Julia Gardiner had the grace and stature of a goddess. Submissive brown eyes, tiny waist, perky little nose. Someone he could carry away and enjoy for a long time. Perhaps the child custody blackmail wouldn't work and he'd have the chance to do something more creative to her.

Ambling back toward the parking lot, he noticed a decidedly bitchy female rushing from where Julia had fallen to the ground. The woman glared at Julia as she disappeared back into the kitchen. *Interesting.*

Red hair pulled up into some fancy style, she wore expensive clothes and had the kind of offended air that frequented bored housewives who survived on raising their own status while destroying others. She focused more on pulling money from her purse and on her phone conversation than on where she was walking. John situated himself directly in her way, forcing her to lift her head up and hop to one side to avoid hitting him. She stumbled slightly, her knees bending down as though the ligaments had stretched out like taffy.

"Excuse me." She scanned him from just below his belt to his head, stopping when he lifted one of his eyebrows in his most endearing manner. "Oh. Hi." Her demeanor softened and her eyes dropped back down to his fly. A flirt. He did like free sex. "Have you been out here for a while?" she asked, obviously drunk and trying to hide it.

"Long enough." He acknowledged her better assets with a slow assessment. She smiled and placed a hand on his arm to steady herself. From under a dark green cocktail dress, garnished with some expensive baubles, the diva stuck out her leg, showing off impressively toned calves. The kind that could fit around his waist with a few inches to spare.

"Are you okay?" he asked, all concern.

"Um, sure, why?"

"I saw you fall into some crates. You did fall, didn't you? I can't imagine you'd have pushed them over on a woman. Do you know Julia Gardiner?" Letting her know that he'd seen her sneak up behind Julia.

"Know her?" Her body swayed, unsteady in the too-high heels. "I've run across her here and there. She's too perfect for words."

"Is she?" He nodded, trying to seem impressed. "Has she done anything to give herself such an exalted status in your eyes?"

The expression said more than her words. "That little whore flirted with my husband and then when he rejected her, she sent his cousin Finn to punch him out."

"Did I read about that in the newspaper?" he asked, interested in her husband's take on the assault.

Shaking her head, she moved closer and mumbled, "The media had it all wrong."

He stepped closer as well. "How is your husband?"

"Jaw wired shut. Not much use to me right now." Her hip caressed his leg.

He placed his arm around her waist. He smelled alcohol, the hard stuff. "I can see that. I don't know Julia well, but we have a few common acquaintances."

Her head was now resting on his shoulder; her weight began

to lose its fight with gravity as she relied on him to hold her up. "I can't deal with seeing her here. She's hired help and yet thinks Finn Maguire gives a rat's ass about her."

"Finn Maguire. I thought they were in a relationship."

"No. They did, once. But he dumped her when she starting acting as a mother to his niece."

"Finn is the little girl's uncle?" he asked as though he didn't already know the answer.

"He doesn't want anything to do with either of them, yet she keeps showing up everywhere he is. She's an overachieving caterer. She's not even on the radar of Boston society. Boston is different from her hometown of Philadelphia." The way she pronounced *Philadelphia* made it sound like the worst place on earth.

Her little rant provided John everything he needed to know about this woman. "Trust me; she'll never be in your class. Would you like to get a drink? You look like you need to get out of here and I'm done with this party."

"I'd love to…"

"John." His arm encircled her and guided her back to the valet station.

"Kim."

A black Mercedes sports car pulled up and the valet exited from a gull wing door. Kim started toward it. John's mind began calculating the opportunities he could create by binding her to his plans. She was the wife of one of Finn's business partners. The more information he gathered, the more chaos he could rain down on Finn's entire life. Rayburn had specifically said he wanted John to disrupt the car dealership.

"Why don't you let me drive?" He took the twenty from her hand and placed her in the passenger seat, slipping the valet a two-dollar tip from his wallet.

Kim tilted her head against the edge of the headrest, her

eyelids as well as her defenses lowering. "You're so thought-ful. Thank you."

"Trust me, the pleasure's all mine."

# Chapter 15

The room began to empty. Coffee cups and dessert plates sat abandoned on the tables around the main room in the restaurant. The guests had removed the large centerpieces leaving the room looking like the barest remnants of a beautiful memory.

He'd evaded Jason Stirling and Steve Wilson, the partners of Fresh Pond Security. They were there to support Calvin, but both men took every opportunity to try to persuade Finn to come back. Part of him wanted to return, a big part, but he still had a problem with trusting Jason, had an issue with going back with his tail between his legs, and he'd invested everything into Maguire Exotics and needed to make sure he could get his investment out without hurting Davis. At present, it didn't look good. The team got the message and respected his space, only sharing greetings and the most benign small talk with him before going to mingle with other guests.

Through it all, Kim's cousin Ashley wouldn't leave him the hell alone. She'd accompanied Kim since Richard was still wired shut. He'd tried to get rid of her all night, but the woman was like fly paper. He hadn't been able to have a decent conversation with anyone else since she stood next to him and rolled her eyes and sighed as though the whole event was a huge bore. She seemed like the kind of person who was always bored unless all eyes were focused on her. With less than ten people left at the party, she didn't have much of a shot at being the center of anything.

"Let's head out. I want to be alone with you," Ashley purred into Finn's ear.

She smelled of some musky perfume that should be driving him crazy, but didn't.

"Where's Kim?" he asked, hoping they'd leave together.

"She left. I told her you'd take me home." She leaned in to kiss him and Finn backed five degrees away from her lips in order to concentrate. His patience had dried up a long time ago. He'd been nice and told her he had to speak to various people and to excuse him, but she hung onto his side like a shadow. He'd wanted to spend a few minutes with Julia, not hovering over her as she handled the running of the party, but at least finding out how she was doing.

*Where the hell was she?* She'd disappeared over an hour ago.

Davis, his coat draped over his arm, strolled up to them. He beamed his typical enthusiasm for the world. "Hey, beautiful, why the pout?" He focused only on Ashley, causing her to perk up.

"I'm tired and Finn won't take me home." As though Finn had ever offered to take her home.

"You poor thing. I'm sure he'll be done here in a few minutes." His lifted eyebrows and a subtle tilt of his head asked Finn, *What the hell is wrong with you?*

Finn quickly changed the subject. "Where's Calvin?"

"He left to go to a hospital." Davis turned back to Ashley. "I think the place got hacked. He'll be there all night."

"Wow. I hope he'll be okay," Ashley said, her eyes widening.

"He may develop carpal tunnel, but other than that, I think he'll be fine," Davis said, appearing to stifle a grin.

Finn sat down at an empty table. "We should get him to

update the firewalls on the dealership's systems, now that he's practically family."

"Not a bad idea. If he ever has free time, I'll ask him to use it up on our computer issues. I'm sure he'll love that," Davis said. He stood next to Ashley, who crossed her arms and remained standing, probably in an attempt to motivate Finn to leave.

Finn tried to telepath his need for space to his friend. "Ashley doesn't feel well."

Davis looked her over. "You look great. What's wrong?"

A deep, long sigh followed as Ashley turned into a B-movie actress melodramatically dying from some heinous disease. "I feel very weak and I think I need to *leave*." She held on to the back of the nearest chair and posed like a 1940s pinup with mere moments to live.

"Kim has already left. I can't help her, because I really need to pay the caterer." Finn wasn't sure if Davis understood what he wanted.

Davis's expression lit up at the mention of Julia. The man would love it if Finn and Julia dated again. "Absolutely. The party must be paid for and Finn is the man to do it. Luckily, I happen to be leaving this very minute. Come with me. I need a blonde to decorate the front seat of the Lamborghini."

"Well... I... Are you sure?" She turned her head between Finn and Davis.

Davis nodded.

She straightened and strutted closer to Davis, miraculously cured. "Okay. I really do need to get home. Finn is a buzzkill anyway." In her delusional world, she believed that any man would kill to have her at his side. She was wrong.

"It was nice seeing you again, Ashley. I hope you feel better," Finn replied to her. She ignored him. Now that he wasn't giving her attention, he disappeared from her consciousness.

"Come on, gorgeous." Davis hooked her arm and escorted

her to the entrance. "Let's see if we can cause a few cases of whiplash on the drive."

Finn heard her ask Davis if whiplash was contagious. She was seriously a caricature. There was no way someone that age could be so incredibly dense. In a room of over thirty charming and intelligent women, he had to be noticed by someone so insufferable.

He sat back down and observed the room growing emptier by the moment. The end of a party usually finished like a Sunday service, some people rushing out the moment the minister stepped from the altar, while others milled around looking for some last-minute conversation before returning to their lonely lives.

Julia had disappeared as if she had no part in creating this party. He waved over a young college-age server. The kid had seriously messy hair, which could be considered a style to some, but it looked slovenly to Finn.

"Do you know if the event planner left yet?" Finn asked.

"She's probably hiding out from someone." The kid smirked as if he had some superiority over his boss. "She refused to come back into the main dining room. She's been in the kitchen most of the night talking to the chef. She's wearing a large white apron, so maybe she decided to help with the cooking."

"Can you ask her to come see me? I need to pay her." Finn's face tightened and his eyes narrowed.

The kid's smirk evaporated.

"Yes, sir." He turned and headed back to the kitchen with a brisk walk.

Better.

Ten minutes later, Finn had reached his breaking point. Then he saw her and his throat constricted. She glanced around the room at the remaining staff and then at Finn. Her posture showed hesitancy. Her eyes showed red streaks. Her hair was pulled into a ponytail, a change from her style earlier. Her pretty dress was covered by an apron made for someone the size of a linebacker.

He stood as she approached. "Hi. Long night?"

"The party went well for everyone but me, I think," she said quietly.

Finn waved his arm toward a seat and she sat down. Her elbow rested on the table, but she pulled it back and winced. Her arm had a good-size gash on it, covered with a Band-Aid that was too small for it.

"Are you okay?"

She nodded. "Jonathan, my chef, is skilled at sterilizing and bandaging cuts. According to him, his assistants are pretty adept at slicing themselves with knives." She took a deep breath and went silent.

Finn pulled his chair closer and asked to see the injury. She lifted her arm and revealed a pretty severe gash on her elbow. He also could see a slight tear in her dress. What the hell happened to her? "Did you fall?"

"You could say that, but I just want to go home. It was a long, ugly evening. I don't think I should do any more events with your friends or family. They never turn out well."

"They turn out amazing for everyone but you." His fingers grazed over her forearm and stopped at her hand. She rested her fingers in the palm of his hand but then pulled away as though he was about to cut them off.

"If you're not feeling well, we can settle the bill later."

Julia shook her head. "It's fine. I want to finish this event and put it behind me." She gazed wearily at him. A tear formed and remained nestled in her eye. "Where's your girlfriend?"

Finn placed his hand on the edge of her chair, never touching her. "Ashley? She's Kim's cousin."

"Kim?"

"Richard's wife."

Her face whitened. "I thought I recognized her. Terrific. She was staring at me as though I was a party crasher."

"Kim is an ass and her cousin has the same genetic makeup. Ashley was bored and decided to follow me around the party. I never invited her to do so. Davis took her home."

"Oh."

"I don't have a girlfriend."

She shrugged, her eyes staring at a stain on the tablecloth. "Don't get me wrong. I don't care who you have in your life. I have more important things to worry about, like the guardianship of Lily and a dozen pallets falling on my head."

"Is that what happened to you?"

"A pile of wooden pallets fell nearly on top of me, I almost broke open the gash on my head from the last party with you, then I fell in a puddle of festering garbage sludge and cut my elbow." The tear grew a little into a small shiny ball poised to fall.

"I'm sorry. I had no idea. How did the pallets fall?" He could now smell the lingering scent of something putrid.

"I can't say for sure, but I heard the pitter-pat of high heels before the tower fell. They sounded like stilettos, the kind Kim and Ashley wear."

"You think Kim pushed it over?"

"I never said that," she said, the weariness overtaking her. "I need to go home and maybe take a few days off to focus on Lily. I wanted to make Davis and Calvin's party special, but I'm off my game."

"You achieved everything Davis and Calvin could have wanted for this event. Seriously. You made this party fun, gorgeous and memorable and it had the couple's spirit woven through it. It was an amazing event." He meant it. Julia had a talent for seeing her clients and infusing the whole event with their essence.

Julia's lips pressed together, a move that had Finn wanting to hold her in his arms and take away the bad memories of this evening. "I'm grateful you recommended me to your cousin. And I appreciate the business. This party introduced me to several potential new clients. Davis even asked me to help with his and Calvin's wedding plans. But I'm not in a situation where I care about anything but Lily and her future." The tear fell. It streamed toward her nose and then moved to the edge of the mouth. She pulled out a handkerchief and used it to sweep the tear away. Her constant sadness ripped at his heart.

"I'll going to support you with whatever you need." He backed a few inches away from her to give her space.

She looked at him with a lingering shiny streak on her cheek. "I don't need your money."

He sighed. She had all the money in the world, at least a significant percentage of it. She not only didn't need him, but being in her life made her a target. "I know I refused to take custody of her after Miranda died, but she was in better hands with you. My work pulled me all over the world and she required a stable family. I do love her more than anything. If you let me, I can be there as a backup for you. I was wrong to step completely out of her life. I like you, Midnight, and I'm sure we can work something out. Perhaps we can form a ragtag kind of family for Lily. As friends." Yet friends could be murdered as easily as family members.

As he spoke, he could see her expression shift through a range of emotions. She didn't trust him; she couldn't. He longed to be near her and then when she reacted to their closeness, he always backed away. But this was such a serious matter. Miranda had wanted Lily to be raised by either him or by Julia. He could see her mind working to decipher his meaning.

Her face transformed from offense to distrust to maybe hope. "Friends? I guess we could be friends. For Lily's sake. But no disappearing act."

It wouldn't be easy to stay, but he couldn't imagine not

being close to them anymore. Watching her expression lighten, her mood lift, her exhaustion dissipate, even the slightest bit, eased something in him. They'd once had a future. One whispered on Sunday mornings, and planned with an enthusiasm only the young had. He still remembered their perfect life together before Miranda died. They had sat by the ocean, the warmth of their coffee cups keeping their hands warm, and their long, lingering kisses keeping the rest of them warm. Her well-being set the tone for his own happiness. It had since the day he'd met her. "Let's meet for lunch this week if you have time. As friends. To make a plan together about Lily."

She finally smiled. Not a huge smile, but something subtle and altogether enchanting. "Let me check my schedule. I'm sure that would be okay."

# *Chapter 16*

Three days, eleven hours later, Finn and Julia met for lunch in a sushi bar on Beacon Street. The smell of wasabi and the faint scent of seafood, both fresh and fried, filled the air. The customers' conversations buzzed off the four small walls and servers rushed orders to make sure everyone returned to work on time and satisfied.

Finn hoped they could work out a perfect compromise between them. He could keep an eye on them but not be so intimately involved that it would put them at risk.

After being served a combination plate of sushi and sashimi and talking about the weather, Davis and Calvin and the next moves in the custody case, Finn studied his friend. Julia dressed in a cheery yellow blazer with brown pants. She'd pulled her hair back into a low ponytail. The redness in and around her eyes the last time they'd seen each other was gone, although signs she was not getting enough sleep persisted.

"Have you seen Ashley since the party? She's seems your type," Julia asked, changing the subject from Lily's need for a role model, before popping a small piece of salmon into her mouth. Her lips lifted into an impish smile.

Finn laughed. "I don't need clingy and pathetic in my life. I prefer solitude."

"Right. I guess you're going to end up a reclusive bachelor, alone with three cats and a Ferrari." Her lips still tilted toward a smile.

"I like being alone," he said, although the truth was, he'd love to have the woman across from him fully in his life. "And cats aren't bad, although someday, I'd love to get a dog."

She hesitated, picked at her sushi, tapped the chopsticks on her plate and then said, "A dog? I can see that. You definitely need a dog."

Finn put down his chopsticks and lifted an eyebrow. "Please tell me what sort of dog you think I need."

Julia took a sip of her water. "Well...to begin with, you need a dog who can protect you. Maybe a pit bull?"

Finn bit back a grin. "I like them, but my apartment building wouldn't."

"You need one that can go to work with you and look like a dog that would be comfortable riding in a luxury car. Sporty, but protective. One that would be equally comfortable in a hunting blind and on a private jet."

"Of course."

Julia seemed to relax for the first time in days. "You don't have time to care for an Irish setter."

"They're too friendly and need lots of space to run. Besides, I don't have time to care for anyone but you and Lily." He craved more time with her, a better understanding of the woman she'd become in the past two years.

"What's your favorite television show?" he asked.

"Mine? Are we speed dating now?" Her eyes narrowed. They had small streaks of green throughout them. Emerald veins in orbs of amber.

"Just curious." He shrugged, but continued staring at her waiting for her answer. "I picture you a Martha Stewart disciple."

"I'm more of a Weather Channel addict." She shrugged. "It's practical, entertaining and provides me up-to-the-minute weather reports."

"I can't argue with that."

She shrugged. "I've been known to stay up all night following a hurricane. Sort of a geeky obsession, but I'm addicted." She smiled. "Do you remember getting caught in the blizzard together a few years ago? You ended up stuck at my house two nights in a row because we couldn't get out of the neighborhood."

They'd spent two days and two nights with no work obligations. They ate, watched movies and made love in every possible location in her house. He could see her in his mind sprawled out on her bed, a furlike blanket the only thing covering her body and waving him over for more. The memory seared through him. "I wasn't stuck at all. I was exactly where I wanted to be. I wish I could go back."

She stared at him. She didn't believe in him anymore.

"If you wish you could go back to a time when we were together, then what's holding you back? Your new job isn't exactly sending you around the world."

"It's complicated."

"What the heck are you talking about? You're giving me whiplash. You want to be part of my life, but only under your conditions."

"I wasn't in a good place after Miranda died and I screwed up. I can't go back, but I can be there for you guys now. I'm trying to be what's best for both you and Lily." As much as he could.

"Then tell me, Mr. Maguire, what is really keeping you and me from getting back together?" She leaned forward, her face calm, her voice perfectly modulated for a restaurant.

Finn wasn't sure what to say. "It's just… I can't… It's complicated."

That answer wasn't good enough. She stood up and threw down a hundred-dollar bill. "You're hiding something from me. Changing the subject whenever I get too close, but not letting go. If you can't tell me what's going on with you, I can't be with you. It's too confusing. You can stop by to see Lily occasionally, but stop messing with my heart. I'm not as strong as you think I am."

After she left, Finn sat for a few minutes wondering how his life had gotten so off course. He should tell her, but part of him held back. The secret had been dragging him down for the past two years. Then he saw her sunglasses on the table.

# Chapter 17

Julia returned home that afternoon exhausted. She'd met with a potential bride the night before until eleven and woke up early to head to work by seven. Lunch with Finn should have been relaxing, but her feelings for him and his unacknowledged feelings for her threw her emotions onto a roller coaster of ups and downs. The way her heart thumped harder in his presence took its toll.

As soon as she arrived home, she sent Dianne on her way, sat down to cuddle Lily and eventually fell asleep reading a story. When the doorbell rang, she left Lily napping on the couch and walked to the door. Finn's Bentley stood like a sentry in her driveway. A regal presence in her modest hideaway.

She hesitated. "Finn, what are you doing here?" She tried to whisper so Lily wouldn't wake up. Damn it, she needed a heads-up for his visit.

"You forgot your sunglasses at the restaurant and I didn't want you to have to drive back downtown to get them. Don't worry, I have to pick something up in Lincoln this afternoon, so this is actually on my way." The sincere grin almost melted her heart, but the heat dissipated before any melting could begin. She forced herself to worry about Lily's well-being instead of gushing all over Finn.

"You're an amazing liar," Julia whispered, pushing Finn out of Lily's line of vision. "You should have called first. I don't have the strength to keep playing games."

She started to back away at the same time that Lily woke and called out to Finn.

"Hey, Little Bear. How are you?" Finn asked.

She popped up as though she'd been awake all along. "I have paint." She rushed toward him and pulled on his hand to drag him into the house. So much for Julia's downtime.

She closed the door and followed them inside. Lily had already dragged the small box out to the kitchen island and then ran back to the playroom for paper.

Julia needed coffee and maybe a bit of whiskey. While she buzzed around the kitchen brewing her drink, she pulled out some chicken and began to cut it up and fry it in a pan with some olive oil and garlic. Macaroni and garlic chicken with some scallions mixed in would be easy enough and if Finn didn't leave, she'd have enough to feed him too. He seemed quite settled from the way he was wielding his paintbrush with slow, methodical strokes.

Lily gripped a huge paintbrush and made large strokes across the page, causing the blue of the sky to smear into the brown of her tree. Her brow was furrowed in concentration in the same way Finn's brow was furrowed as he painted a dog on the paper. A red dog…an Irish setter.

"I like your dog. What's his name?" Lily asked. She seemed to speak easier with her uncle than with anyone else.

"Jingles, the Christmas Dog."

"That's silly."

"What did you make?" he asked her.

She lifted the picture up, causing the paint to drip onto the island. "It's a tree."

"I love it," he replied, casually placing another piece of paper under the first to catch the dripping colors.

The enormous grin on Lily's face said it all. She needed Finn. Which meant Julia was stuck in a living hell with a man she loved but couldn't have.

Julia wiped her hands on a dish towel and grabbed three plates for dinner. "You might as well stay to eat, Finn. Because I'm not cleaning up this mess."

"He can stay?" Lily turned to see Finn nodding. She jumped up and down as though she'd been given a lifetime pass to the zoo.

"He can stay." Julia placed the bowl of the pasta on the island between the paintings. "Coffee?"

"That would be great." He looked up into her eyes and she nearly melted. Tonight she was getting the truth out of him. No matter what.

It was the best meal Finn had eaten in forever. Lily sat next to him and Julia sat across the island. They'd shifted the paints to one side. Lily chattered away, her legs swinging back and forth, oblivious to the tension between Julia and Finn.

"I'm getting a dog," Lily told the table.

"You are?" Julia asked, as though this was the first time she'd heard of it.

"I think it's a great idea," Finn replied. "I know a few people who could set you up with a really good dog." One with protection training but was able to be with children. One more barrier between them and whatever threats were out there.

"I'm not entirely sold on a dog yet. Let's get through the next few weeks first. Okay?" She eyed Finn, warning him not to push it.

He took the hint. "Sure. I think waiting until you're at least five is a good idea. Dogs are hard work."

"They are?"

"Sure. You have to walk them, and feed them, and train them, and pick up after them."

"Pick up what?"

Finn made a face before saying, "They don't go to the potty like you do."

"Ewwww."

"So maybe we wait a bit." Julia glanced at him with an appreciative nod.

Lily agreed. She then asked to watch television. Julia let her after she carried her plate to the counter next to the sink.

The room went silent without Lily's enthusiasm. The sound of some television show drifted into the kitchen as Julia cleared the table. Finn helped her and rinsed off the dishes for her to place in the dishwasher.

"You didn't have to stay, but I'm glad you did." Julia focused on the dishes, but he could hear her concern, her curiosity. He should tell her. She wanted him to, but then what? She'd live in fear.

He leaned against the counter. "I like being here. Lily is amazing. She's one part Miranda, but also a huge part you."

"Miranda always wanted what's best for Lily. She'd be thrilled that you're a part of Lily's life again. I always wonder about my relationship to Lily if Miranda had never died. Would I have been like the crazy single aunt, or just an occasional presence in her life? Would you and I have stayed together if Miranda had lived?" Julia leaned against the counter, thoughtful.

Finn rarely mentioned his sister. The topic cut too deep. Miranda had been everything to him after the death of their parents. She'd been the cool and calm sister who always included Finn in all of her plans. His best friend. He swallowed hard. The memory lodged in his throat and he felt as though it was choking him to death.

"No idea. Can I stop by and see Lily on Sunday? Or is that a difficult day?"

"Did you ever speak to Miranda about your time in Afghanistan?"

"What are you doing?" he asked.

"I'm trying to understand you better. What happened during your deployment? What happened when you came home? What did you see at Miranda's murder scene?"

"Don't. They're all memories that are better off in the past."

"For who? I am in the dark over everything. I feel as though I keep bumping into walls. It's uncomfortable and in many ways, I'm getting hurt because I don't have a clue why the hell you're acting like I'm the best thing in the world one minute and I killed your puppy the next. But I know it's related to Miranda. Because you broke up with me the night of Miranda's funeral."

It wasn't just losing Miranda that had precipitated the breakup; it was the way it had happened. So brutal, so fast, so permanent. Miranda had embraced Finn and Julia getting together as a couple, cheering them on with her typical enthusiasm. It had been a perfect time in their life, a window of time where Finn had felt he had conquered the world. Then he was deployed to Afghanistan, and in a matter of months, everything unraveled. He lost his career, his reputation, his understanding of where he fit in. And when he thought things couldn't get any worse, Miranda was murdered. Butchered.

His thoughts had pulled him out of the kitchen and back into the darkness of guilt and what-ifs. When he finally looked over at Julia, she'd stepped closer to him. A whole lot of concern was etched in her expression.

"I'm fine," he said, his voice unconvincing.

She shook her head. "No. You're not good at all. You've lost so much and something is still dragging you down."

He looked down, his hands gripping the edge of the counter. For a moment, he stayed silent. He couldn't reveal his thoughts. He couldn't burden her with all the shit that he'd seen. All the shit chasing him down. But Julia's presence, her patience, broke down some of the walls he'd built. It wasn't as though he couldn't trust her. He could. He trusted her with Lily; he trusted her with his heart. Why couldn't he trust her with the information that was binding him in this hellish reality?

She stepped closer. Her hand brushed over the edge of his neck and rested on his shoulder. She forced his attention, his focus on her and he melted. He should protect her from knowing, but she deserved understanding. It wasn't as though she was weak. She'd faced countless challenges and had stood strong against them all.

Even now, there was strength in her silence. She trusted him and he was protecting her from emotional hurt, but with more information, she could protect both herself and Lily from whatever was after him. If he was her actual bodyguard, he'd never leave her in the dark to potential threats. It was time.

"Can I have ice cream?" Lily asked, bouncing into the room with a smile on. She paused when she saw Julia and Finn looking so somber.

"Ah...sure, Little Bear." Julia pulled away from Finn and opened the freezer.

Lily spun around and danced a bit while explaining to Finn what some princess did to a troll. Finn wanted nothing more than to sit with her and share the moment, but it was time to clear up the storm he'd thrown into Julia's life. He'd take time with Lily later.

"I need to speak to your mom for a bit and then I'll join you, okay?"

"Okay."

Julia pulled on a smile and kissed Lily on the forehead, handing her a coffee mug full of ice cream. "We'll be there soon."

After she was gone, an uncomfortable silence returned. Finn didn't know where to start, how to unknot the tangled stories he'd buried deep inside of himself. Every breath he took felt heavy. He never opened up, not until he'd exploded at Davis, a person who hadn't done anything to deserve such an outburst. It was as though the more he held in the storm, the larger it was growing. Near hurricane strength now.

Julia wrapped both arms around him now, in a patient, comforting way. "You were saying?"

"You make an amazing mother," he said trying to get his thoughts together.

"I'm the best mother I know how to be for Lily, but that's not what's on your mind."

He closed his eyes for a moment, steeling himself to the fact that once she knew, she'd never unknow. Perhaps she'd blame him. Perhaps she wouldn't want him in her life. A wave of emptiness nearly bowled him over. Yet, Julia still held him, both arms stretched over his shoulders, her head looking up at him.

When he gained the courage to finally speak, his voice was barely a whisper. "It's my fault. Miranda."

Julia stepped closer, her body pressed into him, giving him support. "I don't understand. What's your fault?"

He could feel the weight of his guilt pressing down on him. "Miranda's murder. Someone killed her to get at me."

Julia's eyes widened, but she didn't speak. She didn't comfort, but she didn't dismiss his words. She waited.

"When I was in Afghanistan," Finn continued, the words ripping through him, "I discovered someone stealing weapon inventory and selling it to the enemy. We literally found the missing guns in the hands of enemy troops after a raid. I checked the paperwork and it was all convoluted and mysterious. I confronted Major Mark Donner about it. He lied, trying to convince me that I was wrong. I made the mistake of arguing with him in front of other officers. That argument and an unexplained drop of blood on my shoe were enough to convict me when he was murdered that night."

"I don't understand. What does that have to do with Miranda?"

Finn's throat burned as he tried to explain. "After I was co-erced into pleading guilty to manslaughter, I was sent to prison for six months and then dishonorably discharged. I couldn't let it go. I used every resource I knew to try to dissect how the shipments were sent into enemy hands to murder our own troops. If I found out the person in charge, I might find out who framed me. I was close. Then Miranda was murdered," he muttered, unable to meet Julia's eyes.

"How do you know it was related?"

"The mark they'd carved into her chest, it wasn't an *X*. It was the Ordnance Corps insignia, two cannon barrels and a cannonball. It was Donner's unit in the army."

Julia's intake of air broke the silence, as her arms tightened around him. "You didn't know. How could you have known they'd go after her? You didn't put a target on her. They did."

He shook his head, the guilt suffocating him. "I should have known. The sale of the weapons wasn't a one-time thing. Dis-crepancies had come up in the past. This wasn't one person, it was a network. I think Donner was killed because I ques-tioned him in public. He'd become a risk to the operation if he admitted to the scheme."

"Do you know who runs it?"

"No. I'd try looking again, if only to avenge Miranda, but I have to go slower, more methodically, more clandestine. I don't want anyone in my life hurt by this. I have some leads and they're in a secure file that will go to the Office of In-spector General if anything happens to me. It might be the only reason I'm unharmed."

"Which is why you pushed us away. You were protect-ing us?"

"You and Lily are my everything. If I had to separate from you both for you to prosper, I'd do it."

"But we didn't prosper without you. We need you happy and safe and in our lives."

He wrapped his arms around her waist, holding her as he broke. He'd given up so much time for nothing. For the first time, he let out the guilt and sorrow and rage, his body shaking with the force of it all. She stayed in his arms, holding him, grounding him with her presence.

"I'm terrified they'll involve you," he said.

"But now I'll be prepared. As long as we're together, we'll be okay. You don't have to shoulder the burden of this alone. You never had to."

The sounds of Lily's laughter drifted in from the other room, shifting something inside of Finn. The walls he'd erected to keep everyone out cracked a bit. The crack let in just enough light to provide him the first flicker of hope he'd had in a long, long time.

# *Chapter 18*

$S$un filtered through the sheer curtains of the bedroom in the old farmhouse where Kim grew up, waking John. He looked at Kim sleeping beside him. A sheet covered part of her leg. The rest of her naked limbs remained exposed to the drafty air. The house smelled of mouse droppings and dust. Apparently, she'd inherited the farm property after her parents died. She never sold it. She probably needed to be reminded of why she fought ruthlessly to maintain her status.

Former farm girl makes good. How cliché.

John had been surprised when she'd first invited him to stay over, but where else could they go? He told her he had a live-in girlfriend at his North End town house to keep her from discovering his actual basement apartment in Allston. Having spent more time with her, however, he should have brought her to his place in the city. As long as she could get laid without Richard knowing, John doubted she cared where they did it.

He looked over at his newest conquest. Her flawless pedigree a lie. No wonder she harbored so much hatred for Julia. Julia arrived into the world, received a gentle slap on the ass and was given millions of dollars. Kim, on the other hand, had to marry an ass for money and behave within the confines of a prenup.

She must have been beautiful once, before the Botox and the attempts to tighten the loosening skin under her eyelids created imperfections in an otherwise symmetrical face. It didn't matter; he didn't have to look at her face to get what he wanted from her.

She offered him all of Finn's dirty secrets. Like the fact that he needed an investor in the dealership or he'd lose most of his net worth. Finn needed more obstacles in his way. Perhaps more trauma for his ex-girlfriend and niece. For the past two weeks when John had been staked out at Julia's house, the only visitor was the nanny. Not even a bodyguard. She was either incredibly naive or extremely stupid. Probably both.

After he enjoyed some more play time with Kim, she stood up. "I have to get going. Richard will be wondering where I am."

John turned onto his back and pulled up the covers. "You disappeared last night, didn't he care then?"

"No. He was busy getting a special visit from his visiting nurse."

"Have you ever been with Finn?"

"No. He's not my type. He prefers celibacy."

"Why does he spend time with Julia Gardiner?"

"Finn probably wants her money," Kim said with a sulky pout. She wanted Finn much more than she let on.

"Does she know that?"

She pushed out her lower lip, plumped from something manmade. "I have no idea, but why else would he pursue her?"

He could think of a few reasons that Kim's catty little brain wouldn't comprehend. "Maybe you should help her come to that realization." Screwing with Julia's alliance with the former soldier would only benefit John's plans.

"Perhaps I should," she said as she headed to the bathroom.

His phone rang. Colonel Rayburn.

"Yes, sir," he said more out of habit than respect.

"Where are you on this?" Rayburn barked.

"He's knee-deep in both a custody case and a potential takeover of his company."

Rayburn took a breath. "Perfect. I haven't heard any rumblings from above. He has no time to pursue revenge while he has so many other fires to put out. And in the process, I want you to garner a settlement with Ms. Gardiner. A large settlement after you obtain custody of the kid. For the right amount of funds wired internationally, she can keep her."

"Will I get a percentage?" John had to push for a pay increase now, before the final numbers came in.

"Get custody first." The line went dead.

# *Chapter 19*

Finn and Julia didn't have a chance to see each other again until a meeting with her attorney to prep for the case. She invited him back to the house to have a visit with Lily. His relationship with his niece had only blossomed over time. Julia loved how much he loved Lily. And Lily adored him as well.

When Julia saw Lily back at the house, she ran up to her and squeezed her until Lily squirmed away. Lily wanted Finn, causing Dianne's brows to lift. Julia had explained to Dianne that Finn and Lily's reunion had gone well, and he'd been a part of Lily's life when Miranda was alive. It was strange that Lily was captivated by a man when many other people scared her into silence.

"Did the meeting go well?" Dianne asked. Her now-even-shorter hair had had a new color added to it in the past few days, Day-Glo yellow.

"For now, we can breathe. We'll have to wait to meet the guardian ad litem in order to get an idea of which way she'll lean." Julia looked over at Finn, who had come up behind her and placed his hands on her shoulders. She loved having him as her support system. With her mother and sisters scattered around the world, his presence anchored her.

"Guardian ad what?" Dianne asked.

"Ad litem, or GAL," Finn answered. "A person appointed by the court to investigate the case in the child's best interest. A GAL's report can mean more to a judge than the testimony of either of the parties in a case. Hopefully this person will put more stock in the love and stability Lily has living with Julia than in a genetic test that lists some random sperm donor who couldn't be bothered with his daughter for her first four years."

After Lily wandered into the family room to play with some of her Little People collection, Dianne asked, "Did he look like her?"

*Did he?* "I'm not sure. He has dark hair, but so did Miranda. His skin color is paler than Lily's, ghost white, but that doesn't mean anything. I honestly don't know. We'll have to wait for the paternity test."

"Can I ask a sort of strange question?" Dianne looked down at her feet and then over at Julia, ignoring Finn for the moment.

Julia remained anchored under Finn's solid grip. "Sure. What's up?"

Dianne's hands fidgeted together and she shifted her stance. "It seems like this guy showed up right after the news reported that you're from some rich family in Philadelphia. Is it true? Because if it is, could he be looking for money?"

Finn guided Julia to a seat at the kitchen table. He sat down next to her. "He might be looking for money. People do crazy things all the time for a shortcut to riches. If the paternity test turns out to be valid, then we'll have to figure out what exactly he wants."

*We.* Julia held on to that connection.

"But *are* you really rich?" Dianne asked again, a little more insistent.

Julia hated this focus on her money. "My father runs a major corporation, so I grew up with money. But seriously," she said in a light, breezy way, "would a superwealthy person drive a Mini Cooper or live in a three-bedroom house?"

"I'd take any house, and this is Concord, but it is fairly modest." Dianne then acknowledged that those items wouldn't be the choice of someone with the wealth of the world in her pocket. Finn, however, raised his eyebrows at her, out of Dianne's line of sight. He knew the true value of her limited-edition Mini Cooper. Certainly not an exotic sports car, but more expensive than the average minivan. Luckily, she trusted him to keep quiet.

After Dianne left to spend time with Kevin, Finn began showing Lily how to build massive towers with her Duplo. Julia rested on the couch with some tea as they made three- and four-foot-high towers. They continued until each tower fell to the ground, scattering blocks all over the room.

After the last tower fell, Lily ran over to Finn and jumped onto his back like a mouse attacking a stallion. He rolled her off and tickled her until she laughed herself into hiccups. His playful actions provided Lily with her first real interaction with a father figure since Miranda's death. A happy and protective father figure.

The vision of John popped into her mind. The serious, creepy guy who could rip apart Julia's family. Her throat tightened and she put the tea down on the table beside her. Julia needed to keep Lily away from him, if it took every dollar in her trust account.

She threw together a spaghetti dinner complete with homemade meatballs and freshly cut green beans steamed in lemon water. Lily nibbled on everything on her plate as she told Finn about fairies that pretended to be butterflies while creating towers of blocks as high as a tree and complaining about Julia's insistence that she eat all of her green beans. Finn's attention remained riveted on the child. His laughter, revealing those adorable dimples, infused the room with warmth and security. Perhaps together, Finn and Lily could confront their demons and live a more peaceful, serene life.

After a dessert of chocolate ice cream covered with M&M'S, Lily tried to persuade Finn to accompany her to the family room, but he needed to get home. Lily gave him a squeeze around his leg and went off on her own, leaving Finn and Julia in the kitchen alone.

"Thanks for dinner. You're an amazing cook."

"You're welcome. I appreciate you coming to the meeting with me. I could never make it through without your support."

"I doubt that. You have more strength than most people I've met in the past thirty years. You're also a terrific mother." He walked over to her and placed a hand on her shoulder. With his other hand, he lifted her head toward his.

Julia stared up into the most handsome face she'd ever seen. She could get lost in those stormy eyes, in his strong arms. She rose up onto her toes, bringing her face a mere inch closer to his. He moved the rest of the way, his lips touching hers until she kissed him back. Their kiss might have looked perfectly innocent, but it created a spark of energy that could light up Boston.

"Good night, Midnight."

"Good night," she said faintly as he released her. Her stomach quivered at the loss of his touch, but she let him go. They'd found a connection and she could understand all the actions he'd made in the past. She had confidence that everything would work out.

# Chapter 20

Four cold walls, decorated with large photos of the cars everyone wanted, but few could afford, closed in on Finn, suffocating him. He massaged his temples and shut his eyes. What the hell was he thinking telling everything to Julia? He didn't want to put her in danger and he didn't want her to step into the line of fire. Yet, he craved every part of her. And she hadn't sent him any signals telling him to stay away. In fact, they shared an attraction so palpable, they would combust if they continued to ignore the flames. Could they truly get back what they'd lost before he'd left for his deployment?

Maybe Lily's presence would lessen the awkwardness.

His office door flung open and hit the wall. The sound reverberated through his head and he lifted his eyes. Kim waltzed into his space in black thigh-high boots, black leggings and a knit minidress that hung three inches below her navel.

Like a coral snake, she used men, then discarded them, quite possibly eating them in the end. She'd pursued Finn years before at a birthday party for Richard. During the event, her drunk husband tried to pick up some young waitress, so Kim cornered Finn, slid her hands down the front of his pants and asked for a ride home, his home. Finn rejected her.

He never regretted staying away from such a venomous creature, but the rejection hung over all of their interactions. Her hatred of him festered over the years as she transformed their business relationship into a personal vendetta. Finn held the upper hand in their conflict. He ignored her. Kim eventually gave up. Now, however, she and Richard were going after Davis and his livelihood.

"Just when I thought my day really sucked, you walked in. Great." Finn glared at the woman trying to destroy him. He stood up out of habit, not respect.

Kim leaned on Finn's desk in a pose reminiscent of a prostitute looking for business. "Finn, you've never appreciated good breeding."

"In horses or are you talking about yourself?" He spoke softly, allowing her to fully digest each of his words.

"Go ahead, sweetie, be a wiseass, you'll be out in a matter of weeks either way. I've blackened your name so much you couldn't borrow a paper clip without massive collateral," she hissed. "Then again, you have no real contacts. You have a few customers and Richard's friends. Of course, everyone of consequence will take our side in this little corporate divorce."

"I'll be fine, Kim. Even better when Richard and you have no attachment to this company."

Her face tightened. The imperfections of her latest attempts to remain twenty appeared more visible, especially around her eyes. "This company? You conceited son of a bitch. You were off fighting in the sand while Richard was running the company. This would be a used car dealership selling rusty Subarus if it wasn't for us."

"Davis built this company from what his father and your father started. You and Richard have taken from it, but I can't recall you giving anything." Finn stared into her eyes and saw nothing but ice. "Is there a reason you're standing in my office?"

She smiled and her eyes almost looked friendly. "Richard and I want the two percent that we sold to you last year."

Finn's throat tightened. He'd purchased just under half of

Davis's shares and two additional shares from Richard. Richard had no problem giving the shares in exchange for a few thousand dollars. But when he did, he lost half ownership because between Finn and Davis, they maintained a 51 percent ownership of the business. Richard only held 49 percent.

"That's not going to happen. *Ever.* You sold me the shares and I'm not giving them to a sexual predator and his equally heinous wife."

She hissed at his comment. "As I see it, you have no options. You can sell us enough of an ownership interest to give us a majority or you and Davis can lose the entire business when you're forced to sell to pay off the debt owed." She turned her head as Aspen walked in the door.

Crisp copper pants and an ivory blouse made his office manager far more classy than Kim. Aspen had a solid understanding of both the sales figures and the financials. She had stood in for Finn or Davis at more than one meeting. The only thing holding up her promotion to vice president was Richard and Kim. She placed a file and a cup of coffee on his desk, carefully maneuvering around Kim, who showed her resentment for the young woman by scowling.

Aspen concentrated her attention on Finn alone. She seemed to understand the dangers of staring down Medusa. "Don't forget that you have a meeting in a half an hour, Mr. Maguire. Do you need anything before you go?"

"No. I'm all set. Thank you."

Aspen turned to leave. Kim's eyes followed her, hunting for a weakness. Suddenly, Kim grabbed her arm. "You're not offering me anything? I'm as much your boss as this loser is."

Aspen's face blanched. She yanked her arm back and fled from the room as Kim snickered to herself.

"Get out," Finn said. He wanted to remain calm around her, but he hated bullies of every age and social class.

"Just saying it like it is. She has never given me the respect I deserve."

"Aspen can run this whole dealership. You're trying to bankrupt it."

The witch laughed. "She's not going to be employed long enough to run anything when we take over the company or force you to sell it."

"You and Richard will take this company from us when hell freezes over."

Kim gave Finn a condescending wave of her hand as she left, her clicking heels echoing her disdain. "Brrrrrrr. It's starting to get a bit chilly."

# Chapter 21

Julia needed to pick up some dishwasher soap and a box of tampons before she headed home. She could never run to the store with Lily because of her fear of strangers. It wasn't worth it.

Picking up a box of the little plastic packets for her dishwasher, she cut through the hair color aisle on her way to the feminine products. Richard's wife stood in the middle of the aisle, facing her. A middle-aged redhead who wore two-thousand-dollar stilettos and a five-thousand-dollar handbag.

"Julia Gardiner, isn't it?" The honey pouring from the woman's mouth seemed laced with arsenic.

"Yes. And you are?" She wouldn't give her the satisfaction of recognition.

A patronizing smile, more of a smirk actually, appeared on the woman's face. "Kim Maguire. My husband pushed you into a wall." The smile remained as if he'd done Julia a favor. She forgot to mention that she'd sent a pile of wooden pallets onto her head. One hell of a power couple.

Sighing, Julia responded, "That was unfortunate." As she passed Kim to get to the feminine products, Kim put her arm out and stopped her.

"You certainly are a meek little thing, aren't you?" The smirk morphed into a sneer.

"I beg your pardon?" Since when were manners a sign of weakness? Julia could push herself up into Kim's face, with obvious difficulty since Kim had about four inches on Julia, and threaten to take her down, but that wouldn't prove anything and might invite a lawsuit. No, she'd stick with her retreat. Engaging never worked well for her.

Kim's stance, however, blocked Julia from going forward. Julia hated confrontations.

Kim pointed her index finger in Julia's face. "Richard's jaw is wired shut. He drinks his food through a straw. He's hidden himself in the house until he's healed. He's miserable, because you couldn't keep your mouth shut. Let me tell you, sweetheart, the old society of Philadelphia has nothing on Boston and if you think you can accuse a good man of assaulting you and think you'll keep your business afloat, you've seriously misjudged our family's power and prestige."

Julia stood there, silent. She'd received a threat to her business and had no idea how to respond. She pushed through Kim's arm and continued down the aisle.

"Looks like Finn's latest piece of ass doesn't have a backbone," Kim called out after her.

Julia stopped, clenched her hand on her pocketbook and turned to look at Kim's narrowed green eyes, focused on Julia like a cobra. "Excuse me?" Julia asked. Her voice was strengthening as a blaze grew within her.

"You heard me. He's a nice-looking boy toy for the average bored heiress. How much are you paying him?"

Julia had never been spoken to in such a demeaning manner. She honestly thought that reality stars had a monopoly on such cattiness while dressed in an outfit that cost more than most cars. Her mother must have either shielded her from this sickening display of crass in-your-face wealth, or Philadelphians held themselves to a higher standard of etiquette.

She should leave, but she engaged instead. "Finn is a friend. That's all."

"Honey, you are one stupid little girl. Finn doesn't befriend women. He sleeps with them. Perhaps you're lacking in sex appeal. Or maybe he doesn't want sex from you. Did he ever mention to you that he's about to lose his investment? He needs money, lots of it. Soon. Good thing that his new *friend* has enough money in her trust fund to help him out. So tell me, Julia, has he asked you for the money yet?"

Julia knew from Finn that he and Davis had some issues at work, but did he really need money? He wasn't the type to ask for anything. Throughout their relationship, he took care of her and she reciprocated. Neither of them felt used or taken advantage of. "I have no idea what you're talking about."

Kim cackled, which was the first cackling Julia had ever heard that wasn't in a movie about witches, tilting her head back as she did it. "He'll ask you. It's a matter of time before he gets to it."

Julia needed to leave. "You're crazy."

"Am I? At least I can show my face at the cricket club. Are you even a member? Poor little rich girl. No quality connections, no real friends and the only date you can find requires you to bail out his cousin's car dealership."

Julia placed the box of detergent packs on top of a box of hair color. She needed fresh air away from this horrible person's accusations and lies. She needed to speak to Finn. Kim was a problem. A loud, obnoxious one.

She fled the store without the dishwashing detergent or the tampons. She'd rather have dirty dishes and wear pads all week than deal with such a bitch.

Her hand shook as she pulled out her phone and called Finn. "Julia?"

Her voice now trembling as well, she said, "Hi. I just ran into Richard's wife at the drugstore."

"Kim?" His voice harbored no affection for his cousin's wife.

"Yes."

"Are you okay?"

"No. She's a pretty disturbing person. As bad as Richard." She took a deep breath to control her anger.

"Go home. I'll meet you there." He sounded concerned. He'd be there for her. She had faith that he'd turned a corner.

"Thanks."

"Drive safely. I'll see you in about an hour."

After she hung up, she watched Kim walk out of the store without any evidence of purchasing something. Kim strolled over to a limited-edition black Mercedes SUV. She obviously had an inferiority complex if she had to flash wealth through her clothes and car choice. Kim glanced over at Julia's Mini with her narrowed eyes and a satisfied grin. Julia volleyed back her best "you're an ass" grin. She'd like to embark on a full assault on the woman's social standing, which obviously mattered to her, but Julia didn't know enough people in the area and she wanted to wait to see what Finn would say about the money.

# Chapter 22

Julia's house appeared deserted when Finn arrived. Its isolation and Julia and Lily living alone sent up red flags.

After knocking, he waited for her to open the door. She really should have better security, even a large dog. Would he be stepping over the boundary she'd drawn if he suggested she hire Fresh Pond Security to evaluate and provide someone to watch the place?

She held the door open for him dressed in jeans and a red T-shirt. Long ponytail and makeup free. She had the appearance of a college student. Absolutely breathtaking. Not gorgeous, glamorous or elegant, although put the hair up and drape an evening gown over her and yes, she'd be that too. More like the perfect form of stress relief for tired eyes after a long day at work.

Lily ran up to him before he could enter. After all the trauma she'd been through, he felt privileged to be a man she liked. He stood taller than most men and rarely smiled. Lily should have been scared of him. Not that he tried to be scary, but four-year-old little girls tended be less drawn to gruff old grizzlies and more toward the teddy variety of bear. But he liked her too. She had a decent attitude, not all whiny and complaining like some kids he'd been around.

Julia, in the hour since calling him, had whipped up a stir-fry dinner with shrimp, broccoli, red peppers and bean sprouts over wild rice. Of course, she cooked a full dinner after a long day of work and having to deal with Kim.

After they finished eating, Julia sent Finn to the family room to play with Lily, while she cleaned up. He tried to argue, but she was right; Lily needed more time with him. He honestly didn't mind. Lily rode him around the room like a pony, until he bucked her off and onto the soft sofa cushions. Then he proceeded to tickle her until she cried, "Uncle."

*"Uncle!"* she screamed. She sat up on the couch giggling and looked at him with the sweetest face he'd ever seen.

"I'm the luckiest uncle in the world."

He walked over to turn the television on. He sat down with Lily, who promptly jumped on his lap and leaned her head back against him like a human cushion. Finn rubbed her shoulders a few times and started to relax.

Julia strolled in with some tea and a beer for him.

"You didn't have to stock up for me," Finn said while reaching out for it.

"Hospitality is my business."

"You're damn good at it too. Thanks."

"You're welcome."

She sat down next to him and Lily squirmed onto Julia's lap, leaving her legs across Finn. Eventually, however, Lily decided that Julia and Finn bored her. She jumped down and picked up Julia's iPad to play on.

Julia and Finn remained side by side. "You shouldn't have raced over here. I probably overreacted."

Finn ignored her downplaying of the events at CVS. "Nonsense. What did Kim say?"

Julia's eyes became glossy and she said soft enough for Lily to miss it, "She called me your current piece of ass."

"She's the ass, Julia. Petty and vindictive too." Finn tried to control his response, but Kim had already screwed with his work life; she wouldn't get away with harming his personal life as well.

"Shhhhhh." She pointed to Lily, who sat staring at a screen covered with little pink unicorns. "She also told me that I'm not your typical type."

"Did you tell her that we're friends?"

Julia shook her head. "Yes. I lied and didn't mention how much more we are."

"We're more?" he said with a grin, placing an arm over her shoulder.

"One subject at a time. Kim doesn't seem to believe in couples 'who are just friends.'"

"She doesn't. She likes men for sex and money. She's quite simplistic."

"My guess is that she's jealous." Julia turned from him and stared at Lily.

*In for a pound.* "Truth is, she made a move on me years ago, and I pushed her away. She's never forgiven me. You're closer to my type than Kim is and she knows it. I typically stay away from married women."

"Very funny."

"Seriously, that's why she's so jealous of you. She's as toxic as my cousin. Her marital vows symbolize an economic alliance more than a mutual partnership between two people in love."

Julia sat quietly for a few minutes, then leaned her head on Finn's shoulder. "She told me that your business is in trouble. That you want my money to bail it out."

*Leave it to Kim to create additional issues between us.* "My business is in trouble, but I don't want your money. I don't need your money. When I bought into the partnership, I ended up with twenty-five percent of the company, and combined with Davis's twenty-six percent, we hold a majority. The agreement, however, stipulated that Richard could sell his shares to us with a sixty-day written notice. He's given us notice."

"Can you afford to buy him out?"

"All of Davis's and my money is tied up in the business and we owe too much to the bank to get a loan. So no, we can't afford to buy Richard out, but Davis and I have a plan. We've found a few potential investors and if Kim doesn't poison them with lies, we should be able to secure the financing before the deadline."

"When's the deadline?"

"We have a few weeks left."

"Do you have any serious investors?" Her skepticism annoyed him.

"We'll be fine. This has nothing to do with you and it never will. I would never use our relationship to get investment money."

"I guess I feel bad because Richard and Kim hate me and maybe that's why they're selling."

"I broke Richard's jaw, not you."

Julia didn't look appeased. "You broke his jaw to help me. I'm sorry."

He turned to her, so close he could feel her breath on his cheek. "This has nothing to do with you. Richard and I have had issues since I moved into his house during high school," he repeated. "He went to college and I bonded with his parents. The business will survive without his money. The company has a solid reputation mostly because of Davis. Richard and Kim can try, but I won't let them tear everything apart."

She placed her head on his shoulder. "I've always trusted you."

Finn reached up and put his fingers through her hair. He leaned over and kissed her on the top of her head. She felt soft and smelled of oranges and teriyaki sauce.

She rested her hand on his leg and snuggled in closer. "I

feel like the world is caving in on me. First Richard, then John, now Kim. It's like the most evil people have found me and are all out to destroy my family." Her body shivered.

Finn felt the same. She needed more protection. Although she also had a great legal team to protect Lily, she needed more protection at the house. It was too isolated. As for the custody case, the GAL should pick up on John's creepiness during their interview. If she didn't, she sucked at her job.

Julia remained curved into his side, her head resting on his shoulder. Lily sat on the rug nearby playing in silence. After several minutes, Julia's steady breathing and deadweight told him she was asleep. She deserved a nap to escape from everything going on in her life. And he deserved a few minutes to hold her close.

# Chapter 23

John watched Finn drive away from Julia's house. So much for driving a wedge between them; Kim had singlehandedly pushed them together. The car Finn drove, something John would be able to buy in cash if he blackmailed Julia when he received custody of Lily, annoyed John. How did Finn, the one dishonorably discharged, get so lucky, while John had left the military honorably?

As darkness blanketed the area, he became more than ready to be done with all of this. Watching two ridiculously privileged people fall in love had not been part of his plan. Julia's security had been upgraded with cameras and outdoor spotlights, but he'd yet to see any physical presence on the property. Rayburn wanted results and he'd get them. If they couldn't blackmail Julia in the custody case, they'd find another way to take her for everything and destroy Finn as well.

# Chapter 24

Julia dreaded therapy for Lily because she hated the idea of Dr. Gupta pushing the little girl's boundaries even when necessary to heal Lily. This custody-related session had even higher stakes. This wasn't about helping Lily; it was about the guardian ad litem finding a baseline of Lily's trauma. Neither Julia nor Dr. Gupta would be allowed in the interview. Julia hated that Lily had to go through this. She hated John for making it necessary.

The room held everything a preschool class would want: primary colors, lots of books, toys and a little girl excited by all of the new sights. Julia watched Lily, dressed in striped blue-and-yellow tights under a blue sweatshirt dress, from behind an observation mirror. Lily calmly interacted with a woman in a faded brown jumper with a pale pink turtleneck. Success would depend on what the woman learned about Lily.

Lily seemed to have no idea that the mirror on the far wall allowed Julia, Teena Gupta, Lily's psychologist, Bridget and Gwen, the two opposing attorneys, to see her interacting with the guardian ad litem, whose name currently escaped Julia. Lily also had no idea that everything she said and everything she did would be recorded and analyzed both good and bad. Julia had no idea if this one interaction would result in her losing her little bear to a man that creeped her out and never gave a rat's ass for his daughter.

The GAL took out a few Barbie dolls and placed them on

a small round table where Lily sat. A blonde Barbie, a brunette Barbie, a Skipper, a blond Ken, a dark-skinned Ken and
a dark-haired GI Joe holding a rifle. *Subtle*. During the GAL's
interview with Julia, she learned about Lily's fear of being
near men. Did she want to debunk the psychologist's claims
in order to clear the path for John to take Lily from her? Julia's gut tightened, and she held on to the wall to prevent from
sliding down and curling into a ball.

"Lily, let's play dolls."

Lily stared at the stranger and replied, "Can I color some
more?"

"Don't you want to play with the dolls?" The woman's voice
sounded cheerful, like a kindergarten teacher encouraging her
children on to the next activity of the day.

"No."

"I'll let you choose whichever dolls you want to play with."

Lily never looked up from her drawing. She continued to
scribble in a circular pattern. "I don't want to play with dolls.
I want to color."

The GAL glanced toward the mirror and then back at the
dolls. Lily continued coloring. Julia couldn't see the picture
on Lily's paper, but her choice in colors included pink, green
and orange. Happy colors. Nice.

The GAL reached over and took Lily's drawing from her,
stood up and held it toward the back wall for the benefit of the
mirror crowd, while trying to appear as though she needed to
view the picture from a unique angle. The picture contained
three circles of different sizes: a small pink one, a small green
one and a large orange circle.

"Very nice." Fake smile, lots of nodding.

Lily stared at the GAL and her mouth dropped open in a
slight grimace. "I'm not done," she exclaimed. Lily reached
up for the picture and grabbed it out of the GAL's hand. The

picture crinkled and almost ripped, but the GAL had the good sense to let go.

She sat back down next to Lily. "How much more are you adding to this picture? It looks done to me."

Lily took a red crayon and gripped it in a fist, crayon pointing down. She then proceeded to scribble an array of $X$'s over each circle. "Okay." She slid the paper back to the woman, who glanced at her watch and sighed.

The GAL lifted the picture and placed it on the table under the mirror. Red $X$'s, visible all over the page, distorted the perfection of the circles, although Julia could envision the red complementing Lily's original choice of colors. Perhaps Lily was an artist in the making, seeing things with the insight of a visionary, far beyond the capability of the average preschooler.

Dr. Gupta scrunched her face up and looked to be conducting a thorough analysis of Lily's crayon marks. "Interesting."

Gwen, the lawyer representing John, seized on the moment to jot down a few notes on her iPad and take a picture of the drawing. The image would be used against Julia, she was certain. Somehow, red cross-outs showed poor mothering skills. Happy circles under siege from angry red marks.

Julia's attorney, Bridget, leaned against the wall staring at her perfect manicure. Perhaps she didn't see the drawing as the crucial piece of evidence that would convince Judge Miller to grant custody to John.

The GAL wandered back to Lily's table. "Why don't you pick a doll and I will too and we can dress them up?"

Lily picked up the blonde Barbie. She didn't seem enthusiastic, more bored but compliant.

"Would you like a different doll?" The GAL tried to get back to kindergarten-teacher happy banter.

"No." Lily placed the doll in front of her and looked back at the woman tormenting her.

The GAL tried to lighten the mood by using a higher intonation. "I choose this one." Of course, she had to choose GI Joe and the weapon. "Is that okay?"

"I don't like him. Can you take her?" She pointed to the brunette Barbie. "They're friends."

"Don't you like Joe?" She pushed the soldier in front of Lily.

Lily picked up her chosen Barbie and turned away from the GI Joe. "No. I like Barbies." Her forehead tightened and her lips squeezed together.

"What about this one?" She moved the blond Ken in front of her.

Lily stood up. "I like Barbies." Her volume increased and so did her frown. She dropped blonde Barbie, reached over to the GI Joe doll and the Ken in front of her, picked them up and flung them against the wall.

The viewers behind the mirror all perked up at Lily's insolence.

"Why would you hurt them? That's not nice." The GAL's voice was raised enough to cause Lily to back away from her and go toward the door.

Lily had had enough trauma in her life; she didn't need a threatening woman to emotionally scar her as well.

"This is ridiculous. She has no clue how to work with children. She's deliberately baiting her," Julia said directly to Bridget, who had lifted her head in time to see the male bashing in the other room.

"Dr. Gupta? What's your opinion?" Bridget asked.

"Let it go for a few more minutes. If this woman can't control the situation, I recommend we terminate the session."

In the room, Lily had walked over to a small rocking chair and sat down with her arms crossed over her chest. She rocked back and forth asking for Julia.

"Ms. Gardiner will be coming to get you in a few minutes." She squatted down to Lily's level. "Why would you hurt the dolls?"

"They hurt people," Lily said, still rocking. "They would hurt the Barbies." Tears dripped from her eyes, leaving small wet dots on the front of her dress. She jumped off the chair and started asking for Julia again. "I want Mommy." Lily walked to the door, turned toward the table, turned toward the book-cases and then back to the door. "Mommy!"

Dr. Gupta looked at the court psychologist in charge. "It's time."

Julia didn't wait. She pushed open the door into the hall and ran to the room. Opening the door, she slowed her pace and stood as calm as possible after seeing her child's pain. "Lily?"

Lily lifted her head at hearing Julia and sprinted over to her. "Mommy. Mommy."

"It's okay. I'm right here." Sucking in a deep breath that filled her lungs with the scent of strawberry shampoo and some milk left on Lily's dress from breakfast, Julia squeezed her tight. "Did you have fun?"

"I drew you a picture." Lily, still sniffling, let go of Julia and found her picture on the table.

Julia knelt down and regarded the masterpiece. "Nice. What is it?"

"That's Auntie Maureen," she said, pointing to the pink circle, "and green is Dianne, and that's you."

Big and orange. "I'm the biggest?"

"You're the mommy."

"Right. I'm the mommy." *Forever, no matter what happens.* "What are these?" Julia, unable to stop her eyes from watering, placed her finger on the red lines.

"The fireworks."

"The ones we saw on Martha's Vineyard last summer?" Julia asked, seeing the *X*'s for they actually were.

Lily nodded, her tiny curls bouncing slightly. "At the beach."

So much for her crossing out the beauty in the world. What

would Gwen's notes reflect after this revelation? Four-year-old child forces fireworks over the three people she loves the most?

She'd never know, because Gwen left the building to share her observations with John.

# Chapter 25

Finn couldn't help feeling more and more interwoven into Lily's and Julia's lives and he actually loved it. Part of it was a fierce protectiveness for both of them and another part of it was the natural feeling of belonging that he hadn't felt, truly felt since his parents and then Miranda died. His aunt and uncle did a wonderful job opening up their homes and their lives to him. But with Richard's demands on their time and attention, he always had one foot out the door, ready to search for a family of his own. In another world, Julia and Lily would be his family, the kind of family that smiled when you entered a room, acknowledging a deep sense of connection and love without saying a word. No matter what, he'd be there for them in whatever context helped them the most.

After two days spent in bliss with them, he headed back into the dealership, ready to secure this investment as well. Aspen met him at the door, as though she'd been standing there waiting for him.

"Good morning."

"Yeah," she replied, her mind not on pleasantries. "The gentleman doing the appraisal was here. Kim accompanied him. I tried to get them to delay until you arrived, but I couldn't reach you." She handed him a business card. "This is the man's phone number. He said to call him if you had anything else to add before he made his final valuation."

"Thanks. I'll call him after I speak to Davis." Finn put the card on his desk as Aspen turned and went to Davis's office.

"It doesn't matter what we tell this guy," Davis said as he sat down. "He's going to come up with some crazy price that helps Kim and Richard take control."

"We'll have our own valuation done. The judge will end up splitting the difference if it goes to arbitration."

"We have to bribe an appraiser as good as this one," Davis replied.

Finn looked out the window. "We're not bribing anyone. The company has serious financial issues even without Richard pulling his investment. Our sales are flat and we're carrying too much debt on our balance sheet. Those issues aren't going away and you and I need to deal with them."

"While you were out trying not to fall for the perfect woman, I spent the past day kissing a few asses and promising things I have no power to promise," Davis said.

"What more could you promise?"

"You'd be surprised. I offered to have you marry George Hatwell's twenty-four-year old daughter. She's a medical student, plans on being a surgeon, so you won't see her much, but he wouldn't take it unless he could name all of his future grandchildren. I told him that you drew the line on names. Too bad, he would have been a great father-in-law." Davis slapped him on the back with a smile on his face. At least he could joke about the situation.

Finn remembered meeting Mr. Hatwell's daughter Destiny. A very smart woman and quite the athlete as well. "George Hatwell's daughter would be as interested in me as you are in her. She's been living with a significant other, a beautiful model from what I hear, for the past three years."

"Ah. That explains his desperation. He always was one to wish unhappiness on his family if he could financially benefit from it. We're better off without that kind of investor."

Davis frowned, mirroring Finn's expression. "I met with another group of investors, the Bancroft brothers. They tend to invest in technology but surprisingly want in with us. They hoped to meet you yesterday, but you were out."

"It couldn't be avoided. I needed to help out a friend."

Davis cocked one eyebrow and smirked. "Is that what she is to you now? Interesting. Anyway, they're willing to invest enough to buy out Richard after they perform some due diligence."

"Seriously?"

"Say the word and I'll send them all the financials." Davis made a bow so flamboyant, he'd have made the Musketeers proud.

"Absolutely. You, my friend, are a miracle worker. My only caveat is to keep this information away from Kim. She's so caught up in destroying us, that I can see her pulling some shit behind the scenes to tank the deal."

"That's the beauty of the Bancrofts, they seem to hate Richard and Kim more than we do. Richard wanted to take up with Sandy, Jack Bancroft's wife. Richard, being the idiot he is, failed to obtain Sandy's consent before groping her at a fundraiser for battered women."

"He's the devil's spawn, but hatred could benefit us in these negotiations. Sounds perfect. Call Bill and have him run some due diligence on them. I don't want to jump from Richard, the partner from hell, to partners we can't trust."

"Now you're being paranoid. This is the answer to our prayers."

"God hasn't really been answering prayers for me lately." And he didn't have the strength to manage any additions to the mountain of burdens he was carrying.

# Chapter 26

John arrived at the conference early. He was in no mood to see Julia. For this appearance, he kept his look immaculate and modest. A navy blazer and beige pants with a white shirt and no tie. Gwen met him at the door.

"Are you ready?" she asked.

"Yes. After everything you told me about the guardian ad litem, Ms. Pearson, I think I can handle her." He could handle anyone, although he was apprehensive about meeting Lily. If she recognized him, he'd be screwed, but he'd worn a beard back then so the chances of a four-year-old recognizing a man from two years ago would be slim to none.

Gwen looked him over and nodded her approval. "Use your usual charm and you'll have her eating out of your hands."

Gwen filled John in on some more of Ms. Pearson's background when they entered the building. "Her husband is a local pediatrician. She worked as a social worker for one of the poorer inner city elementary schools. She left after the birth of her third child and now takes occasional court appointments. She's not doing it for the money. More of a noble calling. As I expected, she definitely has a bias toward fathers. In five of her last eight cases, she favored the father over the mother. When she sided with the mother, the fathers included two drug addicts and a convicted felon."

John nodded and concentrated on appearing empathetic.

He'd win this woman's favor by merely caring about Lily. Easy enough.

Ms. Pearson's office was located in a new executive building. Everything looked modern and temporary as though the people using the offices only worked there occasionally. Ms. Pearson arrived in the reception area wearing navy pants and an oversize pink sweater. Short of stature and a bit rotund, she needed makeup, a new hairstyle and some nicer shoes than the loafers she had on.

"Mr. Holland, it's nice to meet you." She reached out to shake John's hand and then turned to Gwen. "Ms. Holt, thank you for coming in."

"We're glad to have this opportunity to actually see Lily," he said without too much honey. "Where is she?"

"In due time. We need to go over a few things, and then you can head to the observation room."

They followed Ms. Pearson into a neat and tidy office void of anything personal other than a Boston Bruins mug and some reading glasses. Even her laptop appeared generic. After they were seated, she pulled out a pad of paper and a pen.

"I'd like to get started with some basic information." She then requested his name, birthdate, schools attended and work history.

John gave her every bit of information requested with a smile and a humble attitude. His memory on the *facts* he'd created was exact.

"The next questions are a bit more personal," Ms. Pearson said.

He sighed and then nodded, appearing slightly embarrassed. "That's fine, Ms. Pearson. My life is pretty much an open book." His eyes darted between his lap and Ms. Pearson and then he locked his gaze onto Ms. Pearson's face. A faint smile traveled to the opposite side of the desk, but once connected to her, he looked down to his lap again.

As expected, Ms. Pearson blushed. "Well. I guess we need to start with how you met Miranda Maguire."

He recalled the backstory Rayburn had given to him. "We met at a nightclub in April five years ago. The Starcatcher was the name, I think. I bought her a drink, we danced and ended up at my place for the night. That was our only contact."

Ms. Pearson wrote down a few notes and then motioned to him to continue.

"I ran into her that December outside of City Hall. She was huge. The baby looked ready to pop out. I asked her if the baby was mine. She denied it, but I knew. I can't explain it, but I was certain that life growing inside of her was part of me." John's eyes watered. "Miranda walked away from me and never looked back. I searched for her so I could be part of my baby's life, but I didn't find her until after Lily was born.

"I admit, I forced Miranda to have a paternity test of Lily to confirm my belief. The results arrived the week I received a long-term work assignment to India. I had to go. Miranda told me not to contact her. I couldn't make that promise. Instead, I told her that I would contact them once I returned permanently to the States. She was furious. When I returned a few months ago, I learned of her murder. I'm shocked, but thankful I arrived when I did. I need Lily and Lily needs her father to help her through this difficult situation."

Ms. Pearson nodded. Her eyes shone with sympathy and revealed a caring heart. Gwen reached out and patted his hand. Mission accomplished.

After Gwen described the man-doll-hating scene at Lily's interview to John, he faltered in his push to connect to her. If she remembered him from Miranda's murder, he could not only lose his access to Julia's millions, but he'd also find himself in a mountain of legal trouble, beginning with murder charges.

In the tight space behind the mirror, they all met and introduced themselves to Dr. Gupta, Lily's psychologist and Bridget Kovach, Julia's sexy blonde attorney.

John peered through the glass at Julia talking to Lily. They sat together in the room trying to stack some blocks Lily found in a box in the corner. Lily seemed so innocent dressed in leggings and a long yellow sweater. Lily could definitely pass as his spawn, although she had more of her mother's coloring. She didn't look anything like her WASPy guardian. Lily didn't seem to want Julia to leave, and Julia didn't seem to want to leave. Ms. Pearson, still mousy and as plain as asphalt, seemed desperate to get Julia out of the room.

She pulled Julia aside near the mirror. "Ms. Gardiner, Lily and I will be meeting with Mr. Holland to introduce him without saying his actual relationship to her. If it goes well, we'll set up a second meeting."

Julia turned her head toward the mirror and seemed to be looking directly at John. Her eyes narrowed and her face went from princess to bitch. At least, that's how it felt to him. She then proceeded to kiss Lily on the forehead and leave. Lily stood up to go with her, but Ms. Pearson picked her up and offered her a cookie. Lily, cookie in hand, sat down at the table again and played with the blocks.

Julia walked into the observation room and stood beside her attorney. John stared at her, yet Julia gazed through the mirror at Lily, ignoring him. She'd have to acknowledge him at some point whether she wanted to or not. How could she not speak to the potential father of her little angel? In fact, he began to think about taking the kid from her entirely. A father would win a custody battle over some random unattached stranger. She had no blood connection and he, with papers to prove it, did. When he won, if she wanted to see her, she could barter with her money and maybe something more enjoyable.

After settling Lily down with the food bribe, Ms. Pearson

motioned subtly to the mirror. John picked up a stuffed animal provided to him by Gwen and left the booth.

He entered the room, a calm, confident man to everyone except Lily. To John's surprise, she screamed in terror, her eyes transfixed on the man. He'd been too cocky and assumed she wouldn't remember him, but she sure did. He had seen the same horror in her eyes when she discovered him standing over Miranda, blood dripping from the knife, blood leaching into the carpet and blood covering his and Miranda's clothes. He should have killed her then. Ms. Pearson reached out to try to comfort Lily, but the screams coming out of Lily's mouth continued and she fought against Ms. Pearson to escape from the room.

Julia rushed through the door, pulled Lily into her arms and held her close. She rocked her and kissed her on the head, but the child continued to scream.

His plan was falling apart. He needed a Plan B. Custody would not be easily won, even with a paternity test, if the child couldn't stand to be in the same room with men who looked like him.

Lily's psychologist discussed something with Dr. Santos, the court psychologist, out of John's hearing. She then faced John and asked him if he thought another visit with Lily could be delayed until she calmed down.

John's face constricted, looking to all the world as if his heart had begun to shatter. "My Lily," he said. "She needs better help. My God. I never knew how incapacitated she had become after her mother's death."

Gwen placed an arm on his shoulder. "We'll find every means possible to help this child. Perhaps she needs more than Dr. Gupta has provided in the past."

Dr. Gupta turned toward Gwen without the slightest hint of emotion positive or negative. "The treatment for such a traumatic event may take time. The more we force her interaction with strangers, the longer it will take to overcome these fears."

Bridget whispered something in Dr. Gupta's ear and the room went silent. Session over.

# Chapter 27

After Lily's meltdown at the custody determination, Julia did not want to plaster on a fake smile on Saturday afternoon. Perhaps it was a blessing when the day took a detour after her bride and groom decided to elope to Las Vegas instead of attending the eighty-thousand-dollar wedding Julia had planned. She stood among thousands of white-and-purple flowers in the middle of the Isabella Stewart Gardner Museum wondering what she could do to minimize their expenses, as they still owed her a third of the overall cost of the wedding and reception she'd planned. While premarital jitters often accompanied couples throughout the wedding planning process, she'd never had a bride and groom skip a wedding before. She felt jilted and alone in a room set up for two hundred guests and her favorite wedding band.

She took out her phone and sat at a table lavishly adorned with white roses and purple-painted lisanthus, breathing in the citrus scent, calming her frazzled nerves. She had enough issues to deal with. Adding chaos from work did nothing to keep her grounded.

That morning, the couple had sent her a text to inform her of their plans. She called back immediately, but they'd boarded a plane for Nevada. Their friends and family members all received notification via a Facebook post telling them that they wanted time alone and to send their presents directly to the bride's mother's house. They'd pick them up when they returned.

Helena strolled over, brushing her hand across one of the white linen tablecloths specifically requested by the bride. "Stunning. Simply stunning. At least we can get some promo shots." She pulled out a camera and began taking pictures of the finished room. The floral decorations brought out the craftsmanship in the architecture. Millions of brides could only dream of such an opulent location. This one bride, however, preferred Elvis and five hundred dollars' worth of gambling credit for the Venetian Hotel.

"Thanks." Julia followed the direction of the lens and sighed. So much work, for nothing.

"No problem. It's also nice to have a copy for our portfolio. The caption can read, 'This particular wedding had such an exclusive guest list that even the bride and groom had been excluded from attendance.'" Helena laughed, but stopped when her eyes saw the tears rolling down Julia's cheeks. Helena bent over and hugged Julia, causing more of a downpour.

"Can you send the dinner to the Center for Battered Women?" Julia asked, wiping her eyes.

"Absolutely. A nice thought." Helena headed to the kitchen area. "At least all the food won't go to waste."

Julia tapped her fingers on her phone, trying to get to her email screen. "The groom's parents want the cake sent to their house," she added. "Take a picture of it first." It was a three-tiered chocolate cake with raspberry filling and topped with buttercream white roses.

After Helena left, Julia's tears ran in rivers down to her chin and dripped onto the table. She didn't care about the wedding. She could handle the chaos, although the bride could have stopped Julia from spending her day setting up and then taking down the decorations for nothing but a photo shoot. One phone call to her office one day earlier, and disaster would have been averted.

That issue, however, didn't matter in light of John's pursuit of Lily, two weeks before she would have been Lily's legal mother. John roadblocked that dream. She'd bargain away everything, her business, her friends, her family, even Finn, to protect Lily.

Two hours later, Julia alone remained in the museum lobby. The space appeared unadorned after the huge bouquets and flower arrangements were returned to the large plastic bins that delivered them. The cooks had cleaned up their stations and departed, leaving only the faint odor of the chicken cordon bleu. The rental center broke down the tables, chairs and dance floor, piling them all into a large green truck toward another event on another day. The additional security she'd hired for the venue left the premises as well.

The flowers had been Julia's biggest concern until she remembered that this was the homecoming weekend at Miranda's former high school. In memory of Miranda, buckets of beautiful flowers would create a fairy palace out of a basketball gym.

As she walked from the front office with her pocketbook and her coat, she spotted Finn in the foyer, his back to her as he regarded a black-and-white drawing.

"What are you doing here?" she asked.

"I heard you had the afternoon free and thought we could go for a drive." Finn turned around and grinned. Helena, the annoying matchmaker, must have called him.

"Where to?" she asked. She wanted an escape and he could provide one.

"Chatham."

"Cape Cod?"

He raised his eyebrows. "Is there another one?"

"No idea. You're the local." Julia let out a deep breath. "Let's take your car. I don't think you'd fit in my car."

During the drive, Finn asked her a million questions about the canceled wedding. And she wanted to know what was happening with the dealership. Two hours later, they pulled up in front of a lighthouse.

"Nice view," she said. "Can we climb it?"

"It's closed for renovations."

"It's beautiful."

"She's pretty old, but has been a stable resident here for over one hundred years. Like an old friend."

They parked the car and walked to the deserted beach. The sea churned against a stormy gray sky. A cool, brisk wind forced most other visitors and residents into the nearby shops and restaurants.

"I don't think I'm dressed for this." Her black cocktail dress and sensible heels couldn't be described as sensible when walking in the sand. She shivered.

Finn caught her under her knees and lifted her off the ground.

"Put me down."

"You can't weigh much more than Lily." He swung her around a few times and then headed to the water.

The wind caused goose bumps on her legs. The idea of getting wet made her shiver again. "I warn you, if you get this dress wet, you're buying me a new one."

"It would be worth it." He continued walking to the water as she started flailing her legs.

Two college age boys called to her, "Need any help?"

"Sorry, guys, this one's mine."

*Mine?* "He's just being a jerk. Harmless, but a jerk," Julia replied to them with a smile. Until he kept walking toward the water. "Don't you dare. I'll call those boys back here."

He approached the edge of the surf and began to fling her

from him, but her grip on his neck pulled her flush against the leather of his jacket. Her face pressed into his neck until he loosened his grip. Julia could feel his heartbeat pumping as hard as her own and his eyes darkened as he lowered his lips toward her face. He kissed her gently. On her cheek. Their eye contact never broke. Julia wanted to nibble this ear; in fact, she craved it—she craved him.

Before she could kiss him back, really kiss him back, he hefted her hips up onto his shoulder and started walking back to the road.

"Put me down." Julia hit him on the back.

He laughed.

When he finally brought her back to Earth by the SUV, he smiled like a big brother who had found a way to torment a little sister. "Do you feel better?"

"Yes. Absolutely. The idea of being flung into the ocean always makes me giddy." She shook her head.

"Good." He opened the passenger door for her and drove her down the street to a small diner, where he proceeded to warm her up with coffee and a cup of chicken noodle soup.

They were in a good place. Perhaps everything would work out.

# *Chapter 28*

When Julia and Finn returned to her house, Dianne was talking on the phone and Lily was watching the television.

"What's going on?" Julia asked.

"Kevin. He wants to go away tonight and tomorrow, but I have to work."

"Go ahead. I'm taking tomorrow off anyway."

"Are you sure?" she asked, her expression brightening.

"Absolutely. You deserve a break."

Julia headed to the kitchen to start dinner and Dianne picked up her things.

After Dianne left, Julia changed into jeans and a red Martha's Vineyard T-shirt and made dinner as Finn and Lily played Barbies and then had a tea party. Finn, the holder of more testosterone per square inch than an endocrinologist with a warehouse supply, held the two-inch pink plastic teacup with the utmost poise and dignity. The military would be proud. He'd taken off his leather jacket and sat on the floor with his shirtsleeves rolled up. A gorgeous man playing with a child had to be the biggest turn-on ever. Julia's attraction to him skyrocketed, especially when Lily curled onto his lap and he began to read her a story. Maybe her happily-ever-after could become a reality.

After dinner, Julia gave Lily a bath and put her to bed.

"Mommy?" she asked.

"Yes, Little Bear."

Lily reached for her Smurf and a stuffed armadillo. "Can we keep Uncle Finn?"

"I don't think anyone can keep another person. But we can ask him over for dinner again. Is that okay?" She leaned over and kissed Lily, Smurf and the armadillo good-night.

Lily looked at her with her Maguire blue eyes and pleaded, "Couldn't he live here? He can have the other bedroom."

"He already has a place to live." *And Julia was too scared to want the same thing.* "Go to sleep." Julia kissed her again and brushed her hand over her soft curls.

When she returned to the kitchen, she found Finn rummaging through the refrigerator. "Can I help you?"

"I'm craving a beer," he said without looking up. "Do you have any?"

"No beer. I have wine."

He stood straight and shut the door. "No, thanks. It's not really a wine kind of night."

"How about some mint-chocolate-chip ice cream?"

"The green kind or the white kind?"

He stayed where he was, so Julia had to push through him to get the freezer door open. Their bodies remained pressed against each other. Her entire right side nestled into him.

She smiled and lifted out the box. "Green."

"Now you're talking." He took the carton from her and placed it on the counter.

She took her time shutting the freezer door. She needed to cool off.

After she filled two bowls with the ice cream, Finn devoured every bit in his bowl and then began picking away at the remnants of hers.

He left to place his bowl into the sink. Julia remained seated on the couch thinking about how Finn seemed so put together. Although his whole life seemed generically wonderful, he'd had a difficult time. He'd lost both parents and his sister, had been framed for murder and walked away from a job he really cared about only to now learn that the company he'd invested in might be taken away too. Yet, he'd kept up his calm demeanor. At least in front of her.

He returned to the family room and sat next to her. "I could get used to this life. Ice cream, Barbies and a house full of women." His loud laugh vibrated through her. He so rarely laughed like that, it did something to her insides. "Seriously, I love hanging out with Lily…and you."

"Shhhhhh. You'll wake Lily," Julia said as she placed a finger over his lips.

Her touch froze him in place. After she placed her hand back on her lap, they both sat in silence together for several minutes. In the background, Julia could hear the creek flowing by the house.

She draped her leg over his and leaned onto his shoulder. "I appreciate all of your help with everything. The wedding cancellation annoyed me and, to be honest, John scares the hell out of me. I don't know what I'd have done without your support these past few days."

"I'm glad I could be there for you. That guy definitely is missing some important chromosome."

"I know. I have no idea what Miranda saw in him." She needed to block John from her mind for the next several hours. She couldn't think of him without wanting to scream in anguish over the threat he posed.

He nodded. "The only explanation I have for her picking him out of a bar is that she was drunk."

Even for one night, their pairing was too unlikely. She couldn't, in any situation, see them together. "They don't seem to go together at all."

"I agree." He pulled Julia in tighter toward him.

She leaned in and placed one of her hands on his knee. She wanted to give him a large green light so that he wouldn't mistake it for red, yellow or any other color. "I love looking into your eyes. They're intense with a side of sweet."

"Really?" The edges of his mouth tilted up. He tried to appear skeptical, but he sure as hell knew he was gorgeous. How could he not?

"Really." She nodded, moving her hand farther up his leg.

In for a penny, in for two hundred pounds of pure muscle. "I love that you're built like a boxer too."

His laughter shook her nerves until he placed his hand over hers and squeezed. "A boxer?"

She pulled out her hand and moved it over his shoulder and down his arms. "Pure muscle. Pure power. And even with your fairly sinister scar, I feel perfectly safe with you." One finger traced over the scar on his cheek.

His arms encircled her and pulled her in. She let him. Their mouths came so close to each other that certain words caused their lips to touch. Her temperature revved up twenty degrees.

His breath smelled of mint chocolate chip. "Do you feel safe right now?"

"Yes." She lifted her chin and kissed him.

His lips responded like a caress. Softly. Sweetly. She wanted more and pushed further. Her mouth opening, his reacting. His tongue entered and explored. She could taste the mint and the chocolate. Her arms reached around his neck as he leaned down to kiss her. Never in her life had she been more comfortable, relaxed and completely aroused.

"If I said I wish we never broke apart, would that scare you?" she asked as they both stretched across the couch together.

He grinned and bit the bottom on her lip. "I have few regrets in my life, but letting you go is my biggest." He wrapped his arm around her waist, pulling her closer.

Julia sighed, snuggling into him, her head finding a comfortable place on his chest. She could feel the steady rhythm of his heartbeat beneath her ear, a comforting and constant reminder of his presence.

Inhaling sharply for a lungful of sanity, Julia pulled back as her body's cravings fought with her brain's logic. "I need you, but not here." She backed away from him and instantly felt a chill. She reached out to touch his hand.

He gripped her tight as he rose, never letting her go. "Are you sure of this?"

She placed her hands on his chest, pushed him toward her bedroom and nodded.

"You're absolutely sure?" he asked again.

Julia rubbed herself up against him, feeling how ready he was for her. "Absolutely. Are you?"

"Beyond ready." He pulled her into his arms and kissed the top of her head. "Come on."

They both moved into the bedroom together and shut the door.

They left the light on, forcing them to focus on each other's facial expressions and movements as he lifted her shirt over her head. Finn's eyes rested on Julia's chest. His gaze worshipped, and she'd never felt so beautiful.

She pressed her hands under his shirt and wrapped her arms around his waist. Solid. Protective. Pushing his shirt up and off, Julia melted into his chest.

"I haven't been with anyone since we broke up," she said as they both stretched across the bed together.

He grinned and bit the bottom on her lip. "Neither have I."

She sat up. "Really?"

Finn remained on the bed, waiting for her to climb back over him. How could a man look so masculine lying across a floral comforter? "Really. I've never gotten over losing you, Julia."

"But you gave me up…"

He shook his head. "It wasn't by choice. I couldn't see a

future with you that didn't stain your life. My vision is clearer now and maybe there's a way someday in the future. I'm willing to do whatever it takes to make that happen."

His words pressed straight into her heart. She stretched out over him and then pushed him so he'd be on top, but they missed the edge of the bed and fell onto the floor. Julia cried out, even though Finn tried to grab her to lessen the impact of the fall. Neither one of them noticed the door open.

The shrill cry broke them apart. Lily.

"Mommy, Mommy, Mommy." Screams, sobs, and then she was on the bed hitting Finn to let her go.

"Stop," Julia called out. "It's okay."

Lily sobbed and shrieked as if Finn had been murdering Julia. A scene that Lily understood better than anyone else. Finn's expression turned from passion to horror. He leaped away from the bed and into the bathroom.

Julia quickly pulled her shirt on then sat on the bed and held Lily in her arms. "It's okay, Little Bear. It's okay."

But it wasn't.

Julia awoke in her T-shirt and some sweatpants with her arms wrapped around Lily. The little girl stirred and opened her eyes. Innocent eyes that had seen life's cruelest atrocities. They looked surprisingly clear, but sadness tinged their edges.

Julia pulled Lily closer into her embrace. "Morning."

"Is Uncle Finn gone?" she asked.

"Yes. He left last night."

"Good." Lily kept her head on the pillow and shut her eyes again.

Julia didn't want to speak about what Lily had witnessed and so she kept quiet.

When they both woke up an hour later, Julia took her to an emergency session with Dr. Gupta. She tried to explain what had happened, and felt humiliated for having done such a stupid, reckless act. Dr. Gupta asked to see Lily alone for a few minutes. Julia stood in the waiting room. She wanted to call Finn, but what could she say? Instead, she called Bridget.

"You had sex with your *friend*?" Bridget blasted through the phone.

"No, not really."

"What does 'not really' mean?"

"I guess we were headed in that direction. Lily found us on the floor in my bedroom."

Bridget kept Julia frozen in silence before saying, "I knew this would happen. You two looked like lovers and responded to each other like lovers. It was only a matter of time before you both acted on it."

"I'm sorry. Does this mess up the case?"

"What's the status of your relationship now?"

"Now?" There didn't seem to be a status. More of a void.

"Let me guess? He left, freaked out because of Lily's reaction. You're too embarrassed to call him. Your relationship is going nowhere as long as you're protecting Lily, and Finn's feeling guilty."

The reality of Bridget's words stung. "What can I do?"

"If you want Lily, you need to sever your relationship with Finn, at least for the time being. He's now the enemy. If you'd kept it platonic and she really enjoyed his company, his relationship would have been an asset, but there's no going back. You need to move forward. Especially since John's paternity test is authentic."

Julia's hand squeezed the phone tighter and the empty space in her stomach now felt like it would erupt in flames. "Authentic?"

"I've called the hospital to double-check. It's there in the hospital file. I have no idea how we missed it before. This gives us an uphill battle. For the next week, I need you to forget about Finn and stay focused on the court case."

# Chapter 29

Finn hadn't slept in two days. He called and texted Julia to check on her, but received no answer. Regret followed him into the conference room at the Bancroft brothers' corporate headquarters. Lush green plants, rich navy blue fabrics and huge tinted windows overlooking the Charles River screamed money. A large carved oak table provided the final touch to the Bancrofts' psychological advantage.

Finn and Davis sat next to each other with their backs to the view. Finn wanted his focus to be on the room and its occupants rather than on anything occurring outside. He appeared professional in a Brooks Brothers fitted suit, while Davis wore some designer suit that would impress people who were impressed by overpriced bespoke suits.

He did not want to be there, feeling like a truant outside the principal's office waiting for judgment.

He wanted to be with Julia especially after what had happened with Lily. He should have kept his distance until they were sure Lily would be able to handle it. He fisted his hands together. He couldn't erase the picture of Lily's face, terrified, screeching. The little girl who called him Uncle. She must hate him. One more fiend who attacks women in her presence. *Shit.* He missed them both, but needed to keep his head during the meeting or their staff might be without employment before Christmas.

Davis shifted a pile of papers in front of him. Spreadsheets and financial documents about the dealership that the Bancrofts had already seen. Davis wanted to present the business in the best possible light and prepared for hours to explain every debt on the balance sheet and all income available for dividends on the P&L.

Bill, their attorney, relaxed in his seat next to Finn. He loved conflict and never worried if negotiations became heated. Finn had watched him in action and liked the way his mind could wrap around a problem and pull out a solution that everyone at the table could not only agree to, but would be satisfied that they earned an upper hand.

Robert Bancroft walked into the room. A short man with a huge ego, he sat at the head of the table. Davis wrote in small print on one of his papers that Robert's suit was Armani. Who cared? As long as they received the funding they needed, he didn't care if the guy walked into the room in a Victoria's Secret negligée.

An army of attorneys piled into the room next. Five men of various ages. The Bancrofts wouldn't have a female attorney, only female secretaries and mistresses. Finn didn't care as long as he received his financing. If he received 51 percent of the company with Davis at the end of the negotiations, they couldn't affect how he ran his business.

Jack Bancroft walked in last. An inch or two taller than his brother, he earned his reputation as the biggest prick in the technology field through hardball negotiations and nasty tactics. He rarely lost in his quest to dominate the Boston tech region. A small region, granted, but significant enough to make even the bigwig pharmaceutical giants in the area sit up and take notice. He sat on the end opposite his brother.

Robert leaned back in his chair, no cares in the world. "So Mr. Maguire, Mr. Malone tells us that you're focused on finding a partner. We've been looking for a new industry to expand into. Automobiles seems like an interesting sideline."

"A little diversity for your portfolio?" Finn asked.

"Perhaps. We've gained a few silent partners, an angel network, so to speak, that have recommended this investment. I have a serious issue though." That comment triggered a silent alert in Finn's mind. Silent partners could be anyone. But the effort to gather a group of backers meant they'd already put in the due diligence to assume it was a solid investment. That could only work in Finn's favor.

He reached out and poured himself a cup of water from a pitcher in the middle of the table. "And what's that?" His voice resonated with confidence he didn't have.

"Jack and I don't know whether to invest in a new car dealership or your used car store."

Finn could hear Davis's deep intake of breath. *Steady, friend, he's trying to make us feel unworthy.* "What dealership did you have in mind?"

"We're thinking Ferrari."

Finn nodded. "Amazing company. Ferrari currently has thirty-three independent dealerships. The contracts go back years. They haven't expanded in a decade. The competition is stiff. Even with the recent decrease in sales, they still require a two-year wait to create a new car. We sell Ferraris as well, but our buyers can get the cars quicker. We currently have a six-month-old Ferrari V-12 available today. If you're interested, it may still be on the showroom floor, although we move cars fast, lots of them."

"I wasn't thinking of acquiring a new dealership, just taking one over."

Davis laughed. "Good luck. The main dealers of elite cars have roots deeper than an oil well and I can't imagine they'd sell their business barring extreme financial difficulty."

"That can be arranged." Robert smiled, but Jack shook his head as though he couldn't believe how blunt his brother was being.

"I'm sure you know all about our need for an investor to replace my cousin Richard," Finn said. "We're looking for a purely profit driven silent partner. However, Davis and I also want an influx of new ideas. That's where you would come in."

"You've done well taking over your family's business," Jack said, "but you know nothing about creating long-term growth in Boston. We'll need adequate incentives to preserve your precious dealership. We also expect to have more of a hands-on approach to our investment. You boys seem competent, but getting to the next level requires experience and financial backing."

Finn's fists tightened. "We need twenty million to pay off Richard. That brings with it a fifty-percent split in profits and regular dividends. I think that's more than fair."

"We want fifty-two percent profit and fifty percent ownership."

Finn stood. Davis glanced up at him pleading with his eyes for a few more minutes of negotiation, but Finn ignored him. "I'm not interested in those terms. I'll go to a fifty percent profit, based on net proceeds and less dividends paid, and forty-nine percent ownership, but I won't go over." He tried to move around the table to leave, but Jack stuck his leg out to the wall as he approached, effectively blocking Finn in.

Finn glared at Jack then leaned on the table in front of him and announced to the entire room, "Those are my firm limits. Is that clear, or do I need to call for my car?"

"I like it," Jack said, smiling. "I like it a lot. I also like your no-bull style of negotiation. I think we can definitely work something out so that we're all happy. Sit down."

Robert nodded. "Sit down."

Finn walked back to his chair, his hunch right. But even with the favorable terms, something felt off.

# Chapter 30

The small courtroom smelled dusty. Light streaming through the windows reflected off the dust particles dangling in the air and made Julia feel somewhat dirty. The hollow, sick feeling dominating her torso added to her claustrophobia. She wanted to leave and wait outside breathing fresh air while avoiding the man who wanted to take Lily from her.

Could the judge see past John's sad-father persona? Probably not. Even Bridget had a hard time finding fault with the man.

"He may not be my version of a father, but the guy has sperm and no criminal record. If Lily didn't have psychological issues, this would be a much bigger battle. The court could certainly rule in his favor," Bridget had said during one of their recent meetings. "Even now, genetics could help him obtain visitation." Her blunt approach to her cases provided Julia with heartburn, but the honesty prepared Julia for every possible outcome.

Julia twisted to see behind her. Her mother sat on the bench where Finn had sat at the temporary hearing. She would have gladly traded her mother's presence for Finn's, but that wasn't possible. And she needed someone in her corner. She needed her mom's support.

Finn's absence frustrated her, but she understood that he couldn't be involved after the fiasco of a week ago. What judge would place Lily with a woman who kept a man around that terrified her? He had texted her several times to make sure everything was okay, but it wasn't and would never be. Keeping Lily, she'd lose Finn and if she wanted Finn, she'd lose Lily. She understood how Finn tried to avoid getting into situations requiring connections. Some people must not be placed on the Earth to have a soulmate; they had other responsibilities, like their best friend's daughter.

Although her mother had no family law experience, her presence provided Julia comfort. Her business acumen made her a formidable force in the world and that strength was appreciated. She reached over to touch Julia's arm. "After reading the GAL report, I think you'll be fine. She liked John, but clearly had reservations after he met Lily."

"Thanks." Julia turned back toward the bench as Judge Miller walked in with an intern or someone following him.

After the judge sat on the bench, he spoke to the room. "I read the GAL report and have found her findings very helpful. I'd like to ask each party a few pointed questions to clarify a few issues in order to make a better decision for Lily's immediate future."

Judge Miller asked each attorney to go over their reasons for having custody. Gwen focused on the paternity test. Bridget focused on the loss of Lily's mother and how Julia had helped raise Lily since then. The loss of a secondary maternal figure would be devastating to Lily.

Judge Miller pushed his wireless frames farther up his nose. Glancing down at John, he said, "I understand that the paternity test clearly reveals Mr. Holland's paternity of Lily. I have grave misgivings, however, concerning his lack of interest in her life from the moment of her birth to a few weeks ago."

John shifted his gaze to Gwen, who responded. "Mr. Holland, a highly regarded leader in his field, returned from a business assignment only three months ago. As soon as he learned that Miranda passed away, he immediately sought to obtain custody of his only child. He's been distraught over the lack of proper psychological support the poor child has received. His only wish is for Lily to be able to return to a normal family environment and not be locked in a house with no outside influences."

The judge pursed his lips as though he'd bit into a rotten grape. "That's all fine and dandy, Mr. Holland, but you never paid child support and there is no record of you visiting Lily before your transfer. Coming in as the knight in shining armor at such a late date, where removal of the child from her current home could create further damage to a little girl's already fragile psyche, feels more selfish than sacrificial."

John stood. His face was practically angelic, water pooling in his eyes. "I made a mistake. I left so soon after her birth and Miranda assured me that Lily would have the best of everything. I admit I didn't want to see her at first, because I didn't want her to know her father only to have to leave." Tears streamed down John's cheeks. "And I avoided seeing her so I wouldn't carry her beautiful face imprinted in my mind as I traveled across the globe. I know what I did was wrong, but I'm here to make up for that and give her the father she needs and deserves." His head dropped and he sat down, a wounded and heartbroken man.

After several follow-up questions, Judge Miller turned to Julia and Bridget. "Lily's psychological issues seem to have become worse over time. Are you willing to place her in additional counseling if needed?"

"Absolutely. If we find that Dr. Gupta's techniques are not working to lessen Lily's stress, then we'll certainly obtain the best mental health professionals available to help her overcome her fears," Bridget replied. Julia nodded vigorously at the comment. She wanted the best for Lily, no matter what, even if it broke her heart.

At that point, Gwen stood up and asked if she could question Julia.

"I don't see why not. Ms. Gardiner, please answer Ms. Holt's questions as they may offer more insight for me to take into consideration."

Gwen glanced at some papers on her desk, then looked directly at Julia and asked, "Ms. Gardiner, have you had any men over to your house with Lily present?"

Julia's throat constricted preventing her from answering. Could her answer hurt her chances with the case? She looked at Bridget. Bridget gave a barely perceptible nod. Tell the truth, the whole truth.

"Yes." Her heart increased its pace, causing her ears to feel as though ascending in an airplane.

"How many men do you have come over to your house with Lily home?" Gwen asked.

Julia visibly gulped as she tried to arrest the closing of her windpipe. "One, but he doesn't come around anymore."

Gwen smirked. How professional. "Can you provide the name of that person?"

Bridget stood up and said, "Objection."

Judge Miller looked down at Julia. "Overruled. Please answer the question, Ms. Gardiner."

A deep breath, difficult when her throat had constricted to the size of a fiber optic cable. "Finn Maguire, Lily's uncle."

The judge had this information in the GAL report. Why was Gwen torturing her? "What was Lily's reaction to Mr. Maguire?"

"At first, they got along. She adored him."

"And now?" Gwen's voice was stern, her eyes narrowed with a slight gleam, as though she knew what had gone on inside Julia's house. Did she? But how could she? Unless they had someone monitoring outside the house.

Julia remained silent for a few seconds. Then took a deep

breath and replied, "She's terrified of him, of most men." Julia regarded John, not a great specimen, but a man nonetheless. She'd keep him away as well if she could manage it.

"Does he still come to the house?"

"No. I would never allow anyone near Lily that she had misgivings about." Especially John, if she could help it. Her apprehension around John sent off alarm bells as loud as a tornado siren.

Gwen, however, wouldn't leave Finn alone. "What did he do that scared Lily?"

"Nothing. It was a complete misunderstanding." She dreaded the next question. She wanted to run from the room and throw up. Forget Finn, think of Lily. Julia needed to focus on what was best for Lily at this moment.

"Please explain, Ms. Gardiner," the judge interjected.

"She saw us together and thought he was attacking me, but he wasn't." Escape eluded her, as her face reddened in shame. Her body hunched down trying to hide from the humiliation. Her mother didn't need to hear about her sex life.

"What *specifically* were you doing together?" If Gwen wanted blood, this was how she'd get it.

"We were together in bed."

"Having sex?" Gwen asked, highlighting Julia's shame.

She could feel the burn in her cheeks and the tears pooling, ready to fall. "No, not really."

Gwen shook her head in disgust and sat down.

At the break, Bridget ushered Julia into a small office near the lobby. The moment Julia stepped in the room, her tears fell while Bridget spoke to someone on the phone in the corner.

"That attorney didn't need to rehash your private business in such a forum. She must know that she's going to lose and is trying to make the client feel as though he got some of his money's worth," her mother said as she slowly rubbed Julia's back.

"I feel so foolish."

Gabrielle handed her a tissue. "Why? Because you care for a man? You're not a nun. You're not even Catholic. How many parents have been caught in far more sensitive moments? You're fine, Lily's fine. He's no longer in your life and you've found Lily the best psychological help on the planet."

The sympathy thrown her way by her mother didn't assuage her shame. "I've blown it. How can the judge grant me custody?"

Bridget walked over and placed her hand on Julia's shoulder. "John has a hell of a bigger hill to climb. Lily can't be with men right now. Therefore, he should have a snowball's chance in hell of getting custody. He can definitely work toward it, but he's going to have a hard time convincing Judge Miller to let a little girl that falls into a terror at the sight of any man be placed with a father she's never met."

"I agree, even if John acts as though he'd be the best parent out there," her mother added.

When they returned to the courtroom, John glared at Julia, causing goose bumps to race up her arms and across the back of her neck. He then turned to Gwen and gazed innocently down at the table, as if the weight of the world pushed against this sad and weary father.

The judge opened the door and sat on the bench. "Thank you all for your cooperation over the course of these past few weeks. Now that I've seen and considered the GAL report and the court psychologist's reports, as well as the testimony that I heard today and the positive paternity test that I received from the hospital, I feel that I'm ready to make a decision.

"First, Mr. Holland. Your cooperation in court has been very beneficial. I apologize for your lack of access to Lily. Please understand that we take the best interests of the child very seriously and that the trauma she went through with her mother's murder will take time to heal. I will acknowledge that the paternity test is valid and that your interest in your daughter's welfare is commendable."

Judge Miller turned his attention to Julia. "Ms. Gardiner. You took on a very difficult role upon the death of your good friend Miranda Maguire. As quite a few witnesses have testified, you have altered your life and your work to focus time and attention on Lily. Your acknowledgment of the misjudgment about having a boyfriend in the home, even one related to Lily, during her rehabilitation helps us to see a more accurate picture of the limitations of having the physical guardianship of her. However, according to the GAL report, Lily has thrived in your care. You have been a *de facto* mother since Miranda Maguire passed away. Your bond seems strong and loving."

Bridget reached over and took Julia's hand. The squeeze helped to calm her nerves, but Julia would have preferred the strength of Finn beside her.

"My decision focuses solely on the best interest of Lily. She needs a strong family bond, a nurturing environment and a stable, loving parent. I am declaring Mr. Holland and Ms. Gardiner as joint legal guardians for Lily. Mr. Holland must begin to take a role in his daughter's life and he should be able to help make decisions about school, health and financial considerations.

"Sole physical custody, however, must remain with Ms. Gardiner due to the grave psychological problems that Lily is dealing with. And since Ms. Gardiner has to shoulder this burden alone, Mr. Holland will be required to pay child support to help Ms. Gardiner with Lily's medical treatment and child-rearing costs in the amount of five hundred dollars per month, according to his ability to pay."

At hearing the words, a cascade of tears, pent-up stress and tension poured out. Her sobbing increased as all of her worries about Lily evaporated. The adoption may be delayed, but who cared as long as she could hold her little bear in her arms every night.

Bridget hugged her and Gabrielle ran up to them and hugged them both. Physical custody and child support. John must be livid that he not only received no visitation from his custody suit, but also lost a portion of his income. Julia decided to place the child support in the trust she'd set up with Finn's contribution for Lily's benefit when she became older.

Julia glanced over at John. She didn't like him, but she had no material reason for her mistrust. He wanted to be with his daughter. Wouldn't any father? He nodded stoically as Gwen whispered something to him while she put her computer back in her briefcase and organized a few loose papers. Perhaps he wasn't as bad as she thought.

# *Chapter 31*

John had expected to lose the case after the GAL visit. After all, how could he raise a girl terrified of him? The court knew this. He knew this. Physical custody with visitation, however, would have been the perfect bargaining chip to gain access to Julia's millions. Instead, he owed her. Of all the results possible, the worse outcome came to pass. The surprise he'd received about paying child support burned him up, roasted him and spit his charred body to the ground. Rayburn was going to kill him. What the hell did his attorney, Gwen, do to prevent this? Nothing.

Julia stared across the room at him. He could feel her victorious eyes burn him. He looked back at her and gave a half-hearted nod to her. Acquiescing. Reassuring.

A small crowd had gathered around her. Her elegant mother he recognized from his Internet search on her family. The source of Julia's money.

Dr. Gupta had already left. What a boring sack of flesh. She had remained in the back of the courtroom revealing no elation, no excitement, no energy. The perfect balance to Lily's explosive tirades. He hated her.

Julia remained to speak for a few minutes to her attorney, a pretty blonde thing. Ms. Kovach not only beat out a paternity test, but she won the child financial support to boot. Child support to assist an heiress raising a stranger.

Finn had been Julia's support over the past few weeks, but

he no longer stood by her. Watching him leave and overhearing Julia calling her mother on her back patio had provided the perfect means to torment Julia with the most embarrassing story possible. Finn's absence provided John with the one positive note of the morning. If her testimony had any truth in it, she couldn't have him around Lily anymore. Perfect. They'd be more vulnerable.

Gwen picked up her briefcase and turned toward him. "We can appeal, John. Although I'm doubtful that anything will change until Lily gets better, you do have the right to request a new psychologist if you don't think this one will help Lily. Someone with a different method of helping her. A new method could show different results. I don't think her issues would become worse. If she improves, we can come back to court to request some form of visitation."

Typical lawyer, she wanted more money after badly botching the case. *Sure, bitch, let's take this case to the Supreme Court. I'll still lose and you'll make a bundle.*

"My priority is Lily right now." He projected his voice loud enough to be heard by most of the people in the front of the courtroom, a slight hitch in the voice holding back the inevitable sadness, hiding the rage. "I need time before making any new decision. Thank you for all of your help." He placed his hand on her shoulder. "You tried everything you knew to improve my chances to have some involvement in her life. It's not your fault. The dynamics of our family are complicated."

"Would you like to go to lunch? We can discuss the details of the decision?" Gwen asked, clearly looking for redemption. She wouldn't get any.

His hand remained on her shoulder, as if holding himself up from the onslaught of grief that any man in his position would harbor. "I'm not hungry and I need some time alone. Give me a few days. I'll call you to go over the details of the support order."

Gwen's face looked older from her failure, creasing her too-young eyes, causing her skin to look mottled and sallow. John wanted her to feel defeated. He handed over his plan to an untried attorney. Rayburn had assured him that anyone would do. Big mistake. He'd hoped that her clerkship with Ms. Kovach would have given him a slight advantage. After all, Gwen didn't seem too ethically bound and had some grudge against the older attorney.

He grabbed his coat from the back of his chair and exited the room and the building, face aimed toward the ground.

John had predicted this outcome after watching Lily's breakdown in front of Dr. Santos. No judge in their right mind would send a girl to a father she didn't know when any man in her vicinity terrorized her. Ironic really. He wanted her to suffer for her mother's sins. He wanted her terrorized. Yet, Lily's psychological issues divested him of success. He could appreciate the irony in the situation. Not to worry.

It was time to begin implementing plan B. He called Rayburn to update him.

# *Chapter 32*

The stress of the afternoon melted away as Julia's house came into view like a Tibetan sanctuary for weary travelers. She placed her hand on her mother's and squeezed. "I'm glad you came. I don't think I could have handled this alone."

"Maybe you should find a husband," Gabrielle stated as if the notion had never crossed Julia's mind. But it had. Often.

Julia thought of Finn. She craved him, but how could she have a relationship with a man that scared the hell out of Lily?

"Someday," she responded to get her mother to change the subject. The court case had already revealed the depths of Julia's humiliation with Finn; she didn't need to relive it.

Gabrielle picked up Julia's cue and didn't continue the topic of Julia's lack of a love life.

When Julia entered the kitchen, she saw Dianne making cookies in her kitchen with Lily. Lily stood on a chair pouring the chocolate chips into the batter.

"Cookies? A perfect dessert," Julia said, placing her hand on Dianne's shoulder and peering into the bowl.

"In celebration?" Dianne asked whipping around. Her eyes waiting for the answer.

"In celebration."

Dianne squealed and hugged Julia. Flour smeared onto Julia's navy dress, creating whitish blue smudges. Lily jumped down from the chair and squeezed into the embrace.

"Are we having a party?" Lily asked.

Everyone laughed.

Lily clearly understood that celebration meant party. She had no idea that her guardian was almost replaced with a very creepy guy.

"Can Uncle Finn come?" she asked.

"Do you want him here?"

She nodded. "He can come back for ice cream and paints."

"He can?"

"Yep." And she bounced up and down as though the other night had never happened. Had she just been tired and Julia and Finn totally overreacted? From Lily's carefree manner now, it was very possible. Julia wanted to call him immediately, but perhaps they needed a little distance, at least until the court order was final.

"Okay. Maybe not tonight. But soon." Julia faced Dianne. "Can you stay for dinner?"

"I can't. I need to leave after the cookies are done. I'm meeting Kevin."

"How is school going?" Gabrielle asked. She liked Dianne, which was amazing since her mother had very few people she liked.

Dianne mixed the nuts into the batter, as Lily twirled into Julia's waiting arms. "I'm thinking about changing majors from accounting to education. I love spending time with Lily and I think I'd be able to handle a classroom of little rug rats." She pointed at Lily and stuck her tongue out. Lily copied her.

"No doubt. You'll have them cowering in the corner." Gabrielle took her coat off and hung it on the back of one of the kitchen chairs.

Julia laughed. "Doubtful. Dianne's a pushover when it comes to little kids. I can picture you with the black hair and Doc Martens having every child love you to death."

"My looks might not go over well with a hiring committee, but I'll cross that bridge when I get to it. I promised my parents that I'll be more polished after I graduate. Right now, however, I can experiment with my look. No harm, no foul, right?"

"Absolutely. Enjoy this time. We love you no matter what you wear," Julia said.

As Dianne baked the cookies, Gabrielle sat on the couch in the family room to play a game with Lily. Julia took a moment to text Finn that she'd retained custody of Lily and would even receive child support.

He replied within a matter of minutes:

Finn: Fantastic. You're a wonderful mother. I'm glad for you.

Julia: Lily asked for you to come over and celebrate. Perhaps next weekend?

Finn: Really?

Julia: Really :)

When Lily jumped off the couch to play with a pile of toys on the floor, Julia flopped down next to Gabrielle. "Tomorrow everything returns back to normal. I can't wait. I was thinking about enrolling Lily in a ballet class."

"Great idea. She loves dancing and music."

Lily walked over to them holding a Ken doll with the blond hair colored over with a brown marker. "I don't like him." She threw it at the wall.

Julia froze. Her stomach tightened. "Little Bear. Where did you get that doll?"

"On my swing."

A chill swept over Julia's body, but she had enough focus to run into the backyard. She looked around the swing and all over the yard. She even jogged the length of the fence. Nothing. The icy tension in her shoulders shot pain through her temples and she ran back into the house.

"Lily?" she called out, hoping the terror wasn't laced through her voice.

"Yes."

"Don't go outside again until I say you can."

"What is it?" her mother asked.

"Mom, Lily freaked out with a male Ken doll at the court interview. We've never owned one, but she found this in the backyard."

"I think you're overreacting. It's a doll."

No, it was a warning or a threat or a punishment for winning the case. Julia didn't know why the doll arrived in her backyard, but something sinister put it there. Julia shook her head, still holding the plastic man. "I disagree. I think you were right earlier. I need security."

Gabrielle strode across the floor grabbing her cell phone on the coffee table. "I'll send my team up here. They're the best."

Julia shook her head. "Finn has a connection to a local security agency."

"I don't think so. Paying a discount for security will always cost you."

# Chapter 33

A week and three days later, Julia's life became a repetitive jumble of work tasks and activities with Lily. Being busy permitted Julia to avoid all the harsh emotions that coiled deep down in her gut. Her fear of someone stalking them followed her like a dark shadow. It existed beside and behind her, but never took physical hold. She attempted to eliminate her concern with her mother's security guards. Katie Garbano, a former FBI agent who wanted more flexibility of assignments and more money than the agency provided. And Todd Hamlin, a retired police officer. So far, however, their presence increased Julia's sense of peace and serenity only enough to allow her to leave Lily at home while she went to work. It didn't enable Julia to sleep soundly through the night.

To add to her stress, Julia missed Finn. They both had crazy work schedules that seemed to be the opposite of each other. Julia worked more nights and he was busy in meetings most days.

Her focus, however, needed to remain on Lily for the time being. In order to sneak more time with her, Julia, having finished a lunch with a very picky bride, decided to avoid the office and go home to take Lily to the park. Sunny, cool days in November rarely occurred and Julia wanted to enjoy the fresh air before the winter forced them both indoors except for quick outings to make snowmen and go tubing.

After she parked her car in the garage, she ran into the

kitchen. The dishes had been washed and put away. Only a small plastic cup half-filled with milk sat on the countertop, Lily's favorite because it had a picture of blue penguins on it.

"Lily, Dianne? I'm home," she called out, tossing her pocketbook on the table and starting to fill the kettle for tea.

No answer. She peered out the back of the house. No one. Perhaps they went to the park themselves. After all, the blue sky and warm sun caused Julia to race home for the same reason. After looking out the back window, Julia realized Dianne's car still sat in the driveway, but Katie's was gone.

A raw, cool feeling started growing through her, an uneasiness, a fear. Her heartbeat picked up its pace and rattled out a thumping that completely divested her of reason.

"Lily? Dianne?" she called again. *"Lily!"* She ran up to the bedrooms. Nothing. She stood in the doorway to Lily's room and her stomach dropped to the floor. The creepy Ken doll was sitting on Lily's bed, next to her Smurf. Bile rose up into her throat. She couldn't breathe. Collapsing on her hands and knees, she pulled out her phone and called 911.

"Nine-one-one. What is the emergency?"

"My daughter is missing and so is the babysitter and their security guard." A huge boulder settled on her chest. Trying to take a deep breath, she only ended up choking.

"Calm down, ma'am. When was the last time you saw them?"

"This morning, before I went to work."

"Have you spoken to either of them?"

"No. They aren't home."

"Calm down. Were you expected at this time?"

"No, I came home early for lunch."

"Okay, why don't you wait until after lunch and see if they return."

"You don't understand. Something's wrong. This isn't the time to wait," she said, her voice cracking.

"What's your address?"

"Twenty-four Creek Road, Concord, Mass."

"Who am I speaking to?"

"Julia Gardiner. My daughter, well, I'm her guardian, she's Lily Maguire and her nanny is Dianne Walter and the security agent is Katie something. Oh my God, I forgot her name." Breathing had become difficult.

"It's okay, ma'am. The police are on the way. Do you know what Lily was wearing this morning?" The voice sounded calm and secure, grounding Julia in something short of reality.

"She was in pajamas. Pink pajamas, but Dianne would have changed her." She ran into the bedroom and looked in her drawers and then in the hamper. "The pajamas are in the hamper, so I don't know what she's wearing now."

Julia heard a knock on the door downstairs. She ran down and opened it, oblivious to any danger to her, merely focused on finding information about Lily. Todd Hamlin, the other security guard, a man in his thirties with the physique of a football lineman in khaki pants and a white polo shirt, stood there.

"What are you doing here?" Julia asked.

"Replacing Katie."

"Where the hell is she?" Her voice boomed. "Lily and Dianne are gone! Where are they?"

"Gone?"

"Yes."

"Let me call the office and see what's going on. I received a call to replace Katie because of a family emergency." She could hear the hesitation in his voice even though he tried to act professional.

"Ma'am. Are you all right?" the 911 operator asked over the phone.

"No. Stay on the line. I need to talk to this person."

At the same time, Katie's red Camry came careening into

the driveway. She leaped from the driver's seat and ran to the front door.

"Where the hell are they?" Julia asked. "Where the hell have you been?"

"I received a call from the hospital. They said my son was in an accident. I called for a replacement and left. Dianne promised she wouldn't leave the house."

"Her car's here, but they're gone. I don't care if your son needed your blood in a transplant to live, I hired you to protect Lily."

"I'm sorry," the woman dressed in black pants and a black shirt said to her, more angry than apologetic. "The call sounded so official. When I arrived at the hospital, they told me that he'd never been there. He's still at his daycare."

Julia wanted to collapse, but she had complete idiots around her and needed to keep her head. "Not good enough."

Full sirens echoed down the road off the small hills that surrounded her house. When the police arrived, Julia began all over again running around to where Lily and Dianne should be as Todd chewed out Katie.

Within minutes a full investigation started.

One officer was recording the entire investigation with a dictaphone and another took notes on a pad of paper. A third officer had a camera and took pictures of everything, including Julia.

In the middle of the search, Julia's stomach finally gave into the stress and fear and horror of the events she'd experienced. She ran into the bathroom and vomited. She stayed there until it seemed like everything she'd eaten for days no longer remained in her body. A female officer stood behind her. Julia didn't know if the woman wanted to comfort her or had been assigned as a guard to make sure she didn't alter any evidence.

When they arrived in the bedroom, Julia pointed to the doll. "Lily found it the other day on her swing in the backyard.

She's never owned a male Barbie doll and because it freaked her out, I threw it away."

"Did you have a trash collection since that time?"

"No, the trash stays in a shed behind the garage."

The police bagged the creepy Ken doll for evidence after taking a picture of it in the bedroom. Some special unit officer sat her in the kitchen and tried to keep her company while police searched the area. They also gave Katie a lecture on work responsibility.

Mr. Hamlin escorted Katie to the police station to give a complete statement and to keep her out of Julia's sight.

Julia called her mother, but Gabrielle was at a meeting in Brussels and wouldn't be home for four days. Even if she caught a flight immediately, it would be at least twelve hours until she could touch down in Boston. She didn't answer her cell phone and Julia could have called her office to get in touch with her, but what would she say? She'd lost Lily?

Julia had never felt so alone. She'd lost her best friend to a crazed killer, nearly lost the only man she truly cared about and now the child of her heart was missing. She needed to move closer to her family. She wanted to flee home to Philadelphia, but not without Lily.

She called Finn's cell phone, but it went to voicemail. She couldn't leave a message. After she hung up, she regretted not saying anything to him about the situation, but she was pulled by another officer into another round of questions before she had time to text him.

Time ticked by as a parade of people asked her questions and searched her house again and again. She sat on her couch, made herself tea and tried not to focus on why they were there. She even found herself laughing at a joke from one of the police officers. Then she found herself dropped face-first into such guilt at having even the slightest smile while Lily could be dead. She could be dead. Julia tried again to refocus on the goings on around her, but her body wouldn't bring in any more stimuli. Squeezing around her waist, she pulled herself into a ball and fell asleep, an escape from hell for as long as she could.

Activity around her woke her up. Half of the town's police force seemed to be rummaging through her house. She stretched and went toward the kitchen to see how the investigation was progressing.

"Ma'am, there is no sign of any struggle or anything unusual. Could they have walked down the creek to the park for the afternoon and become lost?" The police officer looked down at her and appeared sympathetic, but hesitant to do anything else for her until new information came to light.

"I don't know. Dianne never ventured far from the house and she protected Lily from running into strangers. I don't know."

"I'm sorry to do this to you, but until Lily is found, we recommend that you don't stay here."

"Why?"

"First, the perpetrator, if there is one, could come back. Second, you could disturb the evidence inadvertently. Do you have someone to stay with?"

"I don't need to stay with someone, I'll remain here and help you."

"Suit yourself, but you have to limit yourself to the living room only. And only when an officer is present in the house."

"This is crazy. This is my house."

"Please help us help you. We don't want to mess this up and need to close the premises. We'll call you as soon as we hear something."

She sat on the family room couch, a place she had snuggled with Lily so many nights. Her stomach clenched hard again and she started sobbing.

# *Chapter 34*

Finn shook Robert's and Jack Bancroft's hands. He needed this deal to work. So far, everything had moved along smoothly, almost as if his luck was changing. He didn't dwell on the satisfaction building up inside of him; he might jinx his good fortune.

Richard and Kim stood on the other side of the table. Richard still had black-and-blue marks around his jaw where it had been held shut and his eyes blazed with contempt. The asshole probably wanted Finn and Davis to fail. Too bad. Kim, dressed in a bright red suit, likely purchased for this meeting, stood there, posing like an aging trophy wife. Predictable. She remained beside Richard, but not with him. Finn could picture them arguing about something before entering the final meeting and harboring grudges with each other and everyone else in the room.

The sooner Finn rid his life of those worms, the sooner he'd feel better. He wanted to go back to work, without having to deal with all of these side issues. What he really wanted was to return to Fresh Pond Security, but for now, keeping the dealership afloat was his biggest goal.

After the papers were signed, Richard left the room first, discussing something with his attorney. Robert followed on his heels. When Jack left, Finn noticed his glance toward Kim. Kim's mouth lifted slightly. *What the hell?*

With Davis behind him a few steps, Finn pushed up toward Kim.

"Sleeping with Jack now? Or are you merely lusting after him." Finn leaned in and spoke in her ear.

Kim cackled, no modesty, no discretion. "Men come to me, Finn. Jealous? Get in line. I already have enough interest to last me years."

"And Richard, the cuckold, approves?"

"We're free to find new experiences as long as we're discreet." She stopped and grasped Finn's wrist. "How's Julia? She must be thrilled to have custody of the brat. The kid's father is so much more of a man than you'll ever be. In so many ways."

Finn's stomach twisted. What the hell was she playing at? "How do you know her father?"

"I know everything about your pathetic girlfriend or whatever it is you're calling her these days."

Before Finn could reach out and strangle her, Davis cut between them and pulled Finn away. "Kim, why don't you catch up to your husband, your lover or whoever's paying for your Botox this week." He smiled as though flirting with the devil's mistress.

"Davis, are you jealous because I have real men in my bed?" She spun toward him.

"No. I'm not jealous of you, your marriage or your money."

Kim smirked. "You're pathetic, kissing up to me as though I ever gave a damn about you. You're nothing to me. Didn't you know that the Bible disagrees with gay marriage?"

Davis stepped closer, his smile replaced by furrowed eyebrows and a glower. "I thought it frowned upon dishonesty and adultery. I must have misread it."

"Screw you," she spit.

"You're not my type."

"Davis." Finn's utterance broke up Davis and Kim's nose-to-nose confrontation.

"I'm fine." Davis turned away and sped down the hall with Finn close at his heels, leaving Kim several feet behind.

When Finn reached his car, he checked his cell phone for messages from the office. Aspen hated when he ignored his phone, but he had to focus on the meeting and get the financing lined up. This time, however, his phone had three calls from Julia. Three? She didn't leave messages. Perhaps she wanted to talk to him, but felt as conflicted about him as he felt about her.

He walked over to his car so he could have a private conversation with her and called her back.

"Finn?" She sounded hoarse and despondent.

"Yes, what's wrong?"

"It's Lily. She's gone. Someone took her."

The blow that took out his lungs left him speechless for a second. "Lily?" he asked. "How can she be gone?"

"I came home from work and Dianne's car is here but they're gone..." A sob prevented her from continuing.

"It's going to be okay." Finn tried to be reassuring as Julia caught her breath. Her mother's security team was supposed to have watched over them.

He made a quick call to Jason Stirling at Fresh Pond Security and explained everything. He swallowed his pride and told him things he didn't want anyone to know. Lily needed all the help in the world and Fresh Pond was the best.

"Stay with Julia. I'll have every available person working on it," Jason told him. Finn believed him.

Finn thanked him and hung up when Julia called back. "Julia?"

After a few heavy sniffles and a choked cough, she said, "Dianne is missing too. There's nothing pointing out where Lily is or who has her."

"Where are you?"

"I'm home."

"I'm on the way."

When he arrived a half hour later, police cars with lights whirling in circles lined her driveway and blocked off part of the street. He raced from his car only to be stopped by some burly police officer wearing a snarl.

"Sorry, this house is off limits."

Finn looked down at him, trying to force his way through on physical intimidation alone. "I'm here to see Julia. Can I speak to her?"

The officer looked around, as if trying to make this major decision without guidance for the first time. "I don't think so."

Damn it all. He called Julia. "Julia, I'm outside. Just come to the door."

Within seconds, the door opened up and Julia ran into his arms crying. He squeezed her tight. They remained there for a minute, with Finn supporting Julia and trying to pour some of his strength into her frail-looking body. "It's okay, sweetheart. Everything will be okay." He sure hoped it would be okay.

She led him into the family room and to a couch. The stairway had tape across it and the kitchen was swarming with cops and detectives.

"Coffee?" Her voice quivered as she spoke.

He smiled slightly. "Shouldn't I be asking you if you need something?"

"I guess, but I need something to do. They want me to leave, but I can't. What if he calls the house? What if she returns? What if I lose her forever?"

He held her close, and battered his brain for answers.

# *Chapter 35*

Finn never left Julia's side while she struggled to figure out what happened to Lily. His support helped keep Julia calm on the outside, but she still reeled inside. She couldn't forgive herself. She'd provided inadequate security, she worked too much and she didn't take threats seriously. She didn't think she'd have to.

Yet, Dianne and Lily were missing. Almost a day. What did the Amber Alert people say? Something like the first twenty-four hours were the most crucial. What happened after that time? Lily was still missing.

"We have something on your Facebook account," an FBI agent said. He'd been fishing around on her laptop for an hour or so, possibly looking for information to implicate Julia herself.

The FBI arrived soon after the police, probably from a nudge from Gabrielle, who would be rushing to Boston to support her, again. This time guilt would force her to Julia's side and honestly, Julia didn't want her. She didn't need to soothe her mother's ego. Not right now.

Law enforcement had done a complete search of Julia's house and Dianne's car, gathering bits of evidence from everything they could find, hair samples of Lily, an examination of which shoes she and Dianne were wearing and Julia's laptop. The police and the FBI seemed to work seamlessly together.

"Facebook?" Julia repeated as the fog dissipated.

"You have a message from a Kevin Mill on Facebook."

"What the hell has that got to do with Lily and Dianne?" She didn't mean to sound aggressive, but she'd never heard Facebook and missing children come up in the same sentence before.

"Miss Gardiner, who is Kevin Mill?" the man asked, his voice demanding with an attempt to express sympathy as well.

"He's Dianne's boyfriend. He goes to Boston University."

"He has Lily." The voice sounded so matter of fact that what he said didn't register until he repeated himself. "Do you understand? He has Lily. The nanny is now considered an accomplice."

Julia stood with her heart wedged into her esophagus, unable to breathe. She'd been so focused on John, how could she miss Kevin and Dianne? Kevin and Dianne? No, that didn't make sense. Why would they take Lily? Dianne loved Lily. Her gut still told her to focus on John.

"Sal," the agent called out to someone across the room. "Look up a Kevin Mill and Dianne Walter. Every database. He has the kid."

Julia stared at the screen and saw the message.

Julia, I have Lily. She's fine. I need $50 million transferred to the Cayman National Bank. Account number 2211 7575 8359. Don't put a trace on it, I'll know. She'll be returned when the money hits the account.

"When does he want the money?"

"We don't know. Perhaps he's making sure you found this message before giving more details."

"Do I need to send him a message back?"

"Why would he use a Facebook account to give away his identity?" Finn called over to the agent. "Who would do that?

That doesn't seem like a platform a twenty-year-old would use."

"Some college professors require it for easy class communication," one of the officers said.

Julia didn't know if she should be scared that Lily was with Kevin and Dianne or relieved.

"Mark, I found Kevin Hill. He's a convicted sex offender and has been for three years."

Julia couldn't take much more; her body collapsed into Finn's arms. She couldn't cry; she couldn't feel. Her stomach couldn't tighten any further. All she wanted was to run away and hide, but that wouldn't help Lily. She pictured Lily needing her strong. She took a deep breath in and sat up straight.

Finn asked, "Convicted sex offender? What was he convicted of?"

"Looks like child molestation. First offense, suspended sentence, three years' probation."

"I never knew," Julia called out to no one, everyone. "Oh my God. Why didn't I know this? Did Dianne know?"

Finn pulled her back and held her tight. He squeezed her shoulders and around her chest. She let him hold her and then let the tears fall again.

"Why Lily? She doesn't need any more pain in her life."

"We'll find her," Finn whispered into her ear like a verbal caress. "Believe it."

Julia let her head tuck under Finn's chin. She liked hiding in his strong arms. She needed his strength right now.

"So what's the next step?" Finn asked the agents.

"I'll respond for Julia and let's see if we can get a location on him."

Lt. Patrick Martin from the local police department came into the room. "We just sent a unit to his dorm to look over there. Maybe we'll find something."

Julia pushed off Finn. "I need to send the money. That will free Lily."

Finn shook his head. "We don't know that for sure."

"It's worth a try. If he has the money, he'll let her go."

"You have that kind of cash available?" Lt. Martin asked.

"I can get it."

The FBI agents and Lt. Martin looked skeptical.

"Believe me. I'll call my banker for a release of the funds. He'll do it. He's been my banker for years and will allow a transfer from my trust fund. I don't care about the money."

"Are you sure?" Finn asked.

"Am I sure? Lily is worth more than all the money in the Federal Reserve, never mind my money."

"I didn't mean it that way, I mean are you sure you want to send money. It might be a ruse."

"I need to take the chance."

She walked away and called Henry Bishop, her private banker. After explaining the situation, he told her that he needed to confirm the transfer with her mother as a security precaution. Julia called her mother to alert her and then received verification that the transfer could be done.

The FBI, in the meantime, had contacted the Cayman Islands bank and notified them that they wanted the money held, once it landed in the account.

The entire transaction took under an hour.

# *Chapter 36*

After a quick dinner, Finn took Julia, partly by force, back to his apartment. He poured her a small amount of Scotch, but she took over the bottle and drank far too much, refusing his suggestion to slow down.

"I really should be going," she said after she downed the liquid like a college freshman on spring break.

"Why don't you rest a little and then you can go?"

"Finn, I need to get a few things at my house. And the police are probably rummaging through every corner of it." Her body shivered. "And I should contact the police to see if Kevin responded. Things happened in the blink of an eye today and I can't miss anything, not if it pertains to Lily."

Her eyes closed and opened in slow motion as the alcohol began to act as a sedative. She struggled to stand up and had difficulty placing an arm into her jacket. Her body must be fighting everything that happened that day. She definitely inherited some of the fire that made her mother such a powerhouse, standing up to challenges, pushing back obstacles.

The jacket didn't cooperate. She started punching at it to find the hole, then gave up by flinging it across the foyer. It sat by the door, one arm inside out. "Damn it, damn it, damn it."

She pushed herself toward the door without the jacket.

"Whoa. Where are you going?"

"I told you I need to go." She tried to fling the door open but Finn placed his hand on it.

"You aren't going anywhere like this and I'm not taking you anywhere until you rest a little."

Violence spewed from her like the gates of hell had opened and she was first in line to escape. She swung toward his face and struck his shoulder and kicked at his legs. She didn't yell. The sound coming from her sounded more primitive than that. Moans, grunts and heavy breathing. He let her have her moment of insanity. She needed one. The past twenty-four hours had been so draining and she had no way to lash out in public or in front of the police. But she could let go in front of him.

As her actions slowed and the sounds turned into whimpers, he slowly crushed her body to his, keeping her arms down by her sides. Defeated, she melted into him. She stood quietly and sobbed into his shoulders as he stroked her hair and whispered to her. "Let go, Julia. We'll get through this. Rest now."

He picked her up and carried her to his bed. She didn't fight. Stretching out next to her, he held her until she fell asleep in his arms. No need to change her out of the wrinkled beige pants and the soft cashmere sweater that rubbed up against his forearm.

He slid away from her and called Jason. He'd been texting him all night about the situation. Jason had been furious that a professional had fallen for such a scam. He also had Calvin and his team working around the clock trying to track down Dianne and Kevin.

Two hours later, Finn slid back next to her and closed his eyes, his own emotions raging under the surface. They remained curled up together until the morning sun lit up the room and reminded them both that Lily was gone and that they needed to help find her.

Julia called the police and learned nothing new. They stopped at a store for Julia to buy a change of clothes. She needed to look decent in order to handle the new stressors that would arise during the day. She decided on a simple navy sweater dress she could wear with her brown leather boots. Simple, smart and comfortable.

At the police station, Finn escorted her down a short hallway lined with wanted posters and various announcements about worker's compensation and other employee benefit issues. They waited at a reception desk until Lt. Martin came to take them back to a small office. Julia sat down in front of Lt. Martin's desk and appeared as composed as a woman should be while waiting for news on her kidnapped daughter, or almost daughter. She'd tossed around in bed most of the night and a faint darkness framed her eyes.

Lt. Martin also had dark circles around his eyes. He must have spent the night working, as he should have. These first hours were critical.

Martin frowned. Then he turned toward Finn, almost ignoring Julia. "We received a call last night about midnight," he said.

"And?" Finn asked, impatient for the information.

"The Boston police found a woman matching the description of Dianne Walter."

Julia's eyes lit up. "Is she okay?"

"We're not sure that it's her. No ID was found on the body."

Finn felt as though he'd been sucker punched by the tactless police officer.

Julia screamed. Her scream froze everyone in the busy room. Then her repetitive "No, no, no." The tears fell a few seconds later. Finn crouched down next to her and grasped her hands. He couldn't say anything or do anything until she found her balance. He felt her breathing begin to slow and her heartbeat find a less strained cadence.

At that point, he turned to Martin. "Real smooth. Professional, my ass." He shook his head, then said in a hushed tone, "I'll make the ID, Julia needs rest."

Martin nodded, he didn't look particularly proud of his utterance, and he shouldn't be.

Finn released Julia and gently rubbed his thumb under her eyes to smooth her tears. He rose and kissed her forehead and led her to the desk of one of the woman officers that had worked the case the night before. She seemed empathetic and had more tact than her boss. "Stay here for a second. I'll be right back."

Julia didn't say a word, but she released him and stayed put. Her head hung down and her arms wrapped around herself.

Lt. Martin led Finn toward a small conference room carrying a laptop.

The conference room contained a table and six chairs. Not luxurious, but not dirty. Martin opened his laptop and began typing. "Here it is."

Finn looked over his shoulder and saw one of the most pitiful sights he'd ever seen. Dianne, wearing her typical grunge, sat on a park bench near the art museum. If you jogged by her, she looked normal. If you stared at her, however, her features appeared distorted and her head was tilted in an unnatural manner. Her skin had a blue tint and one eye was open. Only one.

Anger swirled through him like a growing storm. He wanted this Kevin kid. The SOB that had Lily, his beautiful niece.

"That's her. Does she have any next of kin?"

"A mother and father who live in Newark, Delaware. We interviewed them last night about the kidnapping. We'll have to contact them again now that we've had an initial confirmation. I didn't want to worry them until we had more evidence. They'll need to corroborate your identification." Lt. Martin stared at the picture and then angled his face to look at Finn. "I'm sorry to have blurted out Miss Walter's death like that.

I sometimes think I have no empathy left after dealing with so much crap in my job."

"I get it, but Julia needs an apology," Finn said. "Have you heard anything more about Lily?"

"No sign of her or Kevin."

After Lt. Martin shut the cover to his computer, they walked in silence back to Julia.

In front of her stood John. Literally in her face.

"Julia, are you all right?" Finn rushed over to her side.

Her eyes squinted as if trying to limit her view of John. She held her hand up, blocking part of John from her view. "Officer Diaz went to get me some coffee. And he arrived."

She tried to smile as Finn approached, but it never quite looked sincere. "I'm okay. John wanted to know how the investigation is going. He's also Lily's legal guardian so the police notified him." A slight flicker of something in her demeanor pulled Finn to stand close to her. Very close.

Lt. Martin strolled up to his desk. "Mr. Holland, nice to speak to you again. I'm Lt. Martin, I spoke to you on the phone last night." He shook John's hand.

"Thanks for contacting me about Lily. I came as soon as I could. What can I do? I need to do something. Thanks for the phone call, Julia," John said sarcastically. Accusations and mistrust ricocheted between them.

Finn stepped between them. "We're fully cooperating with the investigation. Julia has been with them all day yesterday. Where were you?"

Lt. Martin's phone interrupted them and he picked it up. "Martin."

Everyone in the office went silent as Martin spoke to someone on the other line. "Shit, are you kidding? You'd better follow the trail. I thought you guys were the experts." He hung up and sat down rubbing his hands over his worn-out face.

"What?" Julia asked.

"The money. After the transfer, the bank didn't hold it. It's been in and out of three countries and now they've lost it."

"Lost it?" Finn asked. "You lost millions of dollars?"

John's face intensified, turning a more brilliant red by the millisecond. "Money? Is this what you worry about? Lily is missing, and all you care about is Julia's trust fund?"

"No, but if the asshole who took Lily has the money and Lily, we lose a bargaining chip to get Lily back."

Lt. Martin moved back between John and Finn in a weak attempt to control the escalating tension in the room. "We'll find the money. We have police at Kevin's dorm room, his family residence, and are watching some of his friends. If he's out there, we'll find him."

"Or he's on a private jet to some South American country with my daughter," John said between clenched teeth.

Finn never liked John, but his treatment of Julia made him resent him all the more. His intuition told him to not trust this jerk at all, and he always trusted his intuition.

# Chapter 37

After leaving the police station, Julia and Finn headed back to her house. Finn insisted she remain at his apartment and she agreed, so she needed clothes, her toothbrush and anything else to get through the next few hours. She firmly believed that she'd have Lily back by the end of the day. She had to believe that because to think otherwise would kill her.

Finn drove. Her entire body felt heavy, numb and cold. The feelings she harbored now made her emotions at her father's cancer diagnosis seem like an effervescent burst of joy at a birthday party complete with cake and balloons in comparison.

"Shit," Finn mumbled when they turned onto her street.

Lining the street were vans, trucks and satellite setups. Throngs of reporters stood in her front yard waiting. Finn's Bentley drew their attention, and they started toward them like buzzards waiting for the death of their prey.

"I can't handle them now," Julia said.

Finn backed up and turned around onto a crossroad and drove away.

"Thanks."

"No problem." He placed one hand on her leg and squeezed. The pressure comforted her and she shut her eyes.

Her sanctuary had been violated by violence, the police and the press. She'd never return to live there and neither would Lily. Her peaceful life had been severed from her. No miracle surgery or great engineering project would be able to resurrect it.

"Where to?" Finn asked.

Where to? Back to the police station? No. Hiding in Finn's apartment wouldn't help her find Lily. "Your aunt and uncle's house," Julia said.

"What?"

"They need to know and I won't have them learn this from the news."

Finn nodded and followed her directions. While they drove, she contacted her mother, who finally had cell service in Europe. Gabrielle would be flying back as soon as she could get a flight.

Arriving at Aunt Maureen's house, Julia banged on the door. Maureen called out, "Door's open."

Julia led Finn inside.

"Julia, nice to see you. Who is this strapping man?"

"Very funny." He gave her big hug.

"So what brings you both here at the same time?" Aunt Maureen had that "I'm going to embarrass the hell out of you" gleam in her eyes. She needed to be sobered and fast.

Julia said the worst thing out loud, "Lily's been kidnapped."

"What?" Aunt Maureen took a step back, nearly falling over. She placed one hand over her heart.

"Someone took her from the house yesterday while I was at work," Finn replied.

"I told you to get security," she said.

"I did. The security guard had been lured away and the replacement didn't arrive in time. It looks like Dianne's boyfriend, Kevin, took her. Dianne's dead." Tears fell as she spoke the words.

Julia didn't want to spout out the grim details in such a generic way, but Aunt Maureen needed to know everything and Julia didn't have the emotional stability to play twenty questions with her.

Aunt Maureen paled, her eyes almost drooping as tears dripped onto her knit sweater. All her attitude and energy drained away, leaving an older woman who had lived through too much sorrow. "Lily is gone?"

"Yes."

"Dianne is dead?"

"Yes."

Julia moved across the room and away from the entrance to sit in the living room with her. She held her in her arms and their tears fell together. Finn walked to Julia's side and stood next to her without saying a word, without touching her, but his close proximity comforted her.

"First Miranda and now Lily." Maureen shook her head and sniffed, clutching Julia to keep her close.

"No. Lily is alive and we're going to find her." Julia told her about the police efforts and the ransom demand on Facebook and how she paid the requested amount. She didn't spill the exact amount; that didn't need to be disclosed. By the end, they both had stopped crying and had moved to the kitchen for glasses of water.

"Facebook is evil," Maureen spit as she took a sip.

"It's good when good people use it, but you're right, people with evil intent can cause chaos on any platform."

Maureen took a sip of water. "One of my best friends had her Facebook hacked. It seems it happens to so many people. She never got it back and had to open a new one. I've stayed off it since. No use running into trouble."

"Pages do get hacked easily, don't they?" Finn said, his words measured. "If you'll excuse me." He pulled out his phone and started calling someone as he went into the hall.

Julia watched as he barked out orders to someone.

"Lily's children will have whole new technology to complain about. As it should be," Maureen said.

Her comment sobered Julia. She needed to get Lily back so she had a future.

Finn came back into the room. "Sorry, but we need to go."

Maureen stood. "Call me if you find out anything."

"We will. Thanks."

As soon as Julia and Finn sat in the car, Finn turned to her. "What are the chances that someone inside the government with lots of connections could hack into a Facebook account?"

"Really good."

"And what are the chances that a man turns up out of nowhere to claim paternity for a daughter he's never met? Maybe it's a coincidence, but I'm going to Fresh Pond Security and see what Calvin has discovered. While I drive, check in with the police. Explain our theory. We'll start there."

They sped off down the road. Julia couldn't help but think John was involved; she knew it into the deepest part of her soul.

# Chapter 38

A thousand regrets followed Finn into the Fresh Pond Security headquarters. He'd loved his job as a security consultant until Jason had revealed that he'd lied to them all about his past. After being framed in the death of Donner, Finn had refused to work with Jason, someone he didn't trust. The decision had been that easy. Yet here he was, swallowing his pride for the sake of the two people who meant the world to him.

The receptionist gave him and Julia each a visitor pass as they stepped into a sleek, minimalist lobby hidden under a storage facility. "Hi, Finn. We all miss you."

Her words bit at his heart. He wanted to come back, but the walls he'd built wouldn't allow it. "I miss you guys too."

"Jason is expecting you. You can go to his office."

With a nod, Finn and Julia made their way down the hallway, his heart pounding in his chest. Jason's office was at the end of the hall. Finn took a deep breath, squared his shoulders and knocked.

"Come in," came the familiar voice, calm and steady as ever.

Finn opened the door and let Julia enter first. Jason, his long black hair pulled into a ponytail, looked up from his computer. His expression was unreadable, a mask of professionalism that Finn once admired but now found infuriating.

After introductions, Finn got to the point. "I need access to Calvin."

"Finn," Jason said, leaning back in his chair. "You don't need clearance to go into the technology room. You never lost it."

"Thanks." Jason really was an upstanding kind of guy. Finn should have trusted him even when it seemed like he'd betrayed them, because his gut told him he'd been wrong about Jason.

Julia looked at him once they left Jason's office. "This is where you worked?"

"I wasn't in the office that much."

They arrived at the technology room, a large open space that housed Calvin and his team. Monitors covered every surface and one of the walls.

Calvin looked up from what he was doing. "I'm glad you're here. You were right. There are problems with the Facebook post. I've also had someone looking into John Holland. So far we've found nothing on him. He's a ghost."

Finn whispered to Julia, "John, whoever the hell he really is, killed Miranda. I'd bet my life on it."

"I always knew there was something wrong with him."

"It'll take me a bit to get more information," Calvin said. "I'll contact you as soon as I learn any more."

They made an abrupt goodbye and drove to his apartment, but press outside his front door made him turn toward the dealership, where they could find some privacy. He handed his phone to Julia to give the information to Lt. Martin.

The call didn't go as planned.

Lt. Martin was not impressed with their case theory. "Mr. Maguire, we understand the animosity between Ms. Gardiner and Mr. Holland, but that is not a reason to implicate him in this kidnapping. Kevin's car was seen by a neighbor leaving the neighborhood, he has a police record for child molestation and he requested and obtained a sizable ransom from Ms.

Gardiner. Mr. Holland, on the other hand, has been supportive in every aspect of the investigation."

"Where is Kevin now? Do you have any idea?" Finn asked.

"We have a lead. We think he's driving to South Dakota, where he's from. We've contacted the appropriate authorities in the jurisdictions between here and there. If he's still in his car, we'll find him."

"Did they say South Dakota?" Julia asked, lifting her head out of the daze she'd been under.

Finn turned the speaker toward her so she could hear the conversation better. "Kevin might be headed to South Dakota."

Julia nodded. "Dianne told me he lived there. I think his mother is still there."

"We're on it," Lt. Martin said. "Stop worrying about John. He'd been at the police station a big part of the day and has been helping the authorities throughout the investigation. The guy is trying his best."

"What about the information we sent to you about John having no internet footprint?"

"We're looking at it, but I think you are letting your anger interfere with your judgment. Follow the evidence and it leads directly to Kevin."

When they hung up, Julia searched for John Holland and John Holland's addresses. There were a ton of John Hollands but none linked to the asshole who had tried to take Lily away.

"Where is he? And where would he take Lily?"

"Someplace isolated, private."

"I wonder if he has a girlfriend."

Girlfriend? Kim's bitchy image popped into Finn's mind. "Kim, Richard's wife."

"I know who she is. She's not his girlfriend...is she?"

"She said some stuff about John at the meeting yesterday. I just remembered. She hinted that she knew him in an intimate way."

"How is that going to help us find him?"

"I don't know."

They waited to hear from the police. A half hour and a cup of coffee later, Finn called Martin.

"What did you think about the information?"

"Look, I know you two feel pretty helpless, but John's been a great help to us. He left a few hours ago to return to a farmhouse he rented to be near Lily. He sounded disappointed he wouldn't be able to share it with her. Leave him alone, he's been through a lot these past few weeks."

Lt. Martin hung up on them. Bastard. He needed to open his mind to other possibilities. Then Finn thought about what he'd said. John had rented a farmhouse. And Kim owned an old farmhouse.

It made sense. The connections between them became as clear as a laser beam through dust. "He's with Kim."

"How do you know?"

"She owns a farmhouse. Her family's. They rent it out. How many people would say farmhouse instead of renting a house?"

"Not many people around here. Where is it?"

"I have no idea, but maybe Aunt Maureen and Uncle Walter do."

# Chapter 39

Killing had always come easy to John. He tortured a few cats as a kid for the fun of watching the life fade from them and even shot a neighbor's dog with a BB gun because it barked too much in the middle of the night. He never felt remorse or regret. And he didn't when he'd looked down at the nanny dressed like Dracula's daughter. She deserved to die. She'd fought him ever since first seeing Kevin in the front seat of his car with a bullet hole in his head. She tried to run, but she underestimated John's speed. He knocked her unconscious.

Lily had been easier to restrain. She took one look at John and remembered. Her mother's murder was mirrored in the terror found in her eyes. In her scream. Too bad for Lily that Julia's idyllic house was so isolated. No one could hear the little girl's screams except for John.

After placing Lily in the trunk, he twisted the nanny's neck into a very unnatural position and left her limp body on the floor in the back seat.

The entire process took less than an hour. The easiest part of his plan turned out to be disposing of Julia's security. What a joke of a security team. A fake call to Katie Garbano about her two-year-old son and an accident involving a knife and a missing finger and the woman couldn't leave the Gardiner house fast enough. She didn't even wait for her replacement; no wonder she retired from the FBI with a series of missed promotions and eventually a permanent desk job. The woman had the instincts of a murder victim.

At the farmhouse, John found an old Facebook account Kevin had used in high school. He used it to send Julia a message. Within two hours, the money had been transferred. The transfer out of the account had included a few security walls around it.

Julia had tried to screw him over. She was an idiot. His dark web sources provided by Rutland manipulated the electronic barriers and moved the funds to the next country and then one additional jump to the British Virgin Islands before deciding how to repay her for not following his orders.

After leaving the nanny by the museum next to the walking path, he traveled to the police station with Lily locked in the trunk. How fun to see such useless investigation protocols by local and federal authorities. They'd never figure it all out. They had their heads stuck up their asses and would focus only on the easiest theory: Kevin and his criminal record.

John stared at the screen of his laptop listening to Lily wail. Then silence. He looked on the couch and saw nothing but a slight indent of where she should have been. He walked around for a second and heard her breathing and wheezing. Stupid kid.

She'd tried to escape, sneaking to the back door and into the mudroom. He hauled her back to the couch, but a painful spanking didn't deter her. She cried but continued to fight him.

He needed some peace. Gripping her by the back of the neck, he led her to the back bedroom and locked it. He graciously supplied her with a bowl of cereal every few hours and even tossed in a few magazines for her to look at the pictures.

She should have rested on the bed sleeping. No. She cried, wailed, hit the door and even tried to break a window. He finally threatened to kill Julia if she touched the window again. That scared the hell out of her. She cried more, but stayed away from the window. She must care a lot for Julia to remain in the room without any resistance.

Listening to her whimper messed with his concentration. How could he finish his work if he couldn't concentrate? He had to handle the transfers and if she continued to wail, he'd never complete them. Her value diminished with each moan and each whine. How the hell could people parent brats like this? The incessant crying, the smells, the constant interruptions.

Ten, maybe twenty minutes later, the sounds from Lily's room became a repetitive form of torture. If he had to listen a minute further, he would take out his gun and shoot her. Enough.

He pushed the laptop away from him and started down the hall. As his footsteps creaked over the old wooden floors, Lily's cries grew louder. Clearly, she hated him. She was a good judge of character.

When he opened the door, she scurried away to the back corner.

"Come here," he demanded.

She didn't move.

"Now."

Slowly, she picked herself up from the ball she had become and took two tentative steps in his direction. Her face was red and wet and blotchy. Her breathing sounding like a panting dog.

He stepped to her and grabbed her by the arm and brought his face directly in front of hers.

"Listen. You have to be quiet, because I have to work. When Julia comes to get you, we may be going on a trip somewhere together, but I swear if you keep screaming, we're going to have to leave you behind. Understand?"

She nodded her head and gulped in some air. John turned

to leave. As he walked to the door, Lily began her biggest wails yet. Uncontrollable, high-pitched and so damn annoying.

John spun around and grabbed her by the arm and shook her. "Shut up."

She nodded amid hysterics and crying.

John reached down and covered her mouth with his hand. He could feel his hand getting damp from her scream and a chill went through him. Disgusting. He clamped down on her mouth harder and stared directly into her eyes.

He didn't know how long he looked at her. Long enough to see the terror turn to fear. Long enough to see the fear fade into oblivion. Long enough to be holding a very quiet, small, limp body.

The silence embraced him, a warm hug, comforting. He carried Lily's body to the bedroom closet and opened the door. Carefully pushing back the body of Kevin, and making sure that any remaining blood draining from his skull didn't seep under the door, he placed Lily on the opposite wall. When she came to, she better not holler. John didn't want to be forced to kill her until he maximized his profit.

He heard Kim walk behind him as he shut the door and locked it.

She gasped. "What the hell are you doing?" She sounded less sure of herself than she'd ever been. She stepped back.

"Did you bring me what I asked for?" John reached for the large brown envelope in her hand.

"I wanted to mess with them, not hurt anyone."

"You didn't hurt anyone." He opened the envelope and peered at the papers inside. "I did."

"I... I have to go." She bolted to the front door, but John kicked the back of her knee and she fell face-first into the floor.

Her scream sounded like one from an Alfred Hitchcock thriller.

John smiled. "Where do you think you're going? I need you here for a while." He grabbed the top part of her arm and flung her onto the couch. "Sit. Be comfortable."

"John, please."

"Begging, Kim? How plebian. I thought pretend bluebloods like you never begged for anything, not even your own pleasure." He sat down next to her and stroked her hair, enjoying making her flinch away. "That's right, you're not really of Julia's class, are you. An imposter. Should I send your fancy friends the videos of you down on your knees in front of me in the shabby bedroom where your parents conceived you? They may be entertained."

Kim's face tensed, looking grim and ugly. "What do you want? Money? I'll get it for you. Anything. Let me go." Tears streaked down her face. Without money and power, she had nothing. She was nothing.

"I have someone new. She's already given me more money than I'll need to start a new life. Don't worry, we'll be leaving here shortly." He straddled his legs over hers and cupped her face with his hands, as she struggled to go free. "It's been fun." His hands lowered to her neck and as she clawed and fought, he added more pressure to her neck. He continued for several minutes until he could no longer feel a pulse.

# Chapter 40

After a few frantic phone calls, Finn and Julia tracked down the location of Kim's farmhouse. It might not be the right location, but it was the only lead they had.

The farm was located in Warren. A twenty-two-acre farm hidden off the main roads. Kim's family had owned the farm for years.

"With no neighbors close by, he's isolated there. The closest neighbors wouldn't be able to hear a little girl scream." Julia paused. Her face had lost color and she began to rock back and forth in her chair. She took a deep breath and continued. Her voice stronger, more controlled. "I know that area. I worked on a wedding at a little bed-and-breakfast near there. I must have driven eight or nine times to the site trying to make all the arrangements."

"How far is it?"

"Two hours by the highway, but we can get there in an hour and a half following the back roads." She stood up and grabbed her coat from the back of her chair. She still looked shaken.

Finn opened his desk and took out a .38 revolver. He attached its holster to his belt and followed her out the door.

They both stopped in the parking lot and glanced between a practically new black Ferrari 458 Spider and the Bentley. A Thoroughbred and a Friesian. One had gas; the other didn't. At 1:00 a.m., that fact mattered. Finn ran back into the dealership for the key. The Thoroughbred would get them there faster.

When he returned, Julia was standing next to the driver's door. He eyed the Ferrari and then looked back at Julia. Shit. She wanted the key. "No. You have no idea how powerful this car is."

His command didn't seem to register to her. Her face remained dead serious. Her hand outstretched. Her attitude determined. "Give me the keys."

He needed to talk her down. "It's not a manual. This car has the clutch on the steering wheel. Besides, you've never driven anything with as much power as this," he guessed.

"My father's Porsche 911 had 317 pounds of torque and 435 hp. Give. Me. The. Key," she shouted across the parking lot. "I can handle it and I know all the back roads. Please," she said as her intense, commanding voice started to waver. "We need to get to Lily."

Finn still hesitated. He didn't want them wrapped around a tree. He'd seen people take the car around curves too fast and a few didn't live long enough to regret their actions. Their families regretted it for them at their funerals.

Julia stormed up to him and gave him a shove. He didn't move. He grabbed her hands and took a deep breath trying to make the right decision.

"She's my child, you never took responsibility and I know the way. Give me the key," she said. Finn could hear her voice hold back, trying to contain her anger.

His heart beat faster as he handed her the key. Hopefully, he made the right decision. His gut told him to trust her; his brain, however, wanted to shove her into the passenger seat.

Julia sat in the driver's seat and adjusted it forward. She looked over the controls and then at Finn, who had moved his seat back for his long legs. He breathed in the smell of new leather to try to calm his nerves. It didn't work.

She started the car and it roared to life as she hit the gas. Julia accelerated smoothly and pulled out onto the road. At

1:00 a.m., they had the road to themselves and Julia took advantage of the open roads and blinking yellow lights. She barreled down the main road out of town, going over eighty-five miles per hour. She handled the car well, and Finn's confidence increased. They might be able to make it without needing to head to the body shop or hospital after retrieving Lily.

They drove in silence. Finn didn't want her to focus on anything but handling the car. An hour into the trip, she slowed and turned onto a small one-lane country road, leaving the shopping plazas and residential areas behind.

The car held the corner but drifted a little too far to the right as it came off the curve, almost careening into an old stone wall.

The twisting force threw Finn into the door. "Hold the wheel," Finn yelled.

"I am. Don't tell me how to drive." Julia's hands had a death grip on the wheel, but she held the road and continued down the dark, deserted lane.

After about five miles and several more close calls, Finn began to relax again. His hands, which had been clenched tightly into fists, began to loosen. Julia could drive. She held the corners perfectly fine and found cutoffs that Finn would never have found in full daylight. The tension in her face also seemed to decrease as she continued toward their destination.

Finn wanted her to focus on the road rather than on the lunatic who had kidnapped her daughter. If she had time to think about Lily being held by the man who had stabbed Miranda to death and also had killed Lily's nanny, she'd fall apart. To hold the Ferrari at such high speeds in the dark, on country back roads, her mind didn't have the option of dwelling on anything but mastering the next curve.

Finn also wanted to focus on the driving instead of on his own fears about where they were headed. If he failed, Lily and Julia could both be killed. He'd texted Jason with the address before they left. He wanted backup and a group of competent people to do it. If Fresh Pond Security's Fiona Stirling or Meaghan Knight had been the bodyguards at the house, Lily would be with Julia, and John would be under arrest.

He looked up from his thoughts to see them closing in on a small steep hill ahead.

"Slow down," he cried out.

Julia braked in time to keep the four tires from going airborne. She remained silent as she continued to drive down the road with a finesse he reluctantly acknowledged.

Her eyes remained on the road, two hands on the wheel. "According to my directions, the farmhouse is a half mile ahead."

She slowed the car and pulled off onto the shoulder. She looked at the GPS and then at Finn. "The farmhouse must be down that driveway. We can't drive up, because he'll hear us. I don't want to place Lily at risk." Red-and-yellow dashboard lights illuminated the tears that started flowing down her cheeks. She shut off the engine. Everything went silent.

Julia had no idea how brave she could be. Finn knew. She possessed a calm demeanor that many saw as the carefree attitude of a socialite. They missed her strength, her intelligence and her keen eye for observation.

She'd weathered major storms in her life and had come out in control. She'd come out of this too. Although Finn preferred her staying back in a safe location, he understood that she alone could bring Lily some calm after the trauma she'd suffered. Lily would need her as soon as she left John's possession. Julia was her rock, her anchor.

He reached over and pulled her closer toward him. She gazed up at his face and responded with a kiss. Sweet, gentle and full of love. They'd deal with their relationship after they had Lily safe. For now, all they could do was give each other support and then do what was necessary.

Finn pulled away first. He kissed her forehead and ran his fingers through her soft hair. "I need to go to the house alone. I can move pretty quickly and quietly. I've been trained to do exactly that. You need to trust me."

"But Lily needs me." There were no more tears. She was focused and ready to rescue Lily. But she was an event planner and didn't have years of training backing her. He had to take this one alone and then call her to be with Lily.

"That's why you need to wait. Lily doesn't need to lose another person she loves." Throwing Miranda's and Dianne's deaths in her face made her vulnerable, but it would also make her safe. *And I need you safe too.*

"I'm scared," she said. She grabbed his hand. "I can't lose either of you."

"We'll be fine. Stay put." His handgun should protect him and hopefully Lily too. John had already killed two people, and probably three if the boyfriend had become a liability. He doubted Kevin was still alive, but didn't share that information with Julia. She had enough carnage circling around her thoughts.

As he left the vehicle, he told her he'd call when he had Lily safe. "Turn off the lights in the car and lock the door." Before he shut his door, he saw Julia nod. He squeezed his eyes tight to diminish his last view of her and to refocus on the danger ahead. Then he headed to the woods next to the driveway.

# Chapter 41

Finn looked back at Julia in the car. He hated that she was so close to a murderer. It made sense for her to be there for Lily, but the help to Lily might be outweighed by the risks of contact with a murderous psychopath. His shoulders tensed as he thought of her in danger. She'd better stay put. Following him could place both her and Lily at risk. His focus on their safety could weaken his instincts and could jeopardize them as well, so he tried to clear his mind of everything but finding Lily.

Turning down the lane, Finn skirted inside the tree line just out of sight. His only problem was the damn leaves on the ground. The autumn woods created a natural alarm around the perimeter. They cracked and shuffled as he tried to make his way along the perimeter of the woods. He looked around and found an area next to some large pines and headed there. His vision was limited and he relied on moonlight and shadows to guide him. An owl called out to him perhaps in warning and he found himself stopping to listen to everything around him in the woods making sure he wasn't walking into a trap.

After what felt like forever, the house came into view. A typical old farmhouse. Maybe a hundred years old or more. Two lighted windows at the bottom of the farmhouse illuminated his way to Lily. A garage stood about fifty yards away from the house. A car, perhaps the gray Acura that Dianne's boyfriend drove, appeared to have been hastily covered by an old brown drop cloth.

Something could be hidden in the garage or in the car it-self, but Finn decided to check the house first. He moved as silently as he could with the leaves slowing his approach. In the kitchen window, he saw John sitting at the table with a laptop, drinking a beer. Bingo. He crouched down and made his way to the back entrance. Finn's heart accelerated as he approached a person who wouldn't hesitate to kill him.

A mudroom buffered the back door from opening up di-rectly into the kitchen. He opened the door slowly, silently, preventing even the slightest squeak. He crouched down, his heart thumping louder in his chest. The anticipation and the feelings that surrounded him pushed him back to Afghanistan and that numb anticipation of danger always a step away and wondering who would try to kill him next. After stepping in-side the door, he went through the same excruciating process to shut it without sound.

The mudroom stank of rotting food, sour milk and a musty smell that the strongest bleach would be unable to penetrate.

He reached for his gun at the same time a flash of light wid-ened his eyes, a deep blast echoed in his ears and sharp pain exploded in his chest under his right arm. The force knocked him back and he lost balance, hitting his head on something behind him. His lungs contracted and he tried to take some breaths, but his throat had constricted. His gun had flown from his hand. Finn instinctively reached up to the wound he'd received. Blood dripped off his chest and covered his fingers. *Shit.*

John stood on the other side of the door, looking through the hole the bullet made. Wood had splintered in a three-inch circle. The idiot must have used a hollow tip and it exploded on impact with the door, with only the shrapnel piercing his skin. Perhaps that's why Finn felt somewhat functional with what felt like a flesh wound.

"Welcome, Mr. Maguire. It took you long enough to walk

down the driveway, but trying to be stealthy must have expended all of your energy. It was amusing to watch." John opened the door with his gun fixed on Finn's face as he reached across the mudroom for the gun lying on the floor. "I'll take that. Thanks."

John had blood on part of his sleeve. Finn prayed it wasn't Lily's blood. He tried to sit up, perhaps leap toward John to take the gun away.

His last image, a foot heading straight for his temple and pain torpedoing through his head.

# *Chapter 42*

Stupid moron. Did he think he could wander into the house and take Lily back without resistance? Or did he grossly underestimate John's ability to make a plan and stick to it through the end?

He rummaged through Finn's pockets and found his wallet and his cell phone. Perfect. This guy made everything too easy. His biggest mistake was leaving Julia in the car alone. Obviously, he overestimated his own ability. Julia would be punished for his foolishness.

John tried to drag him into the back room with everyone else, but the ape must have weighed over two hundred pounds. John kicked him again in his side just for being such a heavy pain in the ass. He thought about possibly hacking off a few limbs. It would be easier to move smaller pieces, but then he remembered the dolly in the barn.

He went out and pulled it up through the mudroom doors. The thing had been created to move refrigerators; it could move this deadweight. When he finished pushing, pulling and arranging his body on the cart, he manipulated it through the door and dragged it to the back bedroom. Once he burned the house down, the bodies would be charred beyond recognition.

He unlocked the back closet and pushed the entire dolly inside, dumped it and then pulled it out. He could hear whimpering in the back corner, and saw a small hand sticking out from under the coats along with a Converse sneaker attached to a foot. He shut the door again and locked it securely with a newly installed bolt.

Walking calmly back to the table in the kitchen, John looked over Finn's handgun and laughed. He didn't even get to point the thing. Some soldier. No wonder he left the service; he probably couldn't handle the pressure. John placed it up on the counter next to his own gun.

He picked up Finn's phone again and quickly tapped out a text to Julia. She'd come roaring up to meet up with her hero, because she seemed that stupid.

Once he had Julia, he could finally kiss Boston goodbye and start over. Anywhere.

# *Chapter 43*

Julia remained in the car, despite her urgent need to run after Finn to help him locate Lily. The proximity of her little girl made her fingers twitch, ready to open the door and go to her. Finn, however, knew what he was doing more than she did. She'd never had a self-defense class, shot a gun or done anything especially heroic. Her presence would create more of a roadblock than an assist.

Fear started pulling at her energy reserves. Julia forced her sagging body to sit up straight. She refused to rest her eyes, in order to remain alert to any sights or sounds that would help her understand the story unraveling outside the car. Her surroundings, however, began to creep her out. The leaves had already fallen from the trees. When the empty branches swayed, Julia saw only black bony figures against a navy blue sky. An army of skeletal soldiers keeping her from Lily.

After almost twenty minutes of silence interrupted occasionally by a mournful gust of wind passing through the trees, a xylophone reverberated through the car announcing a new text message. It was Finn.

He wrote, Come down to the farmhouse. Lily's fine.

Julia's energy level lifted and she dropped her head back toward the headrest. *Thank you, God.*

She started the car and took three deep breaths. She wanted backup. If Finn had Lily, then the police would have to believe them. As she idled the car for a moment, she pulled out

Lt. Martin's card. He told her to call if she needed him. She certainly needed him now.

"Martin," he answered.

"It's Julia."

"Where the hell are you? The security detail at your house said you and Maguire went off on your own. You're either with us or not."

"Finn found Lily. We need police backup because I'm not sure if John and/or Kevin are still roaming around."

She tried to disclose everything she knew, but Lt. Martin was furious they went off without notifying him. His lecturing began to burn her ears until she'd had enough. She gave him Finn's cell phone number and told him to call him for more details.

"Ms. Gardiner, please remain in your car. You have no idea what the situation is. We'll have the local police on the scene soon and I can get the state police to provide backup."

"I'll be fine. Send help. I need to go so I can see how Lily is."

"Ms. Gardiner…" The lieutenant's voice sounded threatening.

She hung up. She'd told him a thousand times that she thought John knew more than he let on, but they were the professionals. They sure as heck could handle the rest of their end of the case without her. She punched the gas and drove down the dirt lane. The engine roared, announcing her arrival. She looked around for Finn, hoping he'd be standing outside with Lily. But no one was in sight.

The farmhouse looked pleasant enough. A square brick two-story house. Kevin's car was peeking out of the barn.

Julia rubbed her hands over the soft leather steering wheel trying to calm her nerves. One more large intake of air and she opened the door and stepped out.

John stood ten feet away. He must have been hidden in the

barn as she drove up. The gun in his hand pointed directly at her face. Finn's gun? Julia stood frozen holding the door open. Terror punched up her heartbeat and propelled her stomach up into her throat. She couldn't breathe.

John walked over to her as if strolling in the park with a lethal weapon. He tapped the barrel of the gun on Julia's temple. "Give me the keys, princess."

Automatically, Julia dropped the keys into his open palm. Where were Lily and Finn? If John stood waiting for her arrival, he'd probably sent the text. From Finn's phone.

"And your phone." He stood behind her with one open hand in front of her face waiting for the phone while the other stroked her cheek with the barrel of the gun. He appeared calm. No fear. Like he didn't have to worry about Finn coming to get him.

Julia pointed behind her to the driver's seat. She could barely speak; her throat had constricted to the size of a pipe cleaner. "The phone is in the car," she said with a gravelly whisper.

"Go get it." He pushed her toward the car.

Julia caught herself before she fell.

The pain in her stomach began to numb her movements. She pulled herself up and across the driver's seat and reached for the phone. Maybe she could contact the local police. With her back toward him, she tried to dial 911 without him noticing.

Suddenly, John yanked her out of the car by her hair. Intense pain radiated from the scar above her ear through her eyes. He threw her forward onto the ground. Her forehead hit first, taking the majority of the impact. She closed her eyes, but couldn't escape the throbbing ache now taking over all sides of her head. *Not again.* She didn't count herself as a strong individual. All she wanted was her little girl safe and a comfortable place to live. *Was that too much to ask?*

She looked over at John as he picked up the phone that had

fallen from her hand. He had on faded jeans and the same maroon golf shirt he'd worn to the station. Mr. Perfect. Mr. Utter Nightmare.

He glared at her. "Get up. We need you to make another withdrawal. If you work quickly, I might be nicer to the little brat."

She said nothing. Just stood up and began trekking toward the farmhouse fifty feet away, but the pain from her head slowed her progress. John shoved her in the back to move her along.

She moved as fast as possible, because according to John, Lily was still alive and that was everything.

# *Chapter 44*

John pushed Julia into the kitchen. She landed on the ground, on hands and knees. The wood floor contained a thousand scratches and the dull finish of years of neglect. She stroked her fingers over the boards in an attempt to stabilize her nerves until she saw a drop of blood, still damp, and then another. Several more scattered across the floor, like the mistake of a careless painter. Her stomach lurched up toward her throat, her hand came to her mouth and her body keeled over.

"Finn?" she muttered. Lily? Finn? Where were they? Were they dead?

John grabbed her arm and lifted her up again, throwing her into one of the chairs at the table. "Don't worry, he's in a safe place now."

She sank into her seat, all energy gone. Bile rose up and she began curling up in the chair. She wasn't the warrior type. She hated violence. She wanted safety. A smack on the side of her head forced it up.

"If you want Lily, you need to do what I tell you and do it quickly."

He remained standing as he pulled the laptop in front of him and typed something until Julia saw the Bank of America logo. "We need your mother to make a little transfer from her account. The fifty million wasn't nearly enough to make up for my misfortunes."

Pushing any questions about Finn from her mind, she focused on Lily. If she gave John everything he wanted, he'd have no reason to keep Lily safe. "No," she replied.

John hit her with the back of his hand. Her head flew back. The strike to her cheek didn't hurt nearly as much as being tossed face-first onto the ground next to the car. Perhaps her body was beginning to shut down in order to alleviate the pain.

She looked up at him in defiance. "Let me see Lily first. I need to know she's alive."

"Call your mother, Julia. Now."

She tried to rise from her seat, but a push of his hand forced her back.

"Stay seated," he said before storming away.

He moved quickly down the hall and into another room. She thought about getting up and running to the door. She rose to her feet. A large slam echoed back to the kitchen. Did he kick a door? Then she heard it. A small scream and then Lily's sobs. Julia stumbled toward the sound. John came out of the room that held Lily and stood like a sentinel. Not caring about consequences, she rushed him and at the last second, she tried to drive under his arms toward Lily.

His leg kicked out to stop her. Her body was flung into the side of the wall. Dazed and in pain, she remained on the ground until John pulled her up by her hair. She tried to fight, but every time she struggled, he wrenched her hair tighter.

When he manhandled her back into the kitchen, he pushed her into the chair again.

"Sit down." He spewed venom. His eyes displayed cold, calculating hate. He backed away from her, never taking his eyes from her.

Julia's scalp burned from the brutal treatment. She wanted to strike out at him, but she'd be no good to Lily dead. He placed a hand on her shoulder and squeezed. Julia winced as his nails dug deep.

He placed his face directly in front of her. "Perhaps you

aren't understanding me. I need you to call your mother. I think another twenty million will be adequate. I'll see exactly when the funds hit my account. I graciously set up my account in the same bank as her. Convenient. Quick and easy."

She looked at her phone. One button would contact her mother. Would she even answer? John was giving her a chance to contact her mother and get help. Would the police arrive in time? Her own death seemed imminent and not altogether scary. Except she needed to be alive, alert and aware for Lily and Finn, if he still was alive.

Julia hesitated. Her voice calm and controlled. "I need to see her first."

"No. You heard her."

"Then I'm not continuing," she said. Her hands began to shake. She needed to see Lily and maybe get her away from here before she had any more money transferred. Once he had what he wanted, they'd be dead. There was no question about it. It was a fact.

John walked over to the cabinet and took out a steak knife. "I'm not sure how sharp this is, but it'll do." He positioned the knife to the side of her face, by her ear, and pushed.

Julia could feel the serrated edge depress without piercing the skin. It didn't hurt, yet. She had to delay. "Please don't."

"I'm pretty sick of you negotiating. Make the damn call."

The blade bit into her cheek. She squeezed her eyes tight and sought strength from the ruins around her. Revenge for Miranda and Dianne, retaliation for any harm done to Lily and vengeance for whatever he did to Finn. "Let. Me. See. Lily."

John began to pull the blade down her cheek, the stinging turned to agony, involuntary cries projected from her vocal cords and she reached up to stop him. He grabbed her hand with his free hand and forced it back to the table. She could feel the blood beginning to drip down her face, onto her shoulder, a small stream of thick liquid. "Kill me now, because I will not call my mother until I know Lily is safe. Away from you."

The blade continued until it grazed her chin. As John backed away, Julia's hands lifted up to try to hold the blood in. A coldness took over her body and she shivered uncontrollably, but held the tears at bay.

"Bitch. Wait there." He pointed the knife at Julia and then turned toward Lily's sobbing. "You have one minute with her and then I begin again. On her face."

# *Chapter 45*

The bang on the door and Lily's screaming and unrelenting sobs roused Finn from his unconscious state. He could hear her within a foot of him, but he couldn't see anything besides a band of light streaming under the door. He tried to move, but his body had been dumped awkwardly. One arm had twisted behind him and the other slumped against the wall. He needed to straighten out, but pain hindered his movements.

Reaching to the ground for support, he felt a small cold hand. At first, he thought it was Lily's, but the size of the hand was too large and cold dead skin felt thin and bony like an adult woman's hand. *Julia?* His heart sank and his lungs tightened. He reached down again. The fingernails had length. Lots of length. Julia only had short nails. Whoever was sharing this space with him and Lily had been dead for a while from the feel of the skin. He moved it away from him until he found the rest of the body. A thin cold woman. He pushed her toward the back of the closet. Her presence must be scaring the hell out of Lily, who seemed to be seated near the light streaming in. As his eyes adjusted to the darkness, he saw the outline of Lily's legs, sitting cross-legged and her arms hugging her torso. Her face, however, still hid in the darkness.

After the footsteps of the person on the outside faded away, Finn lightly pushed at the door. If he used all of his strength, he could get them out of the closet, only to be shot again by John. He needed a better plan and first aid. First, he needed to calm Lily, who sat beside him still crying and wailing. He could understand her fear. Banging doors, the darkness and the stench of death overwhelmed the enclosed space. The surroundings fired up Finn's adrenaline and gave him the strength to begin planning their exit, but at four years old, Lily couldn't do much but absorb the carnage around her.

"Are you all right?" he whispered.

"Uncle Finn?" she whispered back, her voice trembling.

Finn sighed at her voice, relieved to hear her alive. "It's me, Little Bear."

Despite his words, Lily pushed herself farther toward the door, away from him. The limited space hindered her efforts. "The man who hurt other Mommy came back."

He could feel her foot shaking against his thigh. "Your other mommy? Miranda?"

"She's under the stone with the heart on it." She was a little girl speaking about Miranda's murderer. She saw him murder her mother.

"Is Mom here?" Lily asked, still sniffling and rocking back and forth with her arms holding herself for support.

"I don't know." He had no idea what had happened to Julia. Hopefully, she stayed away.

"The man hurt the red lady too."

"The red lady?" Probably the woman at the other end of the closet.

"She has red hair. She's with Kevin." She pointed to the other side of the closet.

Red hair. Kim. He lost his breath for a moment trying to wrap his head around all the carnage around them. John had killed Kim and Kevin and left Lily in a closet with them. He killed too easily. Negotiations wouldn't work with such a cold bastard.

"Are you going to sleep again?" Her leg steadied and she spoke with less hesitation.

"I don't want to." Finn reached over to touch Lily's shoulder. He still couldn't see her face. "Are you cold?"

She pulled back at first, but then accepted his comfort and support. "No. I want my mommy."

"We'll get out of here. We just need to wait for the right time." He couldn't lose Julia, nor could he lose this amazing child. His sister's daughter. He tightened his fist and blinked down hard, pulling himself together. Focus. It was his only hope. "We're going to work together to get out of here. Can you help me?"

"Okay." She cautiously reached up for his hand. The tiny size overwhelmed him. Such a little thing to be caught up in more violence than most people ever experienced, even in a war zone.

He leaned toward her and spoke softly. "If we hear the man come down the hallway again, I want you to move back a little. Behind me, okay?"

"With the other people?"

"Just for a moment, not to stay there."

She didn't respond, and he didn't want to push it. Hopefully, she would follow his orders when the time came.

They remained hand in hand for a few minutes. Finn's head started to ache and he could feel the stiff muscles in his back tense further. He tried to lengthen each of his limbs and stretch his body out, but he didn't want to invade Lily's space. Instead, he pushed toward the back of the closet across a sticky liquid and into the soft, limp forms behind him. He recognized the metallic smell of old blood. He'd smelled it while waiting for help at a bomb site in Afghanistan.

While Lily shifted back, he went through several scenarios on how to escape. His face hurt like hell, but he couldn't do anything about that, except ignore the pain and hope he didn't scare Lily when she finally had enough light to see the damage John's had foot caused. He fumbled around until he found what felt like a scarf and wrapped it tight around the wound under his arm. A short moan escaped him as he tightened it.

"Are you hurt?" Lily asked, reaching her hand to his knee.

He covered her hand with his again. "A little." He didn't want to lie to her about something obvious. "I'll be fine after we get Julia and leave this place."

In the distance, someone screamed in pain. A woman's voice. His woman's voice. Finn's heart raced and his pain evaporated as he prepared to kill someone.

"Wait there," John yelled, probably at Julia.

Finn gently pushed Lily back behind him. "Stay back, Little Bear. Shhhhh." He placed his hand softly on hers and squeezed lightly. Then he maneuvered himself off the floor and leaned against the wall. He couldn't beat a handgun, and his strength was severely diminished, so he relied on the only asset in his possession—the element of surprise.

The floorboards outside the closet creaked, and the lock slid open. As soon as the doorknob turned, Finn kicked the door with all of his might. John flew back across the room and landed on his ass. Not hurt, just surprised. No gun in sight.

"What the…?" John scrambled to get up while Finn moved toward him to keep him down.

Lily ran out of the closet and wrapped her arms around Finn's leg, tucking her head in for protection. Bad timing. John received a burst of energy probably from seeing the four-year-old run to Finn. He had to choose and Finn chose Lily. He picked her up with one arm and curved his torso around her to protect her as John struck him from behind where the bullet grazed him. The pain shot through him, but he remained standing. Finn turned and tried to swing at him, but missed.

"Julia, get in here," Finn hollered while dodging John again. Hopefully Julia was mobile, because Lily needed to get out of the middle of the fight.

Finn used his leg to block John's kick. Still shielding Lily, he struck John in the chest, sending him back to the floor.

"Finn?" Julia called out.

He glanced toward her. She came running down the hall, with blood dripping down the side of her face. The son of a bitch carved a line down her cheek. Finn turned back to John, who stood on his feet again and took a swing toward Lily in Finn's arms. Finn blocked it then backed up, keeping Lily out of John's range. Lily tucked farther into his arm until she saw Julia.

"Mommy." She squirmed and struggled to get down, throwing Finn off balance. John, the weasel, kicked Finn in the stomach as he turned to protect Lily. He released her behind him and charged John, pummeling him into the wall with his good shoulder. Grabbing him by the shoulders, Finn slammed his head into the wall.

John struggled to stand. Then a gunshot rang out. Finn pivoted behind him to see Julia's shaking arms lower Finn's gun. Lily hid behind her crying.

He looked over at John and saw the hole above his right eye. Blood and debris covered the wall behind him.

"Are you okay?" he asked her.

"I am now." Julia stood, the gun still in her hand, pointing at the floor.

"Give me the gun, and get Lily out of this room." Finn put out his hand, but Julia stood frozen in place, staring at John's lifeless body.

Her face appeared pale, bloody, grim. She took a shaky step backward. Finn rushed to her and took hold of the handle of the gun. He wrapped his other arm around her waist and guided her and Lily to the kitchen, leaving all the carnage in the back bedroom and closet.

# *Chapter 46*

In the kitchen, Julia handed a whimpering Lily to Finn. Actually, she shoved Lily toward him. She then turned and dashed over to the sink where everything she ate in the past twelve hours hurled out of her digestive system. Finn wanted to help her, possibly rubbing her back or holding her hair, but Lily needed him more. He cradled her into his good side and turned her tiny face away from the most important person in both of their lives having a breakdown.

Retching sounds and spitting reverberated against the linoleum splashguards behind the sink. Julia sounded as though she was trying unsuccessfully to calm her esophagus before the dry heaves took hold. "Oh my God. Oh my God," she repeated between gagging and spitting.

Finn placed the gun on the top of refrigerator, away from Lily, and tried to hum a nonsensical tune into her ear, anything to keep her focus off Julia's reaction to her first, hopefully her last, kill. As the sounds slowed to silence, Finn turned around and looked at the woman bent over the sink shivering against her body's mutiny. Blood seemed to flow out of her ear and drip down her chin. Lily reached for her, despite the gore.

The picture of this morbidly dysfunctional family unit should have exacerbated his fear of connection. It should have, but it didn't. He loved them both more than he'd ever loved anyone or anything. There was nothing at that moment that he wouldn't sacrifice to ease their lives.

He guided them to the table and assisted Julia into a chair. Her hair fell onto her shoulders, matted down and tangled. Her sliced-up face took on an ashen appearance and she seemed as though she might faint any minute. Finn rotated the kitchen chair around so she could lean on the table for support. He then placed Lily gently in Julia's lap. She didn't have the physical strength to hold the four-year-old, her entire being drained, but holding Lily would benefit both Julia's and Lily's emotional well-being.

Lily curled her tiny arms around the woman who looked like an apocalyptic survivor. The kid was going to need a hell of a lot more therapy to get over this nightmare.

Finn called the police while trying to carefully clean off Julia's face, then texted Jason with an update. Once her blood was wiped away, the cut appeared thin and straight, increasing the chances that the scarring would be minimal if they could get her the hell out of there. Lily, dressed in a pink Disney T-shirt stained with streaks of blood, stayed seated in Julia's lap sucking her thumb. She had some bruising on her face, but otherwise appeared okay. She'd need a hospital visit to be sure.

"Look at you, Lily," Julia said brushing her fingers over her skin. "You're a mess." Her voice held no vitality. She had given everything to save Lily. "Finn? Are you okay?"

"I'll be fine." He tried to appear strong, but he felt the blood oozing from his shoulder, pulling him down.

"You have a few new scars on your face." Her finger caressed his nose with a featherlight touch.

"Do I?" he asked, more interested in her face and the gash that he failed to protect her from.

He shut his eyes and tried to imagine them alone making love, but too much violence marred any images he could conjure in his head.

"Your face needed some more character anyway. I always

found it kind of bland." She smiled as the tears began flooding her eyes.

Finn reached out and dabbed at the tears, trying to keep them from the open wound. "I aim to please." His free hand caught hers and he brought it to his lips.

Julia's eyes closed, streams flowing down her cheeks, as she rested her chin on top of Lily's sleeping head. They all remained together for a few moments until Finn's legs lost the strength to hold him upright. He let her go and backed away to a nearby chair.

"What happened to your chest?" she asked, noticing the scarf wrapped around him with the large bloodstain.

"John shot me. The bullet grazed my rib cage and under my arm. Trust me, I'm fine." He didn't feel fine, however. The pain in his face warred with the pain ripping through the wound under his arm. He didn't think the bullet went through his rib cage, although it might have lodged somewhere near there, because the burning sensation started to break his resilience.

He tried to look up at Julia and Lily, but his eyes preferred closing. He tried to stay alert, but darkness came in and offered to take the pain away. He fought to stay conscious, but he faded toward oblivion. It felt better there. He heard a helicopter in the distance and, confident that Julia would be saved, melted into the black.

# Chapter 47

Still numb from her stomach's rebellion, Julia didn't know whether to rush to Finn when he went unconscious or cradle Lily, protecting her from any more jolts and terrifying images. He looked awful, beyond awful. He could be dead. His head had fallen forward in the chair and his legs had stretched out before him, possibly protecting his large frame from falling onto the ground, his beautiful face now black and blue and bruised and bloody and distorted.

The trauma had depleted everything from Julia's body and mind. She'd been tortured, killed a man, held her traumatized daughter in her arms and watched as the man she loved passed out or passed away. Her heart couldn't speed up faster, her body couldn't tense further and her throat couldn't constrict more. If she didn't move or feel or think, she might survive another second and then another until the seconds stretched to minutes and maybe if she got lucky, she could survive one more day.

The sound of propellors hummed over the nearby fields. When the encroaching roar stirred Lily, Julia squeezed her a little tighter and kissed her head. A few minutes and she wouldn't have to be a warrior—she wanted to be herself. Small house, simple life, happy family.

Spotlights beamed blinding rays of light into the farmhouse and around the outside. Finn never moved. Julia couldn't see him breathing, but she was seated too far away and had blood dripping in her eyes, making them cloudy.

A megaphone called into the house, and Julia saw faces in the window. She sat still, holding Lily as tight as she could without harming her, afraid that strange movements would cause some inexperienced officer to panic and shoot. When they entered, one burly-looking guy in SWAT gear rushed to her side and began asking questions as others holding large assault rifles ran past her looking for the enemy, but the enemy was dead. Instead, they found carnage. Lots of blood on the floor and Finn fading fast.

A medic crew helped Finn and placed his unconscious body on a backboard. Thank God. If he was really dead, they might not have bothered.

"There are three in the back rooms. We need the photographer," someone yelled.

Three? John was dead. Who else? Kevin? Dianne's body was found in Philadelphia, so who was the third? She didn't really want to know. She wanted to go home.

Julia struggled to get up, to take Lily away from this hell, but her legs didn't hold her and she began to fall to the floor.

Two strong hands grabbed under her arms and pulled her up, returning her to the chair, with Lily still secure at her chest. "Whoa. Stay here." A short blonde woman in black gear turned away and hollered, "I need help over here." She squatted down next to her. She had nice eyes. Kind, concerned. She put an arm around Julia's shoulders.

"I'm Fiona, your temporary bodyguard. I'm not leaving your side until I'm confident you have the best of the best for you and your little princess."

"I'm okay." Julia held Lily tighter. She needed to protect her from the chaos. Lily stared at the woman and then the SWAT team rushing around, and never panicked. Perhaps she didn't need to. After living through hell, what could she fear now?

Still, Julia didn't want to feel trapped; she wanted to leave. She tried to squirm out of the woman's grip. She was surprisingly strong.

Fiona leaned in and whispered in her ear, "You have two choices. I hold you while you sit here until a stretcher comes, or I remove the little girl to a safe place and lay you on the floor."

Julia's fight response simmered and she allowed Fiona to keep her propped up in the chair for a few minutes while she whispered to Lily, "It's all good now. The good guys are here. Okay?"

Lily didn't reply. She kept her head tight against Julia and held on.

A few more people came into the kitchen. One person carried another backboard like the one Finn had been placed on.

Her new bodyguard spoke to her softly. "Ma'am, we're going to place you on your back now, so you need to give the little girl to Meaghan."

"No. It's okay, I can keep her," Julia said.

"Ma'am. Let her go, we'll take good care of her." Her command must have scared Lily, because she finally reacted and fiercely.

Lily kicked at the tall woman who tried to remove her from Julia, and kicked at Julia as well in her fight to remain with her. One good blow to her rib cage, and Julia had to let go to get some air. After a quick breath, she tried to reach out to Lily, but the woman named Meaghan carried a screaming Lily away.

"Bring her back," Julia called out.

"You're making her nervous. Let her get the medical help she needs," Fiona, holding her back, said in a voice made to calm a hysterical victim.

Julia didn't want to scare Lily, but she didn't want to lose her again.

"Please. She needs to be with me." Her tears started again.

"On the count of three. One, two, three." The woman holding Julia and another person lifted her and placed her on a board. Julia tried to rise and go after Lily, but no one was co-operating.

They buckled her in and she fought. Fiona held her head in place and secured it with a neck brace attached to the board. Julia couldn't lift her head and she couldn't see Lily.

"Lily? Where's Lily?" she called out.

Fiona glanced at her from an upside-down position. "Calm down. We're here to get all three of you to safety. And then back together. Lily is outside getting looked at. She'll be in the helicopter with you. I promise."

Feeling helpless, tied down and unable to help Lily through the aftermath of her second life tragedy, Julia started thrash-ing within her bindings. "No. I'm the person who can keep her calm."

A prick in her arm enraged her further. "Lily! Lily! *Lily!*" she screamed. Then her body began to quit, her anger began to dissolve and the world became unclear.

She felt hands dab something on her face, covering part of it including one eye. "No," she whimpered, but stopped talk-ing because she was too tired. She overheard several people speaking together about the urgency of getting Finn medical treatment, maybe being flown to the closest hospital. As she lost her ability to fight, she calmed down. Finn had to be alive. Dead people didn't need treatment.

# *Chapter 48*

Finn woke several times through the night in a hospital room and spoke to a few nurses and a doctor and a couple of technicians or phlebotomists or some such thing. Then, he fell back asleep. When the sun broke through the curtains, he felt more awake and alert.

"Julia?" he said, turning his head to the door.

Out the small window in the door he saw the top of a blond head that he'd know anywhere. There was no one better in the field than Jason's wife. He wasn't 100 percent sure why she was there but he appreciated her presence.

Julia, her face partially covered in bandages, partially covered in bruises, sat in a chair by the window. She wasn't in a hospital gown, which gave him hope that her injuries were limited to the cut on the face.

"Hey there."

"Hey." Her arms crossed in front of her as though she needed to hold herself together. Her face looked bad, but the rest of her looked healthy.

"Are you okay?"

She laughed. "You're the one in the hospital bed and you're asking me if I'm okay?"

"You are so much more important than I am."

She smiled but a sadness lingered in her eyes. "Not to me."

He reached out to her. "How is Lily?"

Julia rose slowly and sat on the edge of the bed. She leaned over and kissed him. Softly, sweetly, sensually. He kissed her back and only backed away when she winced from her bandage twisting.

"She's with my mother. Dr. Gupta thinks she should remain isolated until she has time to decompress."

"If it will help her heal, I'm all for it." He wanted only the best for Lily, although he would have loved to see her.

Julia sidled closer and placed her head on his good shoulder with her non-bandaged cheek.

"How are you really?" he asked, gently touching the bruises near her nose.

"I'll live. The bruises should go away and I have nothing broken. I don't know about the scar on my face. It went pretty deep. I'm hoping the plastic surgeons were miracle workers. We'll know in about two weeks when I can take the bandages off."

"It doesn't matter. You'll always be the most beautiful woman in the world."

She blushed. A perfect rose color. "You're saying that to get me in your bed."

"Not at all. I'm pretty confident about that without resorting to false compliments." He held her tight and she melted into his side.

"What about you? How are you really?" she asked.

"I feel decent. How's my face?"

She examined it for a long time finally nodding to herself when she finished. "Pretty interesting."

"Interesting?"

"Bruised. Swollen. He must have had a hell of a right hook."

"He kicked me in the face."

She blanched. "Oh my God."

"I'll heal. The gunshot wound is more painful. The doctor insists it will heal in time. They had to remove part of the rib to get the shrapnel out, but it didn't travel through anything necessary, so that's good."

"When can you leave?" she asked.

"In a few days, but I may push to heal at home tomorrow. What are you going to do?"

"My mother is taking care of everything. I can't go back to my house. It will never feel safe again."

"Move in with me."

"I couldn't. What about Lily?"

"I have a room we could decorate any way she wants. Princesses, pirates, penguins. It doesn't matter. I want you both with me. I feel better when we're all together."

"That sounds like heaven, but after everything that happened, I think we should take it slow. We don't know if she'll be able to interact with anyone."

"Julia." A woman raced through the doorway wearing a red power suit. Julia's mother. She appeared exactly the same as all of her publicity shots in the press. A grande dame. Finn couldn't help but be impressed by her calm demeanor dressed up with an elegance that spoke of old money and power. Her chestnut hair framed her face and gave her the appearance of a much younger woman. Julia had good genes.

"Mom, this is Finn." Julia turned to introduce them.

"I'm sorry that my security team failed and you ended up hurt. I'll never forgive myself." Mrs. Gardiner shook her head slowly.

"It wasn't your fault. John Holland was not a run-of-the-mill stalker. He had resources behind him."

"How do you know?"

Julia hesitated. "I just do."

She looked as though she wanted to tell her mother, but Finn shook his head. He didn't want the Gardiner family looking into his past. He had a group of people who could handle this and he should have relied on them sooner. He had one more decent shot at uncovering everything, now that Holland was dead.

Julia looked at him. "I'd like to take Lily somewhere she can feel safe for a while."

"Go ahead. I'll be in touch when I can be." Finn had a few things to handle and Gabrielle would never let her daughter get in harm's way if she could help it. And with Fresh Pond Security watching over them, they'd be fine.

"You're sure?" she asked.

"One hundred percent. I need to focus on solving this once and for all without having to worry about you."

She nodded and kissed him goodbye, then followed her mother into the hall.

Before the door swung shut, a guy in a black suit and an attitude strolled inside. Jason followed.

"Finn, I want you to meet our most important client. Ron Downes. He runs EON, the Eclipse Operations Network. I've told him about your situation and he's very interested in finding John Holland's boss. He needs your help to do so."

# *Chapter 49*

Julia and her mother sat in silence as a driver took them halfway across the state in a rented Lincoln Town Car. Lily fell asleep within minutes of being secured in her car seat. Julia sat on one side of her; Gabrielle sat on the opposite side doing something on her phone. Probably checking emails, reading the news or staring at it to avoid having to address Julia. Gabrielle had aged since Julia had last seen her. She appeared tired and worn-out. Her eyes showed more lines and her lips seem to have thinned.

She didn't mind that her mother was avoiding her. She had so many thoughts rushing through her head. Finn wanted her gone from his side temporarily. Was he going to try to locate the person who had set him up in Afghanistan and ordered Miranda to be killed? She couldn't deal with any more risk. There'd been so much bloodshed already.

Fiona, her new bodyguard, had sat her down while Gabrielle watched Lily. "It would be best if you kept your distance from Finn for the time being. He'll explain it all when he's able."

"I don't understand."

"He's found some new resources to assist him in clearing his name." For such a petite woman, Fiona had a serious side and did not appear to be someone that could be walked over easily. "Give him time." She slammed the door and walked behind the car.

When Fiona left, Gabrielle hung up her phone and placed her hands on her lap. "I don't know if we can trust Finn. He's got money problems, and he was dishonorably discharged from the military. Not exactly a man with a solid pedigree." She kept the tone low to avoid waking up Lily.

"You don't know him. He's had a rough life and is trying to make it better. I'm going to trust that he has things under control. For now, I need to concentrate on keeping Lily protected and safe."

She looked out the back of the car and saw Fiona following them. She'd always thought her parents were overprotective. She'd been wrong. Lily required the best security money could buy, and Julia had more than enough money. At least she had until she sent half her trust fund to the kidnapper.

Gabrielle looked out the window at the highway signs and asked, "Do you need anything from your house?"

Julia shook her head. "I'm not going back to the house. I can't. I thought we might move to a gated community. Lots of children, limited access." But she didn't want to live near people who moved there to be seen with the *right* sorts of people. People who would befriend her not for who she was, but for what she would bring to their lives. People who would adore Lily, because of her mother's money and social standing, not because Lily was the coolest little girl ever.

"I understand. We're not going to your house right now anyway, we're going to my friend's house on Martha's Vineyard. You loved taking Lily there last summer. It's quiet this time of year. Your sister can come over for Thanksgiving with her children. I'll take care of everything. You need a break."

"Martha's Vineyard?" It was so far away from Finn.

"We'll be walking on the beach in two hours. It'll give Lily the seclusion she needs for the time being."

Lily did deserve a break from all the police and the trauma and the world pushing in around her. Julia couldn't help herself; she relaxed for the first time in what felt like days. "I'm an ingrate. I'm sorry for always complaining about your protective actions when I was growing up. Martha's Vineyard sounds perfect. Thanks."

Julia shut her eyes for the rest of the ride. Her head hurt, but not nearly as bad as it had when Richard had tossed her into the wall. The scar from that still lingered on her forehead. She reached up and felt the bandage down the side of her face. Pushing on it, she could make out the line of stitches from her ear to an inch past the corner of her mouth. John had left a permanent reminder of his twisted mind.

Although grateful for the time away with Lily, she still worried about leaving Finn alone to fight the charges. She shut her eyes, empty of tears, empty of emotion.

# Chapter 50

With a backdrop of white clouds stretching across the blue sky like ribbons, the beach house on Martha's Vineyard seemed magical. The sand reflected bits of the sun near the dunes, tiny sparkles like fairy dust, but turned darker and damper as it flowed toward the ocean. A gray wooden boardwalk led from edge of the water at high tide to the large seven-bedroom Cape Cod house.

Julia, trying to ease her heartache, made her way across the sand and past wisps of dune grass. Her face, still swollen with the stitches, felt better in the cool salty air. The plastic surgeon insisted he'd hidden most of the scarring and only a faint line would remain which could be covered with concealer. Her internal wounds would last forever, however, firmly embedded in her being.

As she headed toward the house, she saw Lily, her precious little girl, playing in the sand with Rachel and Sam, her sister Anna's children. The sight gave Julia hope. Playing with other children had to be the perfect antidote to the horror she had experienced. Lily didn't speak much lately, but with her cousins, she smiled with a sweetness and hopefully someday that spark of contentment would grow and bubble up into real happiness.

Would Lily ever forgive her for the pain she put her through? Julia hadn't hired proper security until after everything went to hell. Julia had killed a man in front of her. And Finn seemed gone from their lives.

The sisters walked along next to each other for a few minutes, keeping the children in their line of vision.

Julia slowed for a few steps, making her sister slow down as well. "I want to reach out to Finn, but I don't know what to say. Everything is such a mess."

"See that little curly-headed wonder playing in the sand?" Anna said. "Focus on her and everything else will fall into place."

Julia nodded. Lily was running toward the water and then squealing when her toes touched the icy waves. She needed all of Julia. "Sounds like a good idea."

"Are you staying here after Thanksgiving?"

Julia nodded. "It's safe here. I can't go back to Boston right now. I'm scared to sleep in the house and if I go back, all I'll be able to think about is how Dianne and Kevin died because of their connection to Lily and me."

"It wasn't your fault. Have you spoken to someone about how you're feeling?"

Julia nodded. "I had some Zoom calls with my therapist and Dr. Gupta came out and spoke to Lily. She feels Lily has a lot of internal wounds but in some ways has a bit of closure because the man she's been afraid of all her life has been killed."

"I'm glad. You both deserve a happy-ever-after. Take your time before you think of your next step. From what you told me about Helena, your business will be in fine form until you return."

"She's been a blessing. She knows every client and has been adding new clients every day. I told her that she's earning herself a share of the business. She'll deserve it, especially if I stay here until the New Year."

"That's good. You have to heal. So does Lily. I'll come up with the kids whenever I can free myself from my work."

"That would be great. Lily loves Rachel and Sam." Julia watched as the two little girls covered Sam with sand.

"The feeling's mutual."

As the sun set, everyone returned to the house. Anna took Sam upstairs to rinse off the sand that had wedged into every body part imaginable, while Gabrielle started to cook a New England seafood dinner, complete with lobster, steamers and baked potatoes.

Julia curled up on the couch in the family room and watched Lily play with her adopted cousin. Rachel pulled out her Lego and showed Lily how to build a biplane.

The front door opening made Julia's stomach lurch in shock and fear. She reached out to grab Lily, to protect her, but Rachel grabbed for her first.

Anna's husband, Nathan, stood by the door with a suitcase. The blond Texan stood taller than most men. Like a strong, lean athlete. Not heavy, but not wiry either. Julia wanted to scream at him to leave so Lily wouldn't have the terrors again. She'd forgotten that he would be arriving late and she neglected to protect Lily.

"Daddy!" Rachel shrieked. She dragged Lily up the stairs to the uncle she had never met. "This is Lily. She's my favorite cousin."

"She's your only cousin," Nathan responded with a chuckle as Rachel bounced into his arms and gave him a hug and a kiss.

Julia stood ready to run to Lily if she began her hysterics.

"Hi." Lily waved at him. She looked from Rachel to Nathan and then gifted Nathan with curious eyes and a face with a happy countenance. Not quite a smile, but close.

"Hi, Lily." Nathan squatted down where he was, not closing the space between them. "Have you been playing on the beach?"

"We covered Sam with sand," Lily replied. It started at the corners of her mouth and grew until finally, a smile arrived.

Nathan turned toward Julia and winked and then he smiled back at Lily. "Sounds fun."

"We're going to cover *you* tomorrow," Rachel squealed to her father.

Lily's smile blossomed and then Julia heard the sound that had been missing since before the kidnapping. Lily's laugh.

"I better stay off the beach then." He waved to them both and then meandered to the kitchen.

Julia made her way to the foyer and her little bear. Wrapping her arms around Lily, she said, "Aunt Anna will get Uncle Nathan onto the beach. And if not, we'll cover him with sand while he's sleeping."

That sent the two girls into hysterics and Julia back into tears. Happy for Lily, while aching for Finn.

# *Chapter 51*

Finn sat in front of Jason like a student waiting for the principal to pass judgment. It had been a week since he'd been released from the hospital and still no word about John Holland. Someone had to know who he was and why he'd tormented Julia. It seemed likely from Lily's identification that he was the man who had murdered Miranda. But who had sent him?

His hatred for John had grown, and at times he wished the asshole had lived so Finn could make him suffer more and then learn the truth of how he'd framed him.

Jason looked over at him. "You look like hell."

Sure, Finn had lost weight and the color in his face hadn't quite returned, but he didn't care. All he wanted to know was how he could protect his family.

Jason turned on the intercom. "Calvin? You here?"

"In my office," Calvin answered in a mellow voice.

"Finn's here and you probably need to get through whatever you want to share with us quickly. Finn doesn't seem able to sit up for more than ten minutes at most."

"I'm not that bad," Finn insisted.

"That's debatable. Follow me." Jason stood and led Finn out to Calvin's office, a large room with too many monitors and a few other people working with him.

Calvin positioned himself in the middle of it all, glancing up between two of the large screens and then down to a laptop. He appeared tired, more so than usual, his hair pointing all over the place and his gray T-shirt and jeans wrinkled and twisted.

"How are you?" Calvin asked. His eyes darted between two of the screens.

Jason answered for him. "He's a mess. Despondent. I've seen him upset many times, but this time he's not fighting back."

"He'll be fine," Calvin said.

Jason shook his head. "I don't know. He doesn't have much fight left in him."

Finn shook his head. "What do you want me to fight? We keep running into dead ends. Have you found anything new?"

Calvin typed a few things into his computer and shook his head. "Our new sugar daddy, Mr. Downes, has granted me access to some computer systems that I'm not sure I should have access to, but I'm enjoying myself immensely. The information you'd gathered on the illegal arms shipments didn't make sense on their own, but when you add that information into the overall database and then look for similarities, most of those sales are originating from one office."

Finn couldn't believe it; Calvin had the information to find the traitor? "Do you have a name?"

"Colonel Alec Rayburn of the 600th Ordnance Corps."

Finn had heard of him. He was a backstabbing son of a bitch who neglected the needs of the units he'd been assigned to keep equipment for himself, claiming he was doing everything for efficiency. It made all the sense in the world that he was the person who had profited off of stolen weapons, and then killed to protect himself. But without solid proof there was nothing.

Calvin didn't look up but said with a calm voice, "You should go meet him. I hear he'll be at the Pentagon for a meeting next week."

"I owe you, Calvin. You've saved my ass on more than one occasion."

"So get the bad guy, then go get Julia. And Lily of course."

"Have you found Julia's money?"

"There were a whole bunch of transfers. The team involved in this, because there's no way John worked alone, had a mountain of experience deceiving the financial system. It was an impressive feat." Jason leaned back into a chair next to Calvin.

Finn frowned. "I'm glad you're impressed with the way they conned me."

"Not admiring them for what they'd done, so much as I'm intrigued how we're going to take them down. They jumbled everything in the system to such a degree, it was almost impossible to detect their interfering without seriously looking for it at a level not many people have access to." Calvin continued to tap on his keyboard. "I found something, but I need to dig a little."

Jason shook his head. "You can't dig too deep. You don't have the authority to hack into the banks."

"I'm working on getting the authority." He looked back toward Finn. "You were definitely on to them. And they knew it. Since they couldn't attack you without fearing the information would be exposed, they attacked those you loved."

That had been Finn's hunch all along. "I'm grateful to you."

"Here's something else. In my search I discovered that John isn't the girl's father."

"It seemed unlikely, but he had solid DNA proof," Jason argued.

Calvin shook his head and narrowed his lips. "I missed it initially. When I first learned about John Holland, I searched his background. Salesman, Mormon, member of several business associations. Nothing unusual. And entirely Rayburn's creation. His former assistant, John O'Donnell. Now, that name has a history. He had a reputation as a bruiser on various military bases. Would create issues, keeping eyes off the inventory that disappeared out of the systems. After he was discharged, he tried to make money in the tech world. Stealing information, breaking and entering. He had an unusual relationship with the Bancroft brothers."

"Davis and my new investors?"

"Yes."

"I haven't linked those moves to Rayburn, because Holland might have been trying to branch out on his own. By providing backup to the Bancrofts, he could free himself of his need for Rayburn. Kim must have given all the details he'd need to make the connection. In fact, I think the second attempted money transfer had nothing to do with Rayburn and his team and everything to do with Holland's greed. Holland wasn't the mastermind. He was clunky, but effective. He'd stay low and not make a fuss, but must have begun to envy Rayburn and his growing stash of money. From Holland's bank account records, he didn't receive much money to kill Donner or Miranda."

The idea that this asshole had murdered his sister for any amount of money ripped into Finn.

Calvin paused and rubbed his temple. "Sorry, man. I'm trying to get you all the information you need to take down Rayburn."

"I get it. And I appreciate it."

"We're almost there," Jason said, pacing behind them. "Once we understood that Rayburn and his team had the knowledge to hack a computer, we challenged everything about him. I spoke to the police a few days ago. They gave me some leads, unofficially. I didn't want to say anything until I proved my theory. My first challenge dealt with the custody suit. If John doesn't really exist, paternity of Lily didn't exist."

John Holland didn't exist. So Lily was truly Julia's. She was going to be more than relieved.

"She was born at Boston General," Calvin continued.

"Your hospital." The hospital Calvin had been assigned to protect.

"Yeah." Calvin shook his head. "I missed it. The night of the engagement party, Rayburn's team had already attacked the hospital system. That breach was what set off alerts and caused me to miss my own party. When they entered the system, they stole a bunch of records. Probably to bribe various people with. But I never noticed that they'd actually left a record as well, the paternity test. I never thought to look for an added record."

"Why would you?" Finn asked.

"I missed Kevin too," Calvin said, not responding to Finn's question.

"Kevin?"

"He's no sex offender. They slipped a made-up file on Kevin in the sex offender registry. If you really look at the entry, it was added only a few weeks ago. Rayburn had everything covered. He created the offense in a nowhere jurisdiction where the long-term prosecutor recently died. So no one would remember the case and no one would go looking too closely at the records."

So the nanny's boyfriend had been innocent. Julia would want to hear that. She needed to hear it, but at present, he had to finish taking out Rayburn once and for all.

"Have you looked into the money transfers?"

"I'm getting there, but going international, I'm running into certain firewalls that are bit tougher to get through."

Jason looked over at Finn. "Focus on Rayburn and Calvin will focus on the money. You and I have an operation to plan."

# *Chapter 52*

Colonel Rayburn's heavy footsteps alerted Finn to his arrival. The officer opened his office door, only to stall at the entrance. Finn sat behind his desk, casually thumbing through a file. Finn didn't bother to look up, savoring the colonel's fury.

"How the hell did you get in here?" His voice was a low, dangerous growl.

Finn finally lifted his gaze from the file to meet Rayburn's. "Security's not what it used to be."

Rayburn took a step forward, his hand moving instinctively to the phone on his desk. He grabbed the receiver and brought it to his ear, only to find silence. His eyes flicked to the cord, detached from the wall.

His expression hardened. "You think this is a game? I don't know what kind of leverage you think you've got, but you're walking out of here in cuffs, or worse."

Finn leaned back in the chair. "You can try. But before security arrives, I think we should have a conversation."

Rayburn's nostrils flared, his eyes flashing with fury. He stepped closer, looming over the desk. "I don't owe you anything, Finn. If you think this little stunt will get you anywhere, you're delusional."

Finn's voice lowered. "Maybe I am. Or maybe I've got enough to bring your entire empire crashing down. Murder, illegal weapons deals, framing me—" He tossed a stack of papers onto the desk, the sharp flutter of documents cutting through the tension. "This is just the beginning."

Rayburn stared at the papers for a beat, then back at Finn, his expression hardening. "You've got nothing."

"Oh, I've got plenty." Finn's voice sharpened as he stood up, moving around the desk, his eyes locked onto Rayburn's. "And you're going to tell me everything. Donner, Miranda, all of it. You didn't just pull strings, Rayburn—you pulled triggers, and I'm done being your scapegoat."

Rayburn's eyes shifted between the scattered papers and Finn. "You don't have the balls to do anything with that," Rayburn spit. "You think you can scare me into confessing? I've crushed men stronger than you."

"Don't pretend you aren't scared," Finn said quietly, stepping closer. "You think just because you didn't pull the trigger yourself, it makes you less of a murderer? You think sending someone else to kill Donner and Miranda keeps your hands clean? I have nothing left to lose." He pulled out a gun.

Rayburn's face tightened; the sight of a weapon made him freeze. Typical desk jockey. He could put all those soldiers at risk by giving them inadequate supplies, but he wouldn't last a day on deployment. "You wouldn't risk a murder charge. You have Julia and that brat of hers, Lily." His voice was cold, devoid of any trace of remorse. "You should never have come here, Finn."

Finn took a step back, letting out a slow breath. "They'll be safer without you in the world. If I have to live in prison for that to happen, so be it."

Rayburn laughed, a low, bitter sound. "I should have killed them immediately instead of playing with them. It would have been so much cleaner, like Donner." Rayburn leaned closer. "And your sister...she was a loose end. Once you went looking for answers, I had no choice. She's dead because of you, Finn."

Before Finn could react, Rayburn lunged for him, his hand

swinging toward his throat. Finn maneuvered away from him and pulled the trigger. The desk clattered as Rayburn fell back.

Before he hit the floor, the door burst open behind him.

Two military police officers rushed in. One put out his hand toward Finn and took the weapon. Rayburn struggled, cursing under his breath, but it was no use.

From the doorway, Director Ron Downes entered, shaking his head slowly as he approached the scene. His eyes flicked to Finn, then to Rayburn. "You shouldn't have attacked Maguire, Rayburn. He had no choice but defend himself."

Rayburn growled from the floor, his face pressed against the polished wood. "You can't touch me. I've got connections, Downes. You'll be finished before this even makes it to court."

Downes crossed his arms, looking down at Rayburn with a faint smile. "It's all recorded, Rayburn. Everything you just said."

Blood dripped from Rayburn's mouth as his struggles ceased for a moment, confusion flickering across his face. "What?"

Finn stepped forward, now standing over the man who had tormented him for years. "I told you, Colonel. This is over."

Downes gave Finn a nod, placing a hand on his shoulder. "We had an agreement. I know you'll live up to it."

Finn barely heard him, his mind still racing, the weight of everything finally starting to settle. For the first time in years, Finn felt a flicker of relief.

He was finally free.

# *Chapter 53*

Julia stood by the window of the house on the ocean and watched tiny funnel clouds of sand move across the beach. Wind whistled through pines and dune grass. Desolation and emptiness coursed through her. She'd failed to protect Lily as well as Dianne and Kevin from John. Both her mother and Finn had told her to increase security so much earlier and she'd ignored them. If she didn't have Lily to care for, she would have preferred to hide away in bed until the torment subsided.

Lily sat on the floor and played with their new dog, Fritz. A present from her mother, the two-year-old black German shepherd had received extensive protection training specifically for a family with a child. Fritz chased a ball across the floor and tossed it back at Lily for more. Lily's laugh broke through Julia's fog and began to lift her spirits.

Julia had been searching for a new home for them when they left the island. A place where they'd be safe and Lily could grow up a normal child. Her paranoia set near impossible standards for homes, schools and entire communities. Evil could be lurking anywhere. *Focus on finding a way*, she chided herself. *We need to move forward.*

Hiding wouldn't help Lily. Julia needed to set up protection for them and then let her daughter live. Life contained no guarantees, but Fritz's ability to sense danger, combined with new armed bodyguards, gave her an increased sense of security. Declan and Tom, the new guards, generally stayed outside of the main house. Fiona had been amazing, but she was required on another assignment and Declan and Tom could remain long-term. That made Julia more comfortable. One remained in the guest house while the other was on duty. Fresh Pond Security had other trained guards at the ready during the men's time off.

Lily threw the ball again, but Fritz stopped his run and looked at the front door. His ears propped up and he growled as though muttering under his breath.

Julia's phone lit up with the number from one of the security guards.

"Hello?" Julia answered.

"Ms. Gardiner. It's Declan. There's a guest at your front gate."

Not many people knew where she'd hidden out. She wasn't ready for any social calls. "Can you find out who they are?"

"I know who it is," Declan answered. "You should probably answer it. He's from our team."

Julia's nerves calmed; perhaps it was Jason here to go over new details of their security.

"Lily, can you go play in your room for a little while?" Julia asked.

Lily, always the opportunist, asked, "Can I have a cookie and watch TV in my room?"

"Yes. Why don't you take the bag and stay there with Fritz until I come get you?"

"I can bring Fritz?"

"Definitely." Julia led the dog upstairs into her room, shutting the door after Lily arrived carrying the bag of Pepperidge Farms Sausalito cookies.

She walked back downstairs and looked at the security camera. Calvin stood at her door. Why was he here in Martha's Vineyard?

Taking a deep breath and trying to sound composed, Julia

asked Declan, "Will you answer the door and remain inside with him until I return?"

"Yes, ma'am."

"Thank you."

How the hell had her life fallen to where armed guards stood at her front door? She never wanted the glamorous life of her mother. All she wanted was a simple family in a simple house in a simple community. Instead, she ended up with armed guards, attack dogs and island compounds.

She went to the bathroom and rinsed off her face with cold water and brushed her hair. She had no time to change, so her old jeans and green Dartmouth sweatshirt would have to do. Then the doorbell rang.

Fritz barked at the sound from Lily's room, but Julia left him there to watch over her girl.

Calvin stood in the foyer next to Declan. A tabby cat next to a mountain lion.

"Come in." She gestured into the family room.

Calvin stood until Julia motioned him toward a chair. She sat across from him on the couch. A large coffee table separated them. Julia wanted to ask about Finn, but she knew Calvin would likely keep his answers guarded. Instead, she kept her composure, her eyes only momentarily betraying the emotions simmering beneath her calm exterior.

Calvin cleared his throat, squeezed his hands into fists and began to speak. "I'm sorry about what happened. About everything."

"Why are you sorry?" she asked.

"I should have stopped John at the beginning. I noticed the computer breach at the hospital, but I missed the addition of the new hospital record, the paternity test. I focused on stolen information, not added information."

A memory appeared in her head. Calvin leaving the engagement party before Davis. "The engagement party? When you had to find a breach at a hospital? Someone had hacked into the hospital and inserted John's fake paternity test?"

"Yeah," he replied, his voice full of regret. "I could have prevented the custody suit, Dianne's and Kevin's murders and what happened to you guys." He looked down at his shoes and shook his head slowly. "They stole some patient records and several insurance reimbursement account files to push me off his trail. It worked."

"All of that over Finn?"

"It wasn't his fault. He was trying to stop a lunatic from selling the weapons requisitioned by actual soldiers." Calvin's expression changed. Bolder, all the regret he'd revealed now taken over by a certainty. "Finn and I go way back. I knew him before I'd ever met Davis. We both went to UMass together. He was ROTC, and I was a nerd. A few guys thought it would be fun to torment the gay computer geek and they beat me up pretty bad. Finn didn't find their actions so funny. He stepped in and received a pretty bad black eye and a broken rib to protect me. I owe him a lot. That man doesn't have a dishonest bone in his body. He loses in poker every week because he's the only guy at the table that refuses to cheat. He pays more than what's due on his taxes, because he doesn't trust loopholes. He's never cheated on a girlfriend and I've never heard him lie. He's the best guy I know."

She nodded. "I know."

Calvin stood. "I'm also here to give you some good news. I've been able to track thirty million dollars of your money to an offshore account in a Colonel Rayburn's name. Another twenty million flowed into a Cayman Islands bank account in John O'Donnell, aka John Holland's name. Since Rayburn never set up the account, he never knew the money was stolen from him. Once the money entered that account, someone transferred it to an account in Hong Kong. Within minutes, it disappeared as if it never existed."

"Disappeared?"

"It took some late nights, but I was able to trace the flow of the money out of Hong Kong. It was sent to the Bancroft brothers to help John acquire an interest in the dealership. He was pretty sophisticated in creating these accounts. He was stealing from his own boss."

"He did all that just to get at Finn?"

Calvin paced back and forth with his hands in his pockets. His eyes stayed on the floor. "John was a self-serving asshole, Rayburn had the issue with Finn. I have to admit, the man covered his tracks. I've never seen someone so good at hiding his online presence."

Julia looked at him. "If he's so good, how did you find him?"

"Because I'm better," Calvin stated as matter-of-factly as if he'd just told her his middle name.

"Is Finn okay?" She wanted to get on a boat and rush to his side.

"Why don't you see for yourself?" he asked as though that would be the easiest thing in the world. "And ask him to come in for some coffee—he's bound to be pretty cold by now."

Julia froze. "Invite him in for coffee?"

"He's waiting down the road to see you, but if you don't want to see him, he'd understand."

Julia jumped off the couch and ran toward the door. "Declan, stay here with Calvin, I'll be right back," she yelled as she flew out the front door.

# Chapter 54

Finn paced at the end of the street trying to stay warm. The damn sand kept blowing into his face and the chill caused his worst injuries to act up and remind him of how abused his body had been over the last thirty-plus years. His leather jacket helped, but his fingers and his face became more insensate the longer he waited. The gunshot wound was the only part of him that preferred the cold. Cold felt much better than the pain.

He'd decided to stay at least a half mile away from the house in case she didn't want to see him. She was free of all the violence now and perhaps she didn't want to deal with his baggage. Calvin and he could take a taxi back to the airport and leave without hurting her more.

Man, he owed Calvin for this. Without him and his staggering computer skills, they might never have found the cancer at the bottom of it all... Rayburn.

He heard a door slam and tried to see if Calvin was returning, but the blowing sand made him squint to protect his eyes.

"Finn?" His name floated toward him, muffled by the sound of the ocean, the resonance of the wind and the rustling of seagrass.

He focused his partially blinded gaze down the road. Calvin would never move that fast or that fluid. He caught his breath. The woman he loved more than anything, brown hair fluttering behind her, was running down the street in a sweatshirt and jeans and...socks?

"Finn?" she called out again as she ran closer.

He started jogging toward her.

Her face came into view, tear streaked and red from the wind or perhaps because of him. Finn stopped. He wanted to wipe her tears, to explain, to apologize for the hell she'd been through.

Julia, however, didn't stop. She ran straight toward him, accelerating as she neared and leaped into his arms, wrapping her arms around his neck and wrapping her legs around his hips. Her face nuzzled into his neck. He winced at first, as she'd rammed his shoulder full force where the wound was trying to heal. Screw the pain. She'd come back. He squeezed her and held her as tight as he could. Thank God.

Kissing her on the side of her face, near the thin scar that he'd failed to protect her from, Finn closed his eyes and soaked in her warmth.

She lifted her head back and gazed into his eyes. "What are you doing out here? You belong inside, with me and Lily."

"You still want me around?" he said, his lips brushing against her sweet skin.

"Yes." She kissed the tip of his nose.

"Good. Because I don't know what I'd do without you. And for the record, I've been cleared of all charges. No more dishonorable discharge or manslaughter conviction."

"That's the best news," she exclaimed.

He slowly released her and she slid down his legs, her feet maneuvering onto the top of his shoes. "Cold?"

"I forgot my sneakers in my hurry to see you. Calvin wanted me to ask you if you wanted some coffee. There's some brewing in the kitchen." She placed her cold hand over his frozen cheek as her smile melted his heart and ignited every neuron.

"I'd love some, Sunshine."

"Sunshine? What happened to Midnight?"

"I want us back in the light, creating a beautiful future for Lily and us."

"I'd like that, but can you still call me Midnight occasionally? At home, in bed, doors locked."

He laughed. "Definitely."

Her lips parted slightly, her breath visible in the cold air. Finn cupped her face in his hands. Julia clutched at the fabric of his jacket as if anchoring herself to him.

Then, with a soft exhale, Finn leaned down, closing the gap between them. His lips brushed hers. But then the kiss deepened. His hands moved down to her waist, pulling her closer, lifting her slightly so she fit perfectly against him.

Julia's hands slid up, fingers threading through the back of his hair, pulling him in deeper, their bodies molded together against the cold as if trying to banish the chill by sheer will. The scent of salt and sea filled the space between them. In that moment, all Finn could feel was the heat of her kiss.

When they finally pulled apart, their breaths mingled in the cold, the sound of the waves crashing filling the silence between them. Julia's forehead rested against his chest, her fingers still tangled in his jacket. Finn smiled down at her, his heart lighter than it had been in years. He pressed a kiss to her forehead, holding her tight against him, as if he would never let her go again.

Their breath mingled in the cold. Finn reached out, brushing a lock of hair from Julia's cheek, his fingers grazing her cheek an inch above a still-healing wound. Now they both had a scar on their faces, but hers would fade with time.

"Come on. We have a lot of catching up to do." She took two steps then hesitated and stood on the balls of her feet to avoid the cold.

Finn stepped forward and lifted her up in his arms. She snuggled into him as he walked to her house.

An armed brute dressed in black stood as a sentry at the front door.

"Finn, this is one of the new guards, Declan."

Finn laughed. Declan was an old friend and coworker from Fresh Pond Security. "I know him well. The best of the best."

"It's an honor to keep an eye on such a wonderful family." Declan stepped back from the door and Finn could hear him locking the door after they walked past him.

A huge German shepherd lumbered toward Finn as Julia entered the kitchen. She sure as hell had security in her life now.

"Meet Fritz. He's going to hang out with Lily." Julia rubbed the dog's ears as it sniffed Finn and decided he wasn't a threat.

"How many guards do you have on the premises?"

"Two. They're excellent and will continue with us back in Boston, but I have to sell the house. I could never live there again. Too many scary memories."

They entered the family room and Finn froze. Lily was sitting next to Calvin showing him a black-haired GI Joe. He didn't say anything because he didn't want to scare her. He'd missed her so much.

"This is Finn. He's a hero." Lily held the doll up to Calvin and then squeezed it against her heart. "He goes away sometimes, but he'll come back, because heroes always come back."

"They absolutely do, Little Bear," Finn called out to her.

Lily's head spun around and she leaped over the back of the couch and ran into his arms, as welcoming as Julia had been. He lifted her up and slung her high onto his uninjured shoulder. She smiled and laughed. A wide, happy smile and a loud, carefree laugh.

Julia followed him and curled herself into his free arm. She leaned back into the wound. Always causing him some sort of pain, but a worthwhile one.

While Lily dragged Finn over to see some of Fritz's tricks,

Finn observed Julia walking toward Calvin, still sitting on the couch.

She placed a hand on his shoulder and said, "Thanks. If there's anything I can do for you in the future, name it. I owe you so much for helping Finn."

Calvin took out his phone and pulled up his calendar. "I'm supposed to be getting married on May 11. Can you help with that?"

Julia gasped loud enough to draw Fritz's attention. "I completely forgot. You guys didn't reach out to Helena after you picked a date?"

"With the issues at the dealership and everything at my work, we forgot." Calvin looked back at Finn and grimaced. "I'm not so stressed about it, but Davis has been planning this day for years. I want him to be happy."

Julia clasped his hand. "Don't worry about it. I'll take care of everything. The whole wedding."

"You have too much going on in your life. Too bad we can't elope to Vegas—the logistics would be simpler."

"Don't you dare. I have a better idea," Julia replied, looking very much like the woman Finn had fallen in love with.

Finn kissed Lily on the head and tossed the ball for Fritz across the increasingly scratched hardwood floors, waiting to hear Julia's inspiration.

# *Chapter 55*

Finn knocked on the door, ready to beg.

"Enter," Jason called out from his office. When Finn came into his view, Jason put down the phone he was holding and sat back in his chair. "How are you feeling?"

"I've been better, but I'm expected to make a full recovery."

"That's good. How's the car business?"

"It's not security."

"No, I can't imagine it's that interesting."

"It's not. Which is why I'm here."

Jason remained expressionless.

Finn took a deep breath and swallowed his pride. "I'm ready to come back."

"Downes said you'd be back."

"He strikes a hard bargain. And that's why I'm here."

"To give me a wedding invitation?"

"Don't get ahead of yourself, I haven't asked…yet. Let's get through Calvin's wedding first." He sat. "I wanted to apologize to you for walking out on the firm after finding out about your deception. I was angry and I couldn't go through another part of my life where I trusted those around me and they let me down."

"I agree. If you can't trust the team, you shouldn't be on the team."

"But I do trust you and everyone at Fresh Pond Security. And I understand more than ever why you did everything you could to protect those you loved. I did the same thing and have no regrets."

"We're a lot alike, you and I, which is why I need you back. I need someone with your level of competence and integrity to protect the company as it expands. We've grown significantly since you left and our services have changed a bit. Our clients aren't always the people we protect. Our services are looking out for a greater good. And sometimes, to be honest, our work lives in a gray zone."

"I understand. I believe in the mission and would follow the team into hell and back."

"So would I. So are you asking for your old job back? I refuse to offer you any long-term assignments outside of New England. It wouldn't be fair to Lily. She needs her uncle around. I missed part of my own son's life, and it's a regret I'll always have. If you have availability, I need someone to fly to South Korea to check up on a K-pop star. You should only be gone about two weeks."

Finn grinned. "My bags are packed." He turned to leave.

Jason waved him to stop. "One moment. Sit, please."

Finn sat down, ready for his new old life.

# Chapter 56

*A perfect day in May*

The sun began to sink into the ocean, but had yet to change the brilliant blue in the sky to either orange or pink. Julia scanned the area to make sure everything had come together perfectly. She'd acquired permission to use the house on Martha's Vineyard.

Helena waved from the end of the boardwalk. This was Helena's event. Julia was not only a guest, but the maid of honor. Finn, the best man, dressed in black pants and a white dress shirt, held on to the flower girl.

"Let me see you." Julia put out her arms for Lily. The little girl popped to the ground and spun around three times until she almost lost her balance. She seemed like an angel with her warm coloring beneath a pale yellow dress of organza. Small white daisies adorned the skirt and a crown of the same flowers decorated her curly hair.

"I guess I have the prettiest date here." Finn picked her up again and kissed her on the cheek.

"I thought I was your date?" Julia fake-punched him in the arm.

Finn feigned an injury and backed away. "I don't mix business and pleasure, so until I can find an investor to replace your forty-nine percent ownership of the dealership, I'm forced to exchange you for this little bear." Finn touched Lily on the tip of her nose and received a smile and a giggle in return. Julia used some of the recovered funds from the kidnapping to buy the Bancroft brothers out of the car business. Now that Finn had returned to Fresh Pond Security, they all decided that Aspen would step up and take on a larger managerial role in the business. Between Davis and Aspen, the dealership would flourish.

Finn and Julia had been inseparable since December, although Lily did have one other male in her life that she preferred to Finn… Fritz. When she saw Fritz behind her, she struggled to get down so she could play with her dog. Finn let her loose and watched her scamper away.

"I'm not sure I want to sell my investment. Maybe I secretly love exotic cars," Julia said as she took Lily's place in his arms.

"You sold your Mini Cooper for a minivan. Hardly exotic."

She placed her head on his shoulder. "Practical outperforms exotic in real life."

"Then explain the practicality of that belly button ring that appeared last month."

She moved her lips closer to his ear and whispered, "Shhhhh. That's a private matter between me and one of my business partners."

"It better not be with the one getting married today."

"No. It's with the one getting married next summer."

"Good." He pulled her closer and kissed her breathless.

When the brilliant orange sky arrived in the horizon, the guests gathered by the ocean's edge to watch Calvin and Davis declare their commitment to each other in front of their friends and family.

Davis looked fantastic with his wind swept blond hair and blue eyes. He'd picked a J.Crew khaki summer suit and a white button-down shirt to wear for the ceremony, casual for the beach, but a blue-and-green-striped belt added his own style to the outfit.

Calvin wore khaki pants and an untucked blue oxford. With his hair spiked up, he looked very different from the minimalist guy who preferred little more than a laptop and Davis to make him happy.

Lily ran up to the door leading to the beach ahead of Finn and Julia. She stopped at the exit leading outside and backed away seeing the crowd in front of her.

"This could be a problem," Finn said.

"She's made so much progress and has been a fixture at Davis and Calvin's house," Julia replied. "They're her favorite babysitters. Perhaps the wedding was a step too far."

The music began and Finn and Julia grasped each other's hands and started down toward the archway of roses at the end of the boardwalk. Julia looked back often. Would Lily be afraid of the crowds lining the pews?

"Do you want me to stay back here?" Julia asked.

Calvin shook his head. "She'll be fine. She has us."

Davis squatted down next to Lily and handed her a bouquet of daisies and white roses.

Lily didn't move. The people looked backward from their seats to see why the procession had stalled.

Julia couldn't hear them from her spot by the minister, but she could see that Lily would not walk down the aisle alone. It was Julia's fault. She expected way too much of her. Lily had been retraumatized and why would Julia push her to do something even kids who have nontraumatic childhoods hated doing?

Before she could make a fifty-yard dash back up the aisle, Davis and Calvin each took Lily by the hand. They lifted her up off the ground and then placed her back on earth as she burst out laughing. The ocean breeze escorted them as the three of them strolled down the aisle toward the waiting minister. When they arrived at their places, they both bent down to kiss Little Bear.

Lily beamed as she gazed from one man to the other. Then she turned to look at Julia, who laughed and put out her arms to catch her, but Julia's little bear had transformed into a smiling little fairy who ran right by her mother and leaped into Finn's arms. He spun her around, holding her as close as any proud father would hold his own child. Julia's heart nearly burst with love. Eventually, all eyes turned back to the grooms and the beginning of their own happy-ever-after.

\* \* \* \* \*